SURPRISE

Previous Novels by Brian Burland

The Sailor and the Fox
Undertow
A Few Flowers for St George
A Fall from Aloft

SURPRISE

BRIAN BURLAND

London   George Allen & Unwin Ltd
Ruskin House   Museum Street

First published 1974 474287603

© Brian Burland 1974

ISBN 0 04 823115 0

Printed in Great Britain
in 11 pt Baskerville type
by Clarke, Doble & Brendon Ltd
Plymouth

For Rosamond Patricia
and in tender memory of
Les Petits Bateaux Bermudiens

BOOK ONE

I

Surprise had always been a troublesome, uppity nigger, the whites said, and after his master, Nathaniel Darrell, 'The Younger's' death in 1840, he became intolerable.

July 1841

'Even after that flogging damn near tore the black hide off'n the bastard, he still had the trace of that smile – mind you it was only a trace.'

'That child of a bitch's heat don't fear God even – never mind his betters.'

Surprise was a man of average height, but very heavily built – like a thick cedar, and like a cedar, his age was hard to determine. Another factor that made his age indeterminate was that he was partially bald and had, while at sea, adopted the habit of shaving his head entirely. (Indeed, like a good many seamen, he shaved his body too – and let no landsman ask the reason why or he might find himself eating caustic soap.)

In fact, the date being July 1841, Surprise was thirty-two, going on thirty-three, having been born in 1808.

'Yeh, but I hear tell he's the best helmsman Bermuda *ever* did produce – '

'No matter. Some blacks are like that – an angel to one master and then, when he dies, no one can put a yoke on him.'

Truth was, what the whites hated was Surprise's detached independence. He didn't carry himself like a slave, and, although slavery had been abolished seven long years, no black was supposed to act like that – carrying his great head level to the horizon and his sharp brown and white eyes taking in everything like he was some white sea captain ashore looking for a crew.

'He can read and write, too, you know.'

'He can?'

'You're jesting me – no black can learn to read, least not more'n a few words.'

'Well, Surprise can – and that's a fact-truth.'

'You better believe it – he can write better than you and me.'

'Beau Nat Darrell taught him, huh?'

'Yeh, Captain Beau Nat Darrell taught him *everything*, they say – and I don't know what, but it sure was too much.'

'They should've killed him.'

'Keeps on the way he going, he'll kill hisself.'

The lower whites were afraid of him, too – indeed, when the sentence of the magistrate was ordered carried out, no man would stand forward to administer it.

'Twenty-four lashes for his disobedience in being off-shore after nightfall, in a fishing boat, with another negro sailor.'

'They said,' Surprise told his father, 'that no man is allowed off-shore after dark for fear of the Spanish privateers – but no one seen a Spaniard now, not ever, not in my lifetime – and, with Captain Darrell, I been off-shore and clear to America and the West Indies and to Europe – and sometimes gone for upwards of three hundred nightfalls, never mind one night. . . .'

But no white man would stand forward and administer the lashes. And time was short: the magistrate, himself seeming, even to an unknowing eye, uncommonly keen to witness the punishment, had specified that it be carried out that very noon.

They, the authorities, promised pardon to any in the Hamilton jail who would administer the sentence – but there were only three in the jail, the drunk, Black John, who had no right hand anyway, a white petty thief, who refused, and Sara Forbes, the mulatto, who some called the Young Witch, sentenced to two years for selling watered rum and bad meat pies.

Sara Forbes stood forward, grabbing the chance to be free, and had it been any other woman, they might have refused her, but Sara was strong with arms 'like a horse's hindquarters' and the public spirits seemed tickled by the chance of the spectacle of a brown-skinned half-breed woman whipping a dark pure African, and him the recalcitrant Surprise from the Western Isles.

And when they took him to the Whipping Post at the Flag Staff in Hamilton, Surprise himself bade his captors free his arms that he might himself remove his jerkin and shirt. And he took off his dark green jerkin, with its high collar and bright brass buttons, and, folding it carefully, placed it on a handcart standing nearby. (The jerkin bought and given him by Nathaniel Darrell, no less, in Boston and put about him by 'Beau Nat' himself. 'Let every man hear this,' Captain Darrell said, his foot on the taffrail and his hand on Surprise's sleeve, 'This is the Master Helmsman of my ship – and from now on, like it or loathe it, he is answerable to no one save me. And ye two officers may *ask* him, but you may not order him in any way or in any venture.') And he himself bared his back and then they fastened his arms high and bound his legs, both at the knees and ankles.

And Sara Forbes, her arms, too, bare in the noon sunlight, took the whip with the one thin, long and knotted leather cord and thong (called the Cat Cutter) and 'laid it on him' – twenty-four strokes to the slow count.

'It oughta be the other – the Cat 'n' Nine, and that would really straighten him out.'

'Yeh, straighten him out like blooded canvas.'

Surprise, in order to keep a hold on himself against the pain, turned over in his mind the memory of that most salty and rewarding occurrence. For Beau Nat's crew as well as his officers had turned against him for the 'unheard of' 'crime' of making 'a black' an officer. 'I'll not serve under a black.' 'Pay him off.' 'Nor me, neither – you asking us to share our officers' head with him, too?' 'Pay him off, also.' And lastly, with the whites, went one Negro : 'Um not following a black no better'n me – 'twould be bad luck, a black omen.' 'Pay them *all* off.' 'But, Master,' the white first mate said, 'I been with you seven and a half years – what is this?' 'This is *progress*,' Captain Darrell snapped, 'and if you can't take progress, get ashore.' To the man they quit, but, by the turning of the tide, to the man, they returned. A trace of a smile crossed Surprise's pained mouth to think on it : for Captain Nat was cute to play his cards in Boston knowing his crew, Bermudians, were pining to be home, could smell home fires. . . .

As it was, when Sara Forbes had finished, you could have filled a cup from the sweat from her face alone, and Surprise, for all his brute strength and visceral determination, was hard put to gather himself up, when they cut him down, and make it across the wharf and down the long steps to the green moss- and seaweed-strewn giant rocks where his father waited in his old Sandys ferryboat, the *Teazer*, ready to take him, and his daily western-bound cargo, home.

And someone threw his arrogant green jacket after him and his father picked it off the rocks and laid it, too, aboard.

The authorities, and the public, were well satisfied that justice had been carried out and peace protected, but if they had

11

truly known, really understood, what Surprise was up to, what plans that had hitherto seemed mere dreams and were now solidified in his imagination, they would, as the local saying was, have been given 'cause to pause' . . . or, some, 'fifty screaming fits.'

The very next week, the British Royal Navy reported the loss of a valuable brass compass from a pinnace and posted a reward for its return.

The father shoved off from the shore, hauled his mainsail, unfurled his jib, and, the wind, as usual, being out of the south-west, made ready to tack for home.

When they were out of earshot, he said: 'Surprise, you better lie down.'

'Can't.'

'On your stomach, then.'

'Can't.'

'Why so, son?'

'Cut there, too.'

Surprise stood wedging himself in the companionway with his strong thighs, sipping water from a demijohn and wiping his mouth with the back of his hand.

'I told you and I told you, Surprise.' His father steered the old *Teazer* with a very long oar – on calm days he'd often scull the heavy eighteen-foot craft all the way home with it. 'I told you – you can't fight. You can't rebel. You can't fight the whites. I told you – those who rebel and fight are destroyed, utterly destroyed.'

'I know, Senex.'

'Stop that "Senex" – I don't know what you mean –'

Surprise only smiled, he'd told his father that Captain Darrell taught him the word: the Old One, the Wise One – all in one word.

'There is no way to rebel – those who do, are destroyed. My great-great-grandfather, he rebelled. He was put to the gibbet – uh-huh – he rebel, not once, but three times and he put to the gibbet.'

The wind was freshening with the early afternoon, and white and dark clouds forming in the west. It looked like rain or a summer blow, and on the water, it was now cool for July.

'You been to America, *you* know – what happened to the

Indians? Huh, they rebel – some rebellion – burn a barn and the whites take and kill a tribe. Rebel, kill a white family and the whites raise up and kill a *nation*. I told you – there is no way to live but let it all go by.'

'That's living?'

'It is. All you gotta do is obey a few rules and keep your head low and let it all go by. Live, live in peace. There ain't no better living no place – no place on earth, I 'spect – than we got in the Western Isles. Live in peace and enjoy life.' The old man fussed with a rope, dropped it deftly around a cleat, and swept his hand around as if encompassing all to the west, where the sun was moving and the boat, too.

'Live in peace – and enjoy life.'

'And achieve nothing – and live like animals.'

'What is there to achieve? Achieve what? So we get to go nowhere – but to live in peace and enjoy life is to achieve *everything*. You young people think we are fools – but we too have thought. Others too have been young and angry. To enjoy life before it slips by – enjoy it day by day, every day, that's everything.'

'You told me, old one.'

'You ever think, Surprise? You ever consider – consider it might be that here in Bermuda, in the Western Isles, we black people may well live as our ancestors did, before us, long ago, in Africa?' The old man slipped a small piece of board under his buttocks and sat on it (for he suffered from the piles) and looked at his son with a deep frown – would he hear? . . . understand? . . . listen? How could you tell a son anything? It was, as ever, he supposed, impossible.

'Surprise – hear me. I am your father.'

'You told me. . . .'

'Hear me – to live, what does a man need? Just food, shelter, a family – and a little pleasure. Hmm, a little pleasure – whatever your pleasure is. A man needs no more. Here, in the Western Isles, we have food from the ground and fish from the sea – all aplenty. And shelter – what does a man need but a thatched house and a little fire to cook with and to be warm in winter.'

'You told me, Father. I know. I know.' Surprise scooped up salt water in the half calabash and poured it, slowly, down his still bare back.

13

His Africa, Surprise thought, he has his Africa here. But I do not want to go back to Africa – not his Africa or the Africa of the big-mouth talkers. I do not want to go *back* to Africa. I want to go forward and be free.

'It pain you bad?'

'Uh-huh – but I suppose it going to get worse.'

'We fix it at home – I figured we better get good and far away first – from them people. We fix it with a little prickly pear juice and then maybe a little turtle oil.'

'Senex: your Western Isles – look at them. *Look*. Do you not see what has happened? The Western Isles of your young days – the Isles you told me about – have shrunk. The big one, Ireland Island – how many simple independent souls used to live there?'

'One or two hundred.'

'Yes – simple black people fishing and fussing and just living in thatch houses among the palmetto and banana groves – and what you see now? What you see on Ireland Island?'

'You know what you see – great stone buildings and a British fortress and British machines and British convicts – and them treated worse than dogs and worked worse than horse or oxen.'

'You know I hate all that – dirty noise British.'

'Yes – but, don't you see – that Ireland Island was your *home*. Home for the free slaves – home of the free men, the buccaneers. And who got it? – the British. And them all ringed with convict hulks for their Irish slaves. Everything is gone what they call? – "modernised" – there is no end to this modernised, soon all the land be covered with buildings.'

'I know – but we still got home.'

'You got two little islands – Boaz and Gates. What going to happen when the British want those islands, those islands, too, for their fortress? Huh, what?'

'The British don't want no more. They don't want everything.'

'Old man – I sailed practically the whole globe around and everywhere – *everywhere* I seen the British – pretty soon they got it all.'

'They ain't got it all – they ain't got America – they ain't got this United States place you told me about.'

'Senex – you don't know. These Limeys, they just toying

14

with America. You don't know. Beau Nat Darrell told me and I *seen* – against Britain, America is powerless. You see – one day, Britain going to step on America like an ant – step like a giant on a cockroach and crush it and not even *feel* it. You see.'

'Um-huh. If that so – then why you rebel? If white can step on white so easily – where's it for you, and you black?'

Surprise stretched a little, painfully, and said, 'Because they are not coming for me again, the British yellow pigs – not again. They do not take Surprise.'

'But you are big man – you a big seagoing man now – they give you anything – '

'Who?'

'These big sea captains, Bermuda captains – they all would want you. Why even the big man – Captain Hezekiah Fitch, he would want you.'

'Captain Fitch – yes, he a big man, a *big thief*. What kind of Bermuda captain he? He like to sail in big Limey ships. If a Bermuda captain don't sail under cedar he greedy or a fool, or both. Surprise had one captain, one master – one man above all others. Captain Beau Nat Darrell hisself. Surprise never follow no one after Darrell. The Captain was the best – everyone after him is a fool and a donkey and *trash*. Captain Darrell is *dead* . . . Surprise never follow another man. Surprise his own man now. And he going to be *free* – not free to wear a little medal around his neck that *say* he free, when it tied to a chain and he chained – but free-free. As free as a seagull – freer – as free as a longtail leaving for the winter.'

After a while, Senex said: 'I hope you not forget that we are free and let *be*. Bad things can happen – and a real bad thing just happen to you. But I ask you to remember we free and let be, let stay here. It not been long, you know – within not mine, but my father's memory – when a slave freed, they ship him away. Give you freedom and ship you from home – ship you to hell. For hell is a place you don't know – hell is away from home and your loved ones. You understand me, Surprise?'

'I understand. I think it you don't understand me.'

The *Teazer* creaked as the wind nuzzled her and the bow

lapped making its own little wave against the westerly driven Sound.

'She good,' the old man said. 'You see – she laying Boaz now. She sweet. Why I swear, *no* boat can out-point my *Teazer*.'

No boat but mine, Surprise thought. No ship but mine and mine going to out-point everything on the sea – everything on the deep, deep sea.

'Senex – you know what came to me today – today during that whipping and that pain?'

'I sorry, son. Sorry.'

'Everything came to me. You don't tell no one – not even your woman – '

'You know I never tell nothing.'

'I know. I know. Senex: I going to finish that ship and launch her and rig her and outfit her and equip her and man her good – and I going to sail away. I going to sail away to where there are no British and no machines and no potato peelings – nor man shit thick on the water. You hear?'

He looked all around the sky and the sea and clucked his tongue.

'It was like I didn't know until now: Father, what you think we been building this ship for? Just to fish? No, no. To trade? No. It to sail – to sail away. It always been that and I didn't quite understand until now. It is the ship to sail away. And me the black master. To sail away, you hear?'

'Yes, I hear – but I fear, too. T'ain't no black never win over white – not even in the clouds it don't. You're the child of my old age – my old loins. You my Surprise – '

'Stop that.'

'A man's future is his son, Surprise – what you think I am, some youngster of thirty, or fifty? I nigh on eighty years and I lose you, I lose my future, my life.'

Silence.

'You trying to pain me more than that whip – you trying, Deddy, and you doing it.'

The old man, his one hand on the oar and his foot rested, characteristically, high on a barrel, let out the main sheet. Surprise, moving gingerly, let out the jib.

'You going to jump for that sweet prickly pear from St David's?'

16

'I might.'

'You do that. Nothing better. She fine – good woman, one day. She built right for children. I know. You take a girl got legs stick out from her trunk – like so, like a man – no good for children. Die sometimes. Then, you take a girl got legs set wide at the top – like a fowl – good for children. That one from St David's, she good.'

'You told me, Senex. You told me many times.'

'You go and get her then. Pay the man.'

'He want too much. He told me but two days ago : a dinghy – *my* dinghy – and a barrel of rum and a pig and a cockerel. Too much.'

'She want you? Want you good?'

'Yes. I told you.'

'You pay then. Pay the dinghy. You build me a grandson, by 'n' by I build you a dinghy. Yeah, a fine dinghy.'

II

In the most hidden inlet of Ireland Island, a place called The Crawl – unmolested, as yet, by the British; ignored by them, the place being too shallow; and, in turn, ignored by the ordinary Bermudians since it belonged now, these several years, to the Mother Government of England. Deep in the mangrove trees, away from any prying eyes, even from any visiting 'buccaneers' from Gates and Boaz Islands, they had been building, for many months what their close fishermen neighbours, led on by Emilene, Senex's woman, called 'Surprise's Girt Folly.'

Girt she was, for, when the keel was adzed into shape to receive the bow and the stern to receive the skeg pin and the stern frame and scantlings, it was clear she'd be more than four lengths of a man — maybe five.

'What's it going to be, Surprise?' they'd ask.

'The best – the best ship.' Then he'd turn back to work. Only his father, Saul, and his friend August, had seen his drawn plans and his half model – and he kept them well hidden.

April 1841

He himself had first seen his ship, his dream ship, when he was a boy. Over Captain Darrell's desk (the old captain, named Benjamin, the one with the square whiskers – Beau Nat's father) was the picture. It was in many colours and very beautiful : a fine ship with a deep raked mast and a long bowsprit – like many – but this ship was special and set upon the water looking, at the same time, both as light as a mosquito and yet, too, like a sharp knife to cleave the water – a knife to cleave to windward.

And she had but one cross rigging and she set proud on the water, with a proud flag flying half up the bowsprit and down off the stern trailed a cedar dinghy that set the water as light as she.

Always he'd look hard at that picture, and, when he was young, he'd stare and stare and he asked Beau Nat what her name was.

'*Bateau*,' Beau Nat said. 'That's all – *Bateau Bermudien.*'

'Where she to, Master Nat – where she to?'

'Don't know. Never was, I think, Surprise. Never was – just in the man's imagination.'

'What man?'

'The man who painted the picture.'

'What her name again, Master Nat?'

'*Bateau Bermudien.*'

And, years later, when Beau Nat had taught him to read – not everything, but enough, if he took it slow – Surprise made it out with his own eyes : '*Bateau Bermudien*'.

One day, Surprise had promised himself, he would build that ship and sail her himself and be her master. *Bateau Bermudien* : her lines were perfect, he knew them in his dreams, sleeping and waking. Like many a Bermudian sloop, she was beamy – especially amidships – and had no overhang of stern, the overhang that many ships favoured (a sometimes fatal flaw, Surprise knew, for an overhung stern on a small ship was like giving the sea a handle to drive your bow under – poop, and a poop in the stern could drive you to Davy Jones as fast as a steel spike). But, for all her beaminess amidships, about level with her mast step, she sharpened, and, from there forward, she was as if chiselled sharp to point and cut to windward.

The rake of the mast, too, would help her point high –

18

and foot, foot through the water god, foot like a thrown spear.

The problems were, and had been, many : how to get the best cedar, and enough of it, to build her? How to get the copper and brass fastenings; how to get the right wood for the spar, the bowsprit and the boom – then such fixtures as a compass? First off, though, the big essential : the keel itself? Late 1840

James Darrell, Nathaniel's youngest brother, still ran the shipyard on Darrell's Island. Mr James Darrell – who Surprise called 'sire', not because he put him above a 'sir' or a 'master', but because he refused, to himself, within himself and without to all men, to call any 'master' – but the dead captain.

In James Darrell, Surprise saw a trace, a mere shadow, of Beau Nat, but enough – particularly in his voice and gesture – to cause Surprise pain in his chest. A strange contraction that he later realised was grief. And James Darrell had cedar aplenty – it was easy to get the off-cuts. Surprise just worked in the shipyard and asked for the off-cut timber he took to be his pay, or deducted from it. But, how to get the long, thick piece for the keel?

He'd hauled practically enough cedar for the whole rest of the frame, and planking for below water and topsides (in his dinghy and in the *Teazer*) but he still didn't have the keel. Nov 1840 to Feb 1841

Then, on a still winter night, the brand new cedar schooner, *Bee*, caught fire off Hunt's Island in Hamilton Harbour, and, her crew being ashore and leaving no one but a boy, the fire caught hold. And, no sooner had it caught, than a sharp wind grew out of the east, and the *Bee* burned. It was a shame to see such : a brand new ship burning in harbour. She burned so bad that she lit up the whole islands and when they got it out, it was morning and she was burned way down past even her waterline. James Darrell was asked to haul the wreckage away – it was a danger to shipping.

Anchored at Darrell's Island, what was left of the hull, after they stripped the ballast from her, looked more like a dead black whale skeleton than a bee.

Surprise kept looking for a way to get Mr Darrell to let him have that cedar hulk – but whenever he mentioned it, James Darrell just smiled a little peculiar, and, you couldn't March and April 1841 blame him : who would part with a girt hunk of good cedar like that?

And Surprise thought of setting it adrift and then letting the wind take it down by Timlin's Narrows where the new channel was cut. There, of a night, he could haul it home behind the *Teazer*. Hiding it and working on it with adzes, they could cut off the burned timbers and the burn marks on the keel itself – and then claim it was theirs.

But then he imagined Mr James Darrell coming for it – examining it at The Crawl and finding some secret mark. Shipmakers leave funny marks all their own : maybe that man Seon, from Flatts, who built the *Bee*, put some secret mark.

It was too dangerous. Besides, he didn't want to steal it : that was no way to lay the keel of his *Bateau Bermudien*, to steal it. Steal it from Beau Nat's brother.

Work for it? A piece of keel like that (and it was all sound, too – he had tested it with his knife in every part) was worth maybe thirty to thirty-six pounds – a year's wages. Too long, and, all the while, no money would be coming in either.

They had gathered and garnered all manner of things from the sea : from their neighbours, from wrecks and driftwood and flotsam. They had bronze and copper by the keg and they even had a broken gold eagle from a wrecked Baltimore brig. (And Surprise was changing it : recarving it and shaping it to look like a Bermuda longtail. It would make the finest of stern pieces : the proudest decoration. The golden longtail on the stern, above the rudder post, would be perfect and then he himself would carve the words below that : *Bateau Bermudien*. The exact spacing would be tricky.)

Then one day, a Saturday, James Darrell came home to Darrell's Island in his racing dinghy, and he and his crew were all hollering, and, by the sound of them, half hollering hot – had about a pint of rum a man, Surprise figured.

And Surprise went on working and let James Darrell come right up close to him passing by, and he heard Darrell say : 'When we got to the windward mark ahead of the *Diamond*, I could taste that victory and that hundred pounds in gold. Why, you *know* the *Diamond* is supposed to be quicker to windward – and all we had was the downhill run, and the *Coquette* got wings to leeward.'

20

Surprise looked up and stepped out in his way as if accidental. 'You win, sire?'

'Huh? Yes, Surprise, we won – won by a quarter-mile. Come, stop work, everyone is entitled to a little tipple to celebrate.'

Surprise took the tipple and then it simply came to him – came to him right after Mr Darrell said: 'You getting married, Surprise?'

'Yes, sire.'

'That's what I heard. A fine girl, I hear, too.'

'Yes, sire.' And how he hear all that? I ain't even but walked out with the girl a few times – white folks sure do a lot of looking and a lot of listening and a lot of talking. . . . But if that what he hear and that what he think, let him think it. Let him think the wedding settled and strike him, strike him now and hook him good – and hook the girl, maybe, later.

'Well, you got the prettiest dinghy on St David's, I hear – what else you want?'

'That old burned wreck, sire. You give Surprise that wreck and Surprise work for it until you say it paid.'

'That wreck, eh. What the blazes you want that great piece of cedar for?'

'For a new boat.'

'A new boat for your father's ferry, huh.'

It was not a question. Surprise waited. James Darrell started to turn away.

'I want it, sire, for a wedding present.'

'For your wife?'

'No, sire. For a wedding present *from* the house of Darrell.' He looked the man right in the eyes and let the eyes say: I given you and yours my loyalty and my back all my life.

'Man – I never did. Well, I never did.'

'James.' Some white man called.

'Sire?' Surprise insisted.

'Man – take the damn keel and get out of here. Surprise, get clear off this island before I change my mind – or get sober.'

'Thank you. Thank you, Master James.' Piss and smell of a billygoat, that 'Master' just slipped out – who cares. Surprise was already striding for the shore. It would take three good hours to get to Boaz, get the *Teazer* and get back – no, he'd

21

haul it now behind his dinghy and never mind how long it took or if it burned the palms off him rowing.

It was as good as the day you was born, as the old folks would say – Surprise got the backbone of his ship. This is the day Surprise got *it* – got everything. Time he get her built, time he get her launched, he could get the girl. Little Delia, she was the sweetest dinghy on St David's all right, and every blade and buck was after her. She was already sweet on him – and had been since she was about twelve years. Her father was mean and protective and would ask a lot – fact of the matter, he looked like he never wanted to part with her. But if he, Surprise owned the *best* boat in Bermuda, the best boat any black man likely ever did own – why the girl would want him more than ever. Let the girl turn the father's head – and what man could refuse to have his daughter marry the master of such a craft?

And sweet little Delia from St David's was a woman now – even a damn fool could tell that looking through the wrong end of a ship's glass. A woman of fourteen years and all sails set. . . . Delia was something else, some child – as the old folks say – some child: active as a young colt and quick to laugh aloud. Some child, why, just by the way she look at you and smile, and leave her mouth open – and it all the time moist-looking, wet – leave her mouth open in the breeze and look. She was enough to turn a leaf into a banana. The more he thought about it, the more he realised he'd better get her for himself, and quick, afore someone else took her. . . .

The wind veered around to the nor'-west so it was dead ahead of him. He stroking his oars and only making about five hundred yards to the hour – no matter.

He could see her, the *Bateau Bermudien*, riding astern of him now. Furled sails and raked mast and flags flying – twenty-eight feet on the gun deck, ten whole feet of a beam, about thirty-eight to forty tons burthen and drawing near six feet. A whole fathom of draught. She was no ship of the line, as the Limeys said, but then he'd never said she was the biggest, just the *best*. The *Bateau Bermudien* – the best, and she was all his.

To own your own ship and be her master. One time Beau Nat had said about his best brigantine, the *Experiment* (and just like Hezekiah Fitch to *buy* a Limey ship and call it *Experiment* when it was no experiment – Beau Nat's being all new and his own design): 'A man build a ship and he puts his blood and thus his heart in it – a man steer that ship and be her master, that man can feel the sea and the stars, and his soul is in the ship.'

Aye, and that was the *Experiment*, and after that we build the *Improvement*, the schooner – and no Hezekiah Fitch could have even *dreamed* of creating the likes of her. The *Improvement* was the cedar travelling chariot of the deep : on her first voyage we made Land's End from St George's in eighteen days – and not the other way around, that easy. Eighteen days including running into a gale. . . .

The *Improvement*, and, one time, me and Captain Darrell and the *Improvement*, logged more than 12,000 miles in but fifty-two days under canvas – and that including the traverses.

And that last time, Captain Darrell putting to sea and him Sept 1840 sick and hoping the warm weather of the Indies put him to rights – and us only a few hours out of St George's and he call.

Down in his cabin, his face maimed with the pain of his bowels, he say : 'Surprise, it is no good anymore. The motion of my own ship is tearing my guts, my own timbers. Surprise, put about and lay up again for home, for Bermuda.'

'Aye, master, I will.'

'And Surprise,' he called out. 'Lay her close to the wind – not too close to shake me to pieces, mind, but close – close, for I fear I never see home again.'

And he, Surprise, lay that ship for home, and, by his hand, lay her in and out of the ocean rollers as slick as you could slip a dinghy through the inland Sound – as slick as the motion of love.

'Master, Beau Nathaniel, friend of my life, you die and a May 1841 part of Surprise die with you. The shipwright who carved that man, never carve another his equal – but the same shipwright, if he be one, cut him down, too, cut him down with pain and fever as sure as if he a ship and he set afire like the *Bee*.'

Surprise paused in his rowing, stopped the short hand stroke and wiped his palms on his face. Tears, he thought, are even kinder than salt water for the hands chafed by rowing. All other men, beside Darrell, laid beside him, keel to keel, were mere imitations of the man himself. I seen a few men, and

23

women, too, as would turn human heads – but Captain Darrell, when he passed by, even horses would mind.

What other man could log 12,000 miles in fifty-two days? Though the *Improvement* be a girt ship indeed – girt, yet sharp as a dinghy, too, and tall, tall spars and sails as tall as knives. . . .

III

May
and
June
1841
And once they got the keel adzed and laid down good, he and Saul (Senex, his father) and his friend August, took on a new heart and worked like demons.

And weeks and weeks they worked (all the time fishing as well – to eat, to live—and Senex running his ferry service, too) and the frames came up good and each piece of cedar from their precious stock, each piece and every knee were fit together like a Chinese puzzle.

And when they were missing a piece they looked hard : it no good having a knee to brace one way and it grew on the cedar tree another – that weak and bad. Each piece, as it once support a tree, so must it now support the ship.

And if they didn't find just the right piece in their stockpile, then they'd walk the wild places, no-man's land, till they found it growing. Then they'd look around, and if seeing no one they'd lop it off quickly and then head back for The Crawl in Surprise's dinghy.

It got to be the time when she was almost finished – barring her rigging and finishing and equipping – almost ready to launch, to ride the water.

In their little shipyard the smell of cut cedar was heavy on the air, a deep rich heavy perfume, and wherever you stood your whole foot sank deep in cedar chips and shavings – a sweet memorial pile to their long labour.

July
1841
It got to be that time and he and August put out for some deep, deep sea fishing. They took *Teazer* and towed the dinghy and went a way, way out to the sou'-west, to the far, far Banks, where you caught the big groupers. Many times he and August had been out there : the furthest fishing ground

24

that was over six hours' good sailing beyond sight of land. There, especially at nightfall and at dawn, you could catch the big groupers. You only needed to catch two or, perhaps, three, since the big ones, the really big ones, weighed a half as much as a man. (And if you salted them down good and right, the fish meat could last a whole season – and the heads good for chowder on the fire and the parts left over good for feeding hogs and chickens.)

And he and August had been talking, musing, dream and hope talking in the long hours between first light and before it gets hot. They had been talking : 'How come it came to be,' August was asking, 'that men so close when at sea . . . ? I mean, how come so close at sea and so shy and separate on land? Even men like your Beau Nat?'

'It always been that way,' Surprise was saying when he first saw the British brig heave in sight. 'It always been that way – that's what I hear. It always been no black and white at sea – just seamen. And then it change when you step ashore. Deddy always says, you want to tell if a white man is *real bad* – you go to sea with him. If'n he ain't colour blind outa sight of land he ain't got no heart—if'n he still ain't colour blind when the first squall hits, he ain't got no head.'

'I never ship with any that damn stoopid – not the latter,' August said and Surprise could tell that the brig, by the way she was behaving, was laying right towards them with a purpose.

'Myself,' Surprise said, 'I long did figure they *gotta* be colour blind at sea : how long it been that three out of four seamen been coloured? Since the beginning, I reckon.'

'Surprise. Surprise, just say we *did* sail that sweet boat away. Just *say* we did – could you figure?'

Surprise knew what he was asking and the answer before August said : 'I mean, really figure where we been and exactly where we at? Could you?'

'I reckon so.'

'No – no, man. You couldn't stand up on the heaving deck with your legs spread wide apart like a captain and aim that thing at the sun and then go right to the chart, unroll it and put your finger down and say, there. We is right *there*. You couldn't do that.'

'What you mean, couldn't? You never seen me is all. You

25

never seen me at sea with Captain Darrell. He not like the captains you known – he teach Surprise everything.'

'I'd sure like to believe you. How you tell how fast and far your ship gone – how *you* do it, never mind Captain Darrell?'

'Just judgement – knowing your ship's speed on every quarter, knowing the wind. Judging the tides. All judgement.'

'Man, I'd like to believe you.'

'What you talking about,' Surprise snapped, 'is called a sextan – you hear, a sextan. And I got one.'

'You have!'

'Yes – now what you make of that?' He pointed at the brig, bearing down on them on a broad reach, with the white ensign flying, standing out clear off the mainsail.

'She steering right for us. Surprise, that ship is coming right for us.'

'Uh-huh. I known it now for nigh on a half-hour. Question is, what that Limey bluecoat want?'

'He won't take us – he won't press us?'

'Man, don't talk so fullish. Press, hell. You know no British press a negro man. We coloured. To them Limeys we still belong to someone – never you mind. Whatever he want, it ain't to press us aboard in service of no Royal Navy.'

They waited, and, before long, the cry came across the water.

'Heave to. Heave to, there!'

'Just breathe easy, August, breathe easy.'

'It's you who better breathe easy and keep a cool head – *you*, Surprise. It you got the temper, not August.'

'Now ain't that typical of that Navy – "Heave to," he says, and us still on the water, us been hove-to and still on the water for hours and hours.' Surprise moved out of the *Teazer*'s cockpit and waved to the brig.

She was shortening sail but barrelling down on them.

'What ship is that?'

'Fisherman,' Surprise yelled. 'Fisherman from Bermuda.'

'What?'

The brig had gone by and was now making a girt noise, rattling, luffing up into the wind. It took them all manner of time to come about, Surprise noticed – and typical of the Royal Navy, she had not only stopped, lost way entirely, but was going astern, backwards, before she filled her sails again.

26

She started, slowly, to settle on a course that would bring her close by their other side.

'Fisherman – give the number of your crew.'

'Two.'

'Two?'

'Two, only – fisherman from Sandy's, Bermuda.' The brig was sloshing along, creating a great wake, but not getting any place at all hardly, and Surprise could see the seamen curiously watching from her leeward rails. In a while, he knew, she'd be windward of them and then would come the stench – one time on the *Experiment*, a big ship of the line had hailed that she was British and Beau Nat had said, quietly, 'Odour like that, in these waters, you could be no other.'

'Give your names and the name of your owner – your master on land in Bermuda.'

'Surprise. Don't say you own this ship – nor your deddy. Say a white man.'

'Fishermen – two only. Names: Billinghurst, known as Surprise, and August Napier.'

'Who owns your craft?'

'Billinghurst of Sandy's.'

The gold-braided lieutenant was writing it down. Surprise noted that he was an old man – fifty probably. A lieutenant of fifty was a damn fool or a drunk, or both, most likely.

'You seen any vessel?'

'None.'

'You seen any vessel these past several hours?'

'None.'

'How many hours?'

'Been out since yesterday afternoon time and seen none.'

'Name is Billinghurst?'

The brig was almost stopped, in stays again, rattling like an old horse wagon.

'Aye, sire, Billinghurst of Sandy's.'

'You been out overnight and seen no sail?'

'Aye.'

The lieutenant wrote it all down carefully and called over a midshipman and he too wrote in the book.

'Put up for St George's.'

Surprise heard the order as clear as if he were aboard the brig.

27

'Lay north-north-east.'

Surprise paused, looked all about and then hailed:

'Captain. You for St George's?'

The other did not answer.

'Captain. If you for St. George's,' only a few feet of water separated the two craft, 'you'd better sail north-east by east and a half east.'

'Helmsman – Jenkins. Lay north-north-east.'

August said: 'Leave them be, Surprise – why we care?'

'Captain, if you are interested in clear water, sail north-east by east and a half east.'

'Close your mouth, darkey,' a sailor said, 'who do you think you're talking to?'

'Then pray the sea doesn't close over you,' Surprise said and went back to his fishing.

But they both heard the lieutenant shout: 'You'll be logged as lawbreakers.'

Surprise threw over a line baited sweet with shark flesh, the skin and flesh doubled and redouble hooked. 'Shit, these British. Some seamen. He right on top of a bank – he got no more than a fathom under his skeg, under his very arse – and he don't know it. He don't even know enough to have a man on the lead.'

'Must be blind as well as dumb,' August said, pointing at the bright clear coral-tinted water. 'What he think that pale colour is? Ocean?'

And it seemed like, looking back on it, no sooner had they moored up the *Teazer* at The Crawl and got everything put away and washed down shipshape – it seemed like no sooner than that, except maybe that Surprise had had time to think on Delia, and think on that open wet mouth in the breeze and think about what that mouth might do, could do and it be his, than along came the British in a fancy cutter, rowing around fifty strokes to the minute, and, bowswain's whistles flying and a young midshipman decked out in as much gold-braid as you would have thought he was a little cedar tree set afire in a winter squall.

'Ahoy. Are you the black known as Surprise? Ahoy! Ahoy, I say. Are the you the black known as Surprise?'

'Yes. Easy, man, easy.'

'I have here orders from Her Majesty's Magistrate – '

A mouthful, Surprise thought, a mouthful at that. The midshipman must be one of the lucky ones – by the cut of his jib he had more money than manners, never mind sea time.

'Give me the paper,' Surprise shouted. 'Give me the paper.' He sure liked one thing about these official times: showing a white man that he, Surprise, a free negro, could read.

But what he read, first off, gave him a shiver of cold down at the bottom of his spine: 'Perient Reid, Magistrate'. Never mind what else he might make out now or later, Perient Reid was the white man that would most like to flay him, Surprise Billinghurst, flay him alive if he could.

'Easy, sire, easy.' Surprise looked at the midshipman, looked at him hard.

'I'll take you in custeddy – that's what I'll do.'

'Easy, sire, easy.' Surprise looked the youngster up and down, slowly, looking as if he could open his black mouth and eat him like a shark. 'It say here next Friday at Hamilton. I'll be there. Surprise Billinghurst will be there at break of day.'

And, long after the cutter had gone, Surprise's back and lower spine twitched. Them Limeys and that goddamn Perient Reid – God alone knew what they'd do.

'. . . disobedience in being out offshore after nightfall, in a fishing boat, with another negro sailor. . . .' Smell of a billy-goat, he could like as not get August off the hook – his *name* nowhere appeared on the paper – but, he, Surprise was hooked good.

And how the hell did a slippery white trash like Perient Reid get to be a magistrate? He asked Senex, but Senex said, quite rightly, didn't make no never mind, he was – and that was a fact.

And it was just two days later, and still two days before the Friday he was due to appear before the magistrate in Hamilton, that he saw Delia's father, King Jack, of Dolly's Bay, sailing past the mouth of The Crawl. As nice an omen as could be: to have King Jack appear, so far from home, and just two days from the dreaded day ahead.

King Jack himself, sitting, as always, on top of a rum barrel, being steered in his own ship (a real irregular St David's Island craft called by many, an hermaphrodite – she being composed

29

of all types of rigging and sails and even out-riggers) by one
of his tattered and raggedy subjects. King Jack was puffing on
a dead cigar and conning the water – and like as not for bait,
for fry, but, Surprise knew, if you asked him what he was
looking for, he'd like as not say he was looking for gold from
a Spanish galleon – for King Jack, like most of his subjects,
was not given to understatement.

Surprise put out in his dinghy and hailed them and King
Jack had his preposterous, but nevertheless highly workable,
craft luffed up.

'What ye want, Surprise sailor man?'

'King Jack, come into The Crawl and I show you something
from the Western Isles that make you Eastern fellas seasick.'

'If what you got to show me can be washed down with a
little of what's-good-for-what-ails-you, King Jack might just
do that.'

'That easy. I would not ask you to our home, to our little
port, without blessing your visit with some sweetener, King
Jack. Now would I?'

'Reckon not, Surprise. It being July and the days of the
Dog Star upon us – and these Dog Days liable to last nigh
eight to ten weeks, so my weatherman tells me.'

Surprise knew very well that King Jack's weather foreteller
was renowned throughout the whole colony, never mind St
David's, but he said: 'Saul says the Dog Days will be short
this year – and he the best – '

'Best, hell, he couldn't tell a storm if it fell on him and him
looking up a fowl's arse – my weatherman is *the* prophet, you
hear?'

'As you say, King Jack. At any rate, step aboard my dinghy
and I show you something you never seen. And, as you know,
there's no better sweetener than Halcyon's Barbadoes.'

'Is it Nelson's Blood, Surprise? King Jack ain't coming to
The Crawl to taste no yella or white piss liquor, you know?'

'It's dark 'n' stormy, your majesty – who you think giving
you the invitation, some green cabin boy?'

'I come.' King Jack stood up and hitched his trousers – a
difficult task, since he had what was locally known as a no-toes
belly. Indeed, King Jack's belly was so large – though his
heavy and muscular legs could well carry it – that some were
fooled into thinking he couldn't lift it at all, when, though he

often sat still and silent for hours drinking rum and smoking, in fact, he was as agile as a bird, and, when riled up good, had been known to snatch up two men at a time like chickens. King Jack was, the wise knew, as powerful as a bull and his belly only added weight to an argument.

He got aboard without hardly rocking the dinghy and sat quiet amidships.

'You been keeping well?'

No answer.

Surprise sculled fast for the calm bay of The Crawl. The dinghy slipped through the water and Surprise, on purpose, made it look as if he was not working at all, not putting the least effort into it. In fact, with his wrists, he was secretly hefting her through the water – it was a trick, and, doubtless, King Jack knew it and could do as well himself.

'How's the family, King Jack?'

No answer.

He know damn well I'm trying to get him to take the hook so I can strike him, Surprise thought, and said:

'How is Miss Delia?'

King Jack stood up, squirted tobacco juice over the side, without making a sound save what it made in splashing on the still water of The Crawl, where they now were.

'This a almost half good dinghy – where you get it? You musta steal it from St David's.'

'No St David's dinghy ain't ever seen any part of this sweet flyer save her stern.'

King Jack squirted juice again and Surprise sculled around the point and into the mangrove trees close by where the *Bateau Bermudien* lay on the ways, mostly hidden.

King Jack of Dolly's Bay walked all around her, looking, sniffing. The cedar smelled even deeper than before since they had treated it with oil so that the whole of her shone like a new piece of furniture.

Jack paced her out, eyed the bow, touched her topsides, eyed the stern, moved the great thick rudder. In all, after Surprise had given him the earthenware rum jug, he passed a full fifteen minutes in total silence, then he shook his heavy, high-cheekboned head – King Jack, a coloured man, but born free, not freed, and part Mohawk and Mohican and Pequod Indian and part white, too, they said, and proud of it all –

31

shook his head, had another pull of the jug, went down to the water's edge, urinated, came back, walked around again and said:

'Smells like a fucking girt coffin.'

Surprise did not crack a smile, indeed, he struck: 'She mine – and I have min' to marry Miss Delia. What you say?'

'She say you have this girt coffin.'

'How she know?'

'Man, you born in Bermuda and you don't know King Jack of St David's knows *everything* about everybody.'

'All right, your majesty, what you say, I want Miss Delia?'

'You think my Delia is half-witted?'

'Why should I?'

'You think she want you and not know what you got?'

'No.'

'You better not.'

Silence.

King Jack hoisted his trousers. 'No dickering. I ain't no Yankee preacher blown away and washed ashore, you know.'

'Right.'

'No dickering. King Jack say he want a pregnant sow, a forty-gallon keg of high-proof rum – from Halcyon, mind, not yella piss – and, naturally, a cockerel to prove your manhood, and naturally, from you, a seafaring man, this here coffin.'

'Proves what I heard.'

'What?'

'What I heard.'

Silence.

'Goddamn you – what you heard?'

Surprise spat and said, slowly: 'I heard King Jack gone so plumb fullish he drink salt water.'

'That so?'

'Must be – the King ask for my ship.'

'All right, it's settled then: not the coffin but that there St David's dinghy you stole.'

Surprise hid his relief: 'We talk again – but, for the main part – except the dinghy – I agree.'

'Surprise, sailor man. Now I know that, to most men, a dinghy worth a hell of a lot more'n a daughter – but not King Jack. And not my Delia – dinghy or no daughter, you hear?'

'We talk again, King Jack.'

His majesty did some more strutting, kicking cedar chips with his toes. He picked up a sliver of white cedar and put it to his teeth. 'Day you come to Dolly's Bay with the rum – forty gallons – the peeg, the cockerel and that there dinghy – that day you could very well jump with Delia.'

'I give your bargain careful consideration, your majesty. I think it over.'

Jack looked all around the sky, tipped his straw hat over his left eye, looked back at Surprise and said :

'Where the hell you think you are going in this here *sea*going ship ?'

'Any place I have mind.'

'I believe you fool enough to be serious. Surprise, man, let me tell you a truth.' He spat. His face, Surprise noticed, had softened, was almost fatherly. 'You ain't going nowhere except around Bermuda. See me, King Jack. King of Colour. Me, King and me never got a seagoing surety and *licence* – never –'

'Why so ?'

'Surprise – I'm *surprised* you ask. You gotta pass a test.'

'I can read and write –'

'I know – make no difference. They see your skin coming and they make that test written in Roman Catholic scripture –'

'No.'

'Yes – or maybe Chinee. You read Chinee ?'

'No.' Surprise felt a fool.

'Yes. You going no place but around these islands – no coloured man *ever* got a surety and that my surety to you.'

'I get it, King Jack.'

'You never get it – hear me and I give you an engagement piece of wisdom : you want a licence you have to go to goddamn Hispaniola. You prepared to go ?'

'No.' Surprise lied : 'I never leave home.'

'Then that my present to you – wisdom and truth in the face of clear folly, folly most *famous*. You going no place.'

Surprise choked back his disappointment, like swallowing black vomit to windward in a northern gale : 'I going – I coming – to St David's by 'n' by. That where I going.'

'And that *all* – you hear ?'

Surprise never answered.

IV

And so, when he and his father came back in the *Teazer* that night in July 1841, his mind was made up: he, Surprise, was going to quit Bermuda, sail away. As soon as he could rig and finish the ship, as soon as he could get Delia, pay and settle with her father – but without telling Senex or his woman until it was settled – as soon as he could get five other strong men, besides himself and August, he was setting sail.

Where to, could be settled later: he had in mind maybe Jamaica where, he'd heard, a revolt of freed slaves had already taken place, or maybe an outer island of the Bahamas, or maybe even Hispaniola, where he *knew* a black rule existed – but someplace.

Not that Liberty place in Africa. Shit if he, Surprise, a Bermudian master helmsman was going to go back to Africa – shit he was. Not to that wild place and them wild people all a'yelling and screaming some foreign tongue like monkeys in a tree. Shit if he'd go to a foreign place like Africa and be a monkey. Shit he would.

He took his soap and went down to the water's edge to do a sailor's ablutions. Surprise do his ablutions, shave and put on his best britches and jacket and go court Delia. Pay court to the court of her father: King Jack, King of Dolly's Bay, St David's.

The cuts of the whip hurt bad. August had wanted to go with him earlier. Surprise had said: 'Two cut backs don't make one uncut back – besides, conserve. It the law of the sea to conserve.' But it could have been worse, he thought: they could have thrown him in jail. . . . Forget the pain, think of little Delia.

More'n likely he'd have to give the dinghy, his precious cedar dinghy and that would mean a day and a half day's walk home: but if'n he got Delia to be his, he reckoned it wouldn't prove so far: nothing was far when you were happy, no more than an ocean was far when a good ship had a quartering breeze and a bone in her mouth. . . .

Even with the wind from the south-west and freshish, it would take him more than four hours to sail to St David's, he figured. Even with his dinghy, the flyer of the Western Isles, with her leg o' mutton sail.

He got his best cockerel, and, holding him upside down by his feet, lowered him into a lobster pot – best fowl cage made. He put it in the bow – have to be careful not to take too much water, drown the beast. Cockerels are damn stupid.

The sow he lifted and lowered her down amidships – she was the pregnant one all right, she sat down on the floorboards as content as an old woman in church. He took a rope and tied it around her neck and to a thwart – but it wasn't hardly necessary, unless the beast got scared by something.

He got August to help him roll the keg of rum down to the shore and gently over the dinghy's gunwale and rested just aft of the pig.

'Why don't you let a little out, Surprise? Let a little out and add water. No one would know.'

'Too risky. King Jack is no man to get riled up, you know.'

'Reckon not.' August tied a big piece of white cloth around the sow's neck. 'Humm – there you are – she decked out for a wedding now.'

'You coming August?'

'No. I'll come tomorrow afternoon – for the celebrations. What you got to do, you got to do alone.'

'True.'

They shoved the dinghy into The Crawl until she floated.

'Don't tell Saul or his Emiline, you hear?'

'You think I'm fullish?'

'No.'

'Only way to keep Emiline's mouth still is not to feed it nothing through the ears.'

'True,' said Surprise.

August pointed to the mouth of the bay: 'Goes the Death Boat.'

Surprise just looked for a long time. The black pinnace, rowed by convicts, went by often enough – indeed, at least once a week and had been doing so for decades. Surprise knew that, hidden below her topsides would be a rough coffin – or two. Sometimes, when fever was about, the British made the convicts bury their dead daily, and not by ones or twos, but by the score.

The dead were all buried several miles away, on the mainland of Sandy's Parish: on the northern end of Mangrove Bay.

'They don't care what it cost,' August said, 'to build a fort, do they?'

'I seen Gibraltar once,' Surprise said. ' 'Tis reckoned they killed them by the thousand to build that fort – a body for every stone, that's the British way.'

'They have hulks at Gibraltar?' August was referring to the convict hulks, roofed-over aged ships of the line, that the Royal Navy housed their prisoners in.

'Everywhere there's British, there's convicts – modernised slave labour.'

'How come they ain't coloured slaves – I always did wonder?'

'Captain Darrell – he made a sad joke. He said, it's a damn good thing the Limeys know all Bermudians are bone lazy, otherwise they'd enslave us all – never mind coloured, white, too.'

'It's pitiful to think of them all cooped up in the heat – worse than fowls for shipping. Worse than rats. How come we don't set 'em loose, Surprise?'

'Set 'em loose, hell. You want to die. I maybe getting hard, August, but you know how I feel : I just *hate* those convicts. I hate their potato peels and their shit – it make our home like a soil house.'

'Wind in the wrong quarter it do – remember once when I was a boy. Winds in March from the nor'-east – right in The Crawl, you could walk on it.'

'I'm going, August. Going to Dolly's Bay.'

'Good, Surprise.' August shoved him off deeper and stood with the water over his knees, his britches turning dark from the wet. 'And God speed you to your girl.'

'See you, August.' Surprise slipped the handle of his oar through the circular hole in his transom. No sooner had he unfurled his sail than the wind caught him and the dinghy took off across the water like a longtail.

Delia was short, very small-boned, compact, high-breasted and of the darkest complexion Surprise ever saw that still showed freckles. The freckles were, he knew, from her white – or maybe it was her Indian blood.

Standing next to Captain Darrell, Surprise was always conscious that he was shortish, standing next to Delia, he felt like a giant.

First time he could remember seeing her, although she was still only a child, it had flashed through his imagination that he'd pick her up, and her naked, and hang her, tenderly, on his erect member.

She still weren't much bigger than a big doll (such as wealthy white girl children play with) and it sure made a man feel strong and alive and powerful and happy to be looked at with lust by one so little.

And Surprise reckoned Senex was right about the way her legs set her body – good for childbearing. Truth was, the way they set and the way her mound stood out and her belly in, looked like she'd been designed special just to fit a man – and what Surprise wanted was for that man to be him.

And when his dinghy scraped bottom on the sand of Dolly's Bay, he heard a voice out of the half-dark, a small high-pitched voice, 'Surprise,' followed by a giggle. 'Surprise, that be you?'

He stepped in the water, and, no sooner had he felt it, than he felt her, as wet and alive as a new-caught fish – and she pressed against him and she sure fit good. Hugged him and wriggled and squirmed like a little fish.

'I come to court for you,' he said, hesitantly. 'I brought everything King Jack asked after.'

'Surprise,' she said, taking hold with more of a mind of a woman, than, he thought for a moment, he'd quite bargained for. 'Surprise – I'm going with you. Going with you soon. I ain't staying around for no drunken man party neither, you hear?'

'Sure – but the ceremony and all.'

'Ceremony, yes, drunken party, no. We jump, we go.'

'Easy girl. How we going? I gotta give him the dinghy. We gotta walk twenty miles and more, afterwards – after we get to the mainland.'

'No we ain't.' She kissed his mouth – and put her tongue in him too, and pressed hard against him again.

'What you say?' he asked when she broke away.

'We ain't. I got a ride for us – a ship going from St George's to Hamilton tomorrow daybreak.'

'How you fix that?'

'The captain is a man, Surprise. I just asked.'

'What captain?'

'A big white whiskers from New York.'

'How come he say yes – a white man to you? *How he say "yes"?*'

'He say "Ye-eh-ss".'

'You some child, you are.'

King Jack's people were coming down to the bay with a flare – shouting and laughing.

Delia stood proudly by him: the great Surprise from the Western Isles: her man, him with the chest as powerful as the prow of a girt ship. And her dressed in the white frock her mother wove and she, Delia, made: it had arms but no shoulders, was pleated above her bosom, caught in an interwoven blue sash immediately below and then fell, in straight abundance, to her ankles. Now it was a little wet from the water, but she didn't mind that.

An old man came up and put his face only inches from Surprise's chest and looked up at him intently.

'You sailor man? You really been across the beeg sea?'

'Aye.'

'The beeg, *beeg* sea – to Mother England?'

'Aye. And you – you been to England?'

'No, sailor man. I like most everybody else – I stay put. But my grand-daddy go places.'

'Where he go, friend?'

'He go Hamilton.'

'He did?'

'Uh-huh. He go to Hamilton *twice*. Not me. I stay to home where I belong.'

The people gathered up the rum keg, the cockerel, and, after hauling the dinghy clear above high water, led the pig up to the clearing where King Jack sat, outdoors, in his favourite cedar seat with a lighted flare on either side of him.

Surprise, with Delia waiting behind in the relative darkness, went forward.

'I brought all the gifts in accordance with our bargain, your majesty. Brought all and good measure.'

'So I see.' King Jack spat, as usual, and turned his head. 'Woman, is that sow pregnant?'

But he did not expect an answer. He got up – everyone fell silent save the chirping tree frogs. 'Delia will sing.' He sat down and picked up a jug of rum and put it to his lips, all in the same movement.

Delia sang in a small true voice, the long song which ended :

> '. . . my father was a sailor,
> my brother, a sailor was he,
> And the man who'd be my lover,
> A sailor he must be.'

A little silence followed – for there was hardly one present who was not missing a father or a brother or both, to the ever-present element.

King Jack rose again, and said, severely : 'Surprise, sailor man from the Western Isles, you cursed with the evil eye of Adam – ' he spat. 'And, Delia, she cursed too, even as Eve and the serpent. Bring the stick.'

The older women came forward with the broomstick. The wickered end was set alight in the fire.

'Before all gathered here present and before all our kin, living and dead and yet to be – you, Delia and you, Surprise, join hands and jump.'

They joined hands, and, approaching the flaming stick, jumped, single-bounded, together clear over it as if they had rehearsed it many times.

Cheers rang out.

'Before all present, you be man and wife, 'til death.' King Jack sat down heavily. 'Pass the bottle,' he said. 'Goddamnit, pass the bottle.'

Surprise and Delia, when the violin played, danced first together. Then many joined in. Surprise danced with Delia's mother and cheers rang out.

Then King Jack rose, and, with his renowned lightness of foot, danced, with Surprise, they facing each other with hands on hips, a local version of the hornpipe.

Cheers more boisterous followed. King Jack immediately went back to his bottle and cigar.

When Surprise at last found himself dancing again with Delia – and held her close, it being, at last, their right, he said : 'Delia, this as close to heaven as I ever expect to be – but what in hell is hitting me between the legs?'

'My gold,' she whispered up to his ear.

'Your gold?'

'Yes,' she said emphatically. '*My gold*. You didn't think I was going to leave without it, did you?'

'I dunno.'

'Well, I ain't. Neither was no one going to take it – save thee – it being where I hung it.'

Within the span of time as seemed respectable, Delia and Surprise slipped away from the light into the sage and oleander and hibiscus bushes.

The party, they later heard, went on for three days – but, by dawn that first morning, they were in St George's to catch their ride, in the big Yankee ship, up the North Shore, to Hamilton Harbour.

From there, Surprise knew, they could board the *Teazer* – and a good thing it was they were leaving at first light, for a nasty looking black thunderhead was brewing up off over the North-East Breakers.

It was a run-of-the-mill brigantine, Surprise quickly noted, built mostly of pine and oak. Piss poor wood in comparison with cedar. The captain didn't bother them none, and, a kindly soul, he wouldn't take money: 'Not off the Lord's children on their wedding day,' he said, and shuffled off astern mumbling something about 'barefoot in paradise'.

They went for'ard and sat just ahead of the crew's hatch, half-hidden and out of the way of the capstan and any sheets.

Delia, who had been, all the while, touching him, holding one of his great arms with both her hands, whispered in his ear: 'You sure? You sure I didn't hurt you none – touching and grasping at your back? I didn't know it was bad and deep cuts. You sure I didn't hurt you?'

'Girl, Girl, making love to you, I didn't feel anything but you and me.'

'Sure?'

'Girl, you better believe it. You remember: I was rolling on them cuts and didn't notice.'

'You certainly a strong man, Surprise – but you got pain now?' She touched his back with the very tips of her small fingers.

He took both her hands in his left hand – she could feel the rough callouses.

'Girl, Delia, I got you I got everything.'

'Uh-huh.'

'Yeah – and you wait until you see my ship. Wait till you see *Bateau Bermudien*. You wait.'

'I hear it's big – a match to you, Surprise – and decked out beautiful. A seagoing ship, Deddy say.'

'I was just thinking,' Surprise said, as the brigantine began to be hauled clear of the dock.

'Thinking what?'

'Thinking how I gonna lay out the captain's quarters aft. Quarters for you and me. You know, me and Senex can work real good with our tools. I going to make a cedar head with a cedar lid and latch – just like I planned. Only now I'm going to make a little head beside it – down real low to the deck. Make a little round head for children – low, so they can reach easy. Uh-huh, right beside ours.'

She whispered in his ear, he could just see, out of focus, the wind move her close hair about her head – a squall hit them, for a moment, that brisk. 'How come it call a head and it for an arse, man?'

'I dunno.'

'And who said I was bearing any children – and the wedding fire still burning?'

'It burning all right.'

'Stop that. Leave off, now.'

He laughed with a low outgoing breath and she could feel the great rumble of it deep in his chest. Girt and deep sound, as if she were a child making noises in the bunghole of an empty barrel.

'Delia – you want children, don't you?'

His questioning face, so often seen by her as forbidding, knowing, even sardonic, was now so boyish, so tender, that she felt a small ache of her nipples. 'I want your children, Surprise from the Western Isles – and a lot of 'em.'

'How many?'

'No less than ten – and that's a fact. Mamma had nine – gotta lick her record.'

The crew were hauling up the mainsail and it was rattling its hoops; two others hoisted a jib to bring her around.

'Larboard your helm – and hard,' the captain shouted.

Surprise looked anxious – they'd head straight back for the dockface. Then he realised it was a wheel and not a tiller helm. And Yankees gave helm orders that were upside down to Bermudians : the order was to move the helm to larboard, not the ship's bow.

The brigantine came around, and nice, too, and the captain was good, considering it was, doubtless, a strange harbour to him. But, typical mean Yankee, he was not paying for any local pilot.

Surprise turned back to Delia.

'You frown and it go clear back over your head, Surprise – go back like a wave of the sea. What ailing you?'

He whispered to her. 'I'm embarrassed, see – what if you need to make water? These Yankees funny – you never know how they feel.'

'Never mind.'

'I mean – I wouldn't want you going into their forecastle – their man-quarters, see. All manner of rudeness might follow.'

'Never mind. I can hold it to Hamilton.'

'Maybe three hours or more.'

'I hold it.' She laughed. 'One time, when I was a girl – I hold it all day in a boat. An open boat.'

'How?'

'Muscles, man, muscles.'

Out of St George's Cut, the ship jibed and came up smartly and they soon rounded Fort St Catherine's.

'Limey bitches,' Surprise said, gesturing at the great, ancient but newly-restored fort.

She tugged his arm.

'It wasn't what I did, you know – in being out offshore after nightfall. It wasn't that.'

'No.'

'No. It was all this man Perient Reid. The white cockroach.' Surprise felt strangely, newly and happily easy with her – you knew, without ever asking, that she was the kind of female who wouldn't wag her mouth. Not Delia, too proud, too strong.

'It were Perient Reid I beat up on, once. Years ago – right back there in St George's Square. Now you know, a coloured

42

man strike a white man of property and he destined to die – probably slow. But I went fullish. See, this Perient Reid – he a bad man, a bad actor. He one mean bascombe. He whip this coloured woman, see, he whip her bad and she got only one arm – the other withered.

'And she got a suckling child at her breast, and right in the Square he whipping her. And I went blind – it were a good thing no one hardly around at the time. But I go fullish and grip up his whip and start in hitting him. Pretty soon I hitting him with the thick end of the whip.'

Delia was touching the back of his thick neck, very gently, with her fingers. She was wondering, if he frowned hard enough, this girt Surprise man, would his frown go right over and wrinkle the back of his neck, too.

'And, next thing I know, Captain Darrell grabbed me and he start whipping Reid – see. He whip him like a dog. And he tell me, real sharp, but low – go stand by the horse, like nothing happen, hold the horse.

'And he whip Mr Reid and I hear him say to him – him holding him by the collar : "Reid, you see who beat you this day. You see?" And he whip him again and Mr Reid squeal like a stuck pig. And Captain grab him again and say : "Nathaniel Darrell whip you for whipping a helpless woman – and, Reid, I ever hear you say otherwise and you know what will happen. . . ."

'And I could not hear what else he say to Mr Reid – but, I know Darrell, and he likely say he ever hear anything else and he kill Reid. Because Captain Darrell like that : he got a terrible temper. Worstest temper in all creation – and men, white men know it. He a fair man – but you cross him bad. You cross Nat Darrell and he liable to kill you.

'I never seen it, but I heard once he caught a seaman messing with a boy. You know, *bad* messing. Man tell me that Darrell, he seeing the cabin boy hurt bad. He took up a marlin spike and smash this bad man's face right in and throw him overboard and never even look back—just shake, tremble, and hold his course.

'Anyway, sweet Delia. That's how I get them cuts. Perient Reid, he been after me all these years. But he afraid to act when Captain Darrell alive, see. But, last week he got me.'

'It over, sweet man. It over now. All over.'

'It ain't. That's what I *know*. Mr Perient Reid, he never be satisfied till he seeing me hanging. Hanging from a gibbet like my great-great-grandpappy. I know.'

'But who knows – besides you and him, who hit him?'

'Don't know.'

'None, I expect. None.'

'Perhaps.'

'And perhaps, Surprise, he afraid of you, too – '

'Why afraid of me – and him white and a magistrate?'

'Man, you better see yourself in one of them big mirror things in Hamilton. You see yourself. I *afraid* of you and you my love man. So imagine how he feel.

'How big a man is this white Perient Reid man?'

'He a small thing – look like a angry crab. With a red face and nose. He a angry red-faced *land* crab.'

'Then I bet he scared as a little squid squirting black ink – I bet so. All you gotta do, Surprise, is steer clear of him. Give him a wide berth.'

'Where you hear that talk?'

'Deddy. The old king is smart, you know.'

'Delia, I tell you a fact truth. I scared of Reid.'

'Yeah. Who wouldn't be? But he give you trouble – you go talk to King Jack. I figure if this Reid know you *and* King Jack together, he shit hisself.'

Surprise laughed and looked around. Then he put his hand on her soft hair and pushed her shoulder at the same time, and she fell over like a child and got up even quicker, laughing. 'Girl, you don't know. Perient Reid is bad and now he got Limey black British law behind him.'

A sailor in a woollen cap and rough jersey came up. 'Capt'n ask for ye. Aft.'

'I come.' Surprise got up and went back with the man.

It was the exact question he expected:

'Can I cut inside of that there beacon, sailor?'

'It called Spanish Rock, Captain. At high water – inside of it is only four to four and half feet. 'Cept a slim channel – and the wind be out of the north – '

'I go around her, thank ye, sailor. Stand by to come about! Man y'sheets!'

Surprise strode for'ard again – pausing long enough to read, carefully, the name on the ship's bell: *Thos Jefferson*. Oh, yes,

Thomas Jefferson, he was a sort of king, too, president. He knew of Jefferson and Washington and James Monroe – James Monroe was his favourite American king. He felt like a king himself. Delia was indeed a sweet golden thing herself and everything was beautiful.

This ship, he thought, she nigh three times as big as my *Bateau Bermudien*. But his ship, he felt, was the perfect size for him : he wanted no bigger and no smaller. She just fit him right. His ship was the right size for him – it fit his very soul, he felt. In contrast, all other ships were all the wrong size.

It was just the same with his beloved Delia. She was his size : the heft of her just matched his hope and heart. Just lift her and she hefted perfect; and now that he'd known her and the both of them natural naked together, it was as if he'd never made love to a woman before, never even touched a woman – nor known a woman's touch. It felt as if he and Delia had been together since the beginning of time.

It was peculiar, he thought, even like life itself : for we all die and we all are born. Yet I feel as if there never was a time when I wasn't – and though I know, in my mind, I will die, yet I feel there will never be a time when I cease to be.

Strange, and now it felt as if he and Delia had always been naked together, touching each other's bodies in the long grass. Loving and rolling together – and, even as last night, swimming in the dark at Dolly's Bay. Swimming in the dark and a little afraid of what might come out of the dark deep water against them – but not afraid the moment their bodies touched. For Delia's body – her mouth, her head – obliterated all but the sweet and total present. As bright as a falling star but longer lasting, more like the Northern Lights – the Northern Lights he'd first seen as a boy, on a winter's night off Nova Scotia. And those Lights, shimmering, so beautiful because you knew they could not last long – yet they did, they too endured even as if there was never a time when they didn't exist, all beauty shimmering high off the starboard beam, lighting the sails blue-white. . . .

V

Early the following summer Delia bore a son – and Senex, as promised, delivered a new-built Bermuda dinghy. More, he delivered a little miniature dinghy, too, on rockers – a cradle for the child.

Emiline, her tongue stilled for a while, and seemingly caught up with all the building and action and plans, gave to Surprise a strange gift. It was strange, because, when he unfurled it, it was a creation that he instantly recognised as so perfect for his ship that he might have conceived of it himself. It was a large black flag, soot black and six feet in length and wide as the half span of a man. In the left corner she had woven a bright white-winged longtail.

Surprise thanked her but looked hard at Senex and, later, Senex said : 'I told her nothing – but that woman seem to pick things out of the air we breathe.'

'It's all right, Father. It only mean we soon must leave.'

Delia always looked at Emilene warily, and, as if guided by some animal instinct, would not let the woman touch her infant – indeed, if the elder woman went even near the cradle, Delia leapt towards it and grabbed the child in her own arms.

Women were always full of surprises, he thought. Delia : what she do towards the end of her pregnancy time – make swaddling clothes? No, she all the time stealing off in a little boat, all by herself, and, he later found out, throwing loaves of bread up to the Irish convicts in the hulks.

'Them British guards kill you, woman.' He raged when he heard about it. 'Kill you and our child.'

'No, my darling. Even they are men. The time they go to shoot I stand up and show myself and my belly – not even British shoot a small woman and she big with child.'

Full of surprises.

The day he brought her home to Boaz, they went aboard the *Teazer* in Hamilton.

'Senex – this here is my bride.'

'Uh-huh,' Senex muttered and went on coiling rope.

And Delia blurts out, without any embarrassment. 'Father, I need a bucket bad.'

'Below, child.'

It was as if they'd always been family.

The storm from the east was building up that day and it gave them a fast wedding trip home with the wind behind them and the boom wide out and tied. A fast sail home, marred only by the ghastly ship that clanked and belched through Timlin's Narrows.

'Here you are in paradise,' Senex had said. 'Can you imagine a place more like paradise than this?' His hand gave a little wave, as if to indicate it was all too much for him : the deep green of the cedars making a forest all around, even of the little islands, the bright white of the few houses nestled here and there and the flashing colours of the wild flowers.

'It paradise if you are white,' Surprise said. 'If you are coloured, nothing left but our two islands and St David's.' But he too was moved by the scene : especially the black and yellow-tinted storm clouds behind them, raising pregnant fury in the sky, and sea, and exciting their skin – and the bright blue, still remaining in the western sky and reflected in the western sea beneath.

Only the listing, lopsided ugly ship spoiled it. She was fat and high out of the water like a house tipping over – but made of black-painted, rust-streaked, dirty steel.

This ghastly ship clanking towards them, unnatural moving against the wind – even the sound of her defying the wind's direction.

An ugly white cabin house forward of the foremost mast : from there they steered the monster, Surprise knew, for he had seen them before, these hideous modern steamships – new, yet every one always looking old and beaten and ugly however new they were – but he had never known one to invade Bermuda before. And her black smokestack, tall between her tilting, short, useless-looking spars (what sails could they let down to move that thing? She'd move nowhere but to leeward and then no more than a knot with everything set but the captain's stained handkerchief); that smokestack breathing black vomit out of her.

And when she went by, she stank of grease like rancid whale oil and the smoke fell on them, on the sails and Delia's white smock, and, he noticed, fell and even floated on top of the water – like hideous little round black floating coals.

The noise rent the air – spoiled all natural sounds – and, to

47

Surprise's awareness, she was as horrible, as repellant a sight as the five-legged cow once born in Warwick – only worse, for that was an ugly accident of nature and this was a planned creation of man. A thousand Mr Reids, he thought, imagined her and built her – and all of ugly steel.

She flew the British flag – itself grimy, blackened from her bowels.

Across the stern the words, '*Adelaide,* Liverpool'.

'Paradise, Senex,' he called out against her metallic and satanic shatterings: 'You see – behold the black dragon of Britain coming to devour your paradise.'

Senex did not speak. He watched the steamship, and, unlooking, cared for his helm and sheets: but, though he tried to show nothing, even wore a smile and stuck his chin a little forward, his face looked bewildered, scared.

A long time passed before he said: 'How they make it go – that noise in her hold – what make it go? And if that girt thing in her hold, how she carry any cargo?'

'Forget it, Father.'

'Surprise – she don't look like she could stand the sea from here to St George's. How she cross the ocean?'

'I don't know, Senex. I only know I don't want to be where such things are.'

'Changes come. I guess we all gotta accept changes.'

'Not that one. Senex, you don't know. I heard tell that there are now upwards of five *hundred* of those wood and timber and tree and man-eating steel monsters upon the sea.'

'*No.*'

Silence.

'Surprise, what happen when that noise thing stop, break? It not *natural* – God send the wind for ships but God can send nothing for them if they stop. And they *many*, you say – hundreds?'

'Yes. And them mostly British.'

Even Delia could not distract him until they reached Boaz Island.

The plans for their departure in the *Bateau* moved forward, and, through most of Delia's pregnancy, fell into place: like the arrival of her brother Domino, and he, like young men will, sort of attaching himself to them, the newlyweds, as if

48

rehearsing for his own time. But Delia was always full of surprises.

And Domino, young, powerful – as compact as Delia – but man built, being eighteen years old, was definitely to be one of the five. He was anxious for adventure and hot to leave Bermuda. He was also strong and fearless, Surprise quickly assessed, fearless to a fault. But, if guided, Domino was a fine asset : and he was a good lad, reminding all, especially Surprise, of Delia herself.

But, one day, meaning no harm, Delia said : 'You know what *Bateau Bermudien* mean ?'

'It French ?'

'Yes, but what it mean ?'

'A lot of things.'

'Molly from St Kitts – she teach me French. It only mean boat – Bermuda boat.'

Surprise was distraught and refused to believe it and kept saying, long into the night : 'No, *more*. It must mean *more* than that.'

'If you want.'

But he slammed out into the dark winter night and was gone so long she was scared and cold and afraid.

When he came back he grabbed her by the arms and pointed to his skin. 'You know French – what this, my skin, in French ?'

'Skin – I don't know what skin is called in French.'

'No, my skin's colour ?'

'Black – *noir*, I think – something like that.'

'Then what else – who am I if I be French ? I heard it once – and you haven't said it yet. I *heard* it. Years ago I heard.'

'*Negre* – negro – .'

'Yes, that it. *Negre*. Surprise they call *Le Negre*. That it.' He seemed very excited and drank rum, which was unusual and she was afraid.

After a long time, he said, looking into the fire. 'I Surprise *Le Negre*. You understand ? I be no more connected with British – no name meaning British. I be Surprise *Le Negre*.' He drank some more and she kept quiet, only building up the fire and keeping the food hot in the iron pot lest he should want to eat.

D

'You, too – be *Le Negre*.'

'Whatever you wish, Surprise.'

'I wish to be Surprise *Le Negre* of the *Bateau Bermudien* – and our child be called whatever you want first, but *Le Negre* afterwards.'

'Yes.'

'A while later he said : 'Delia, you hurt me bad. . . .'

'How?'

'You say my *Bateau* only a boat. It everything to me. Don't never say it again.'

'As you like. But a name can mean anything – what your name mean to some, only a surprise. To Senex – you are *his* Surprise. To Delia – you are *my* Surprise. Your ship is your *Bateau Bermudien* : and it certainly is the best ship ever, ain't it?'

'It my dream – my hope – my *life*. They call it my folly, I know – but it my *Bateau* and it not be me alone that call it that – but Beau Nat, my captain – he see it. The man who painted the picture, he see it : he have my dream and I build *his* ship and it all be in that ship together : Beau Nat and the painter and me, all our dreams are in that ship and that word-name : *Bateau Bermudien*.'

By and by he calmed down and Delia understood his dream and was relieved, too, that rum, that could make so many men fullish, mad, calmed her man down so that she could reach him.

She held his great head. 'You *my* dream – and the child within me.'

'Aye, you Delia are my dream, too.'

'But I know about man dreams and your ship – women dreams are big, can stretch – I mean, my expectance can contain yours.'

He made a noise of quiet content, like a child, and was soon sleeping.

July 1841 The very first day after their marriage, he had said :

'I aim to be the first coloured man ever really escape from Bermuda. No one *ever* escape before. I aim that we be the first coloured people escape. And I escape, not a runaway slave – but master of the *Bateau Bermudien*.'

'I know, man. I understand.'

50

'Are you *really* coloured – what about that white blood I hear you got?'

'Man, stop. Of course I got white blood – all kinds. Why, there are cousins of mine so light they curse and deny the brown – I long decide, there no way to curse it and it be mine. So I *embrace* it – embrace you, too.'

'You coloured – I am pure African.'

'Two of my grandparents were black Africans. One other was part Indian. Another part white.'

'I ain't got no white.'

'How in hell you know? You been in bed with every one of your ancestors, watching – all those hundreds of years before you born. We are both coloured, that's sure.'

'All right, we both coloured. Now look – we need, for the *Bateau*, powder, guns, charts – but first we must have a compass.'

'How?' she asked. 'From where?'

'I'll show you.'

When the Death Pinnace went by he said: 'From those British – from that boat, somehow, while they bury the dead.'

He rowed her in one of the little punts from The Crawl: they followed behind the pinnace, keeping a safe distance. They followed her past Gates Island and through the channel between it and the mainland and around to Mangrove Bay.

There they watched. The British, armed with muskets, guarded six convicts who carried the coffin and the shovels. One British guard stayed on the pinnace.

Surprise watched through his small ship's glass. 'I know the kind of compass they got. Good. Much better than they need. All little British ships, even ones just for local work, have a fine ocean-going compass. I know the kind. It have two brass fastenings – and, on that old pinnace, they bound to be fouled solid. Somehow I need to get aboard and put fine oil on them. Douse them with fine oil – that oil, left for a day and a night, loosen the fastenings. When I put on the oil, I can measure the size of the fastening – but how to get aboard?'

'Easy,' Delia said.

'How?'

'I attract the British, of course.' She smiled. 'You got oil now?'

51

'Girl – a sailor always got three things: a knife, a splicing pin and oil. He dead without them.'

'Then we do it now.'

'Why not tomorrow?'

'Because, we do it today, tomorrow we get the compass.'

'But they must not be able to put the two together – us and the lost compass.'

'Sure. Let them see only me – a girl – not you. They never figure a girl want a compass.' She thought awhile. 'Say you get overboard and hang, out of sight, to leeward and I row the boat close to the British – you hide, till I distract them, behind this boat, then move and oil and measure.'

'We could try it.'

The water was almost still, just little waves, an inch or so high, refracting green and blue light from the sandy coral bottom.

Surprise slipped over the side and Delia grabbed the oars: he had not expected her ability, she rowed as good as a man. He was hard-pressed to hang on to the slippery skeg of the little boat.

She rowed and rowed, and, without pausing, shipped her oars just as she came alongside the pinnace. Surprise slipped under the larger vessel's stern.

Delia let the motion carry her well along the pinnace and then, using her inward oar, pushed further along it. The guard did not notice her until she was level with the black bow.

'Who – ?' He jumped and grabbed his musket. 'What you want – eh?'

'Nothing. Just passin',' Delia said and shipped her oars again, just gliding a little ahead. Seeing Surprise climbing over the stern, she made a racket in her boat with the bailer against the oar.

The guard watched her. 'Come on back,' he said.

'No.' She smiled. She heard a noise from the pinnace – behind the guard – and, without pausing for thought, simply rolled over and into the water. It was shallow – she came up, dripping water, and saw the guard still watching her.

She felt the sand under her feet, and, at the same time, grabbed the boat's gunwale. She knew very well that her smock, once wet, was transparent.

The guard was watching her like a hungry lizard watching a fly.

Surprise was an awful long time.

She could have stood, on the sea bottom, and let even her waist be out of water – instead she just let herself rise so that part of her bosom was showing in the soaked garment.

'Come back, little missus.'

She moved in the water, splashing a little, twisting her torso. Even from where she was she could see Surprise working away in the stern of the pinnace. Why was he being so long?

The guard made to turn. She popped her whole bosom out: the teats, she thought, that'll stay him.

They did.

Then, to her horror, she saw, to her right, beyond and above the bow of the British craft, the other guards and the prisoners returning. That girt Surprise was still in the stern – working away, as big and as exposed as if he were alone working on a whitewashed roof.

She measured their distance and their speed of movement. The moment they reached the small crest from where they could, if they wanted, see not only her but into the pinnace, she squealed, threw up her arms and went under water.

From the shore they heard and watched and saw a brown girl in a white dress go under the partially transparent sea. Riveted, they watched a strange underwater exercise they did not quite understand until they saw the brown, bare shoulders again break the surface. Dare they hope that she was naked? A bare hand and bare arm emerged and threw the white garment into the little boat. A wild gesture, a gesture of abandon. She was naked.

They could see little but the flashing of brown flesh confused by the flashing silver and blue and green of the sea: but, naked she most certainly was and they watched, transfixed, as she swam and splashed and swam again.

'Come here, missus,' a guard shouted.

'Shut up! Keep quiet,' another said, afraid lest they scare her.

She stood a little in the water, rising slowly, when her breasts were almost exposed, she splashed and went under again.

Again she rose – this time she saw Surprise's dark body

53

disappearing over the pinnace's stern and moving towards the darker shadows of the wooden dock pilings.

She splashed and swam. It occurred to her that her female exposure might be torment to them – especially the poor Irish convicts. Then she thought of Surprise, and, turning herself, let her back rise out of the water : shoulders, shoulder blades, slowly, all the way until her waist. Then she went slowly down again – feeling like one of the wicked women of St George's Town.

Turning back there was no sight of Surprise. She swam, gently, to the boat, reached in, grabbed her garment and went under water. With St David's agility she got back into her smock.

She had now drifted further away from them. They called out. She paid no attention. After awhile they went aboard the pinnace.

She kept her distance till they had gone, rowing – albeit slowly – back towards Ireland Island.

She clambered aboard the little boat and rowed back to the dock. All was silent. Then Surprise appeared, swimming under the dock, bearing aloft in his hands a brass contraption that looked like a hat upside down.

'Take it,' he gasped, spitting water. 'It heavy.'

She took it and he too clambered aboard, rolling his torso over the thin gunwale, almost capsizing them had she not counter-balanced as best her small weight could.

'How'd you get it?'

'It were held by big screws only – see – and I had my knife and I thought, as good now as any other. So, we got it, Delia. Let's scuttle out of here quick and get home.'

It was a beautiful thing : all ringed with bright brass with a white face and all of it suspended strangely : gimballed, Surprise said.

She had never seen such a thing; her father's compass you could hold in your hand and it had only four marks on it.

This was marked hundreds of times, like a sundial she had once seen.

'You tell time with it, too?' she said.

He laughed.

'I mean, as well as steer by it.'

54

'Delia.' He was already rowing. 'We bury it – bury it and tell no one. Bury it until we need it.'

'What they do if they catch us?'

'I never let them catch *you*.'

'But what the British do to you, Surprise?'

'They whip me again.' He knew, full well, that for this they would not only whip him – they'd slit his nostrils or cut his right hand off. 'Don't worry – they do not come again for Surprise, the British yellow pigs.'

That night they lay together, their love salted, like their very bodies, by the actions and danger they had known.

Later he said: 'It's only powder and guns and charts we need now.'

'But the *Bateau* isn't even launched or rigged.'

'Aye, my sweet cabin companion – she isn't. But I know from where I must get all these – and I must get them soon.'

'Where?'

'From Captain Darrell's cellar under the house at Salt Kettle. I still have keys – Beau Nat trust me with everything – except his one key to his gold, he trust no one with that. But I must soon return the keys. Mistress Darrell a gentle lady, she too trust Surprise. I have a mind, Delia, to take the things – but somehow pay Mistress Darrell for them.'

'How?'

'Don't know.'

'Then sleep with the problem in your head – in the morning your problem solved.'

'How?'

'Your head work on it in sleep. My deddy always say such – and he be right.'

He took August with him in the *Teazer*, to Harmony Hall, at Salt Kettle.

Early August 1841

The sight of the house up close pained him: the familiar smell of the cellars was to pain him more.

'Your Mistress to home?' he asked the young house girl.

'No – she away to the Nelmes' house – to tea, she's gone.'

'When Mistress Darrell come home?'

'By and by. You want to wait in the kitchen? I fetch cool water for you – .'

'No, girl. I go and collect my things and then I wait on Mistress Darrell.'

The children, little Miss Susan and young Aubrey, watched from the upstairs veranda. He waved to them.

'Surprise! Surprise, how *are* you, Surprise?' little Miss Susan called. She was the image of her mother – with promise that she might be even more beautiful. And she was as generous and kind as both her parents.

Strange, he thought, where does Aubrey come from – a treacherous little barracuda born in a nest of – what? Herons, he was thinking of.

'I am well, little Miss – and how are you this lovely afternoon?'

'Very well, thank you, Surprise – but Aubrey has the sniffles.'

'Oh,' he said, talking up to the high stone veranda, 'I'm sorry.'

'Yes. And Peter caught the distemper and is put down – but Nathaniel writes that he is doing well, at Harvard College.'

'Good. Good.'

'But he hates Latin and cold weather and all Yankee cooking – save beans.'

'And you, Miss Susan – are you married yet?'

'No!'

'Not even spoken for?'

'No, Surprise.'

'Then, little Missus, they all must be blind.' He started to walk for the cellar, around the house.

'Shall you come back, Surprise?'

'Not even going yet, Miss Susan.' He got around the side of the house – by the cellar steps. Best to get the stuff quickly.

He unlocked the cellar door, then, with August with him, unlocked the heavy inner cedar grated door to Beau Nat's storeroom.

They carried up and out and into the bright light, the small but precious kegs of powder. They carried a keg on each shoulder, two each per load and made four trips. No one was about. Surprise sweated. It was the best powder in the world; not American, not French, but British. Comes to machines or anything to go with them – British always best.

There was a door within the inner door and Surprise unlocked that next and went in alone.

On the tilt-topped rough desk still stood the master's quills – and, hanging on a nail, the old blue gold-braided fore 'n' aft Admiral's hat – it was Beau Nat's father-in-law's hat, Mistress Susan's father. Surprise shivered: the man, an Englishman, had perished in some bad storm in some awful icy northern ocean.

There, too, in its perfect cedar box, was Beau Nat's sextant – next to it the square mahogany box that contained his best calculating log and map instruments. Above, in a many-slotted shelf, lay long tin spools containing all his charts – save those, doubtless, still aboard his four vessels.

Surprise felt tears running down his cheeks – cold in the damp cellar. He shook again and put the heels of his clenched fists down on the desk.

'Master, forgive me. Give me a sign, Master, that I may take them? I, Surprise, your Helmsman. I pay, I steal nothing, as always – but, Master, give me a sign.'

The only answer was a small squeak from a rat – or was it August in the next chamber?

He knew that if he had the instruments and the good sextant – the one he possessed at home had parts missing and the master had never got around to teaching him how to use it, and he, Surprise, was afraid to beg, afraid lest he not be able to learn – he had a chance of finding some captain who would teach him : if not in Bermuda, somewhere else.

He tensed his muscles. An inner voice said, take the swivel guns. Take the American Buccaneers, *now*.

They were in the corner, still in their original packing boxes : two long and heavy crates. They were the very best, he knew all about them. Brass Buccaneers, swivel guns, one-inch bore and with long barrels – for accuracy. Most swivels were only about twenty-four to thirty inches – these were sixty inches long. Most, too, were made for slow fuses : these, Captain Darrell had bought especially because they were flint-locks.

'August, come here.' He remembered loading them in Providence – the crates even contained two dozen shot in each and the man had demonstrated to Beau Nat : no windage, the shot fit tight in the brass barrel. 'We take one at a time –

they heavy.' These swivel guns were the best: they could shoot far and accurate, or up close, loaded with small shot, blast to bits the whole crew of one long boat at a time – if you caught 'em lined up right, longways.

When they were carrying the second crate down the long garden path to the wharf, little Aubrey appeared. He was chewing and sucking on a piece of sugar cane – drool ran down his chin.

'Where you going with that?'

'Watch out, Mister Aubrey – stand back now, lad.'

'Surprise, where are you going with that box?'

'To my boat, Mister Aubrey – watch out now.'

The boy looked into Surprise's eyes: 'That's a gun in that box. A *gun*.'

'No, Mister Aubrey – looks like it but it a ship's telescope. Keep on, August.'

They went on.

'I'll tell Mamma you have Poppa's *gun*.'

'You do that,' Surprise said, matter-of-factly, but sweating hard.

Coming back up the path, he saw Aubrey disappearing into the house. He hurried back to the cold cellar.

In the inner room he hauled out a tin chart tube and took the top off and pulled out the chart. 'The English Channel.' He rolled it up and put it back.

On the third try he got what he wanted. 'The West Indies.' And another tube. 'The Leeward and the Windward Islands. Newest Admiralty Survey of 1746.' That was them.

He had the tall tubes in his arms. He looked with longing at the instrument and the sextant boxes. He could all but see the handsome, but strangely stubby fingers of Beau Nat on them. 'I not take your tools, man. I not know what they worth. Even if I did, I not take them – they are part of you.' He figured, if he'd had his way, he'd 've buried the boxes with Captain Darrell – so as he could find his way.

He heard noises above on the heavy cedar floor.

'August – here. Take these.'

He had the British compass and he had the old sextant – even if it was broken. Yet he was torn: he wanted something else that was part of the man – he couldn't figure what.

Carefully he locked the inner, then the outer and then the cellar door.

Aubrey was there.

'Mamma wants to see you, Surprise.'

'Aye, little mister. I come.'

She was dark-haired, very slim of face and figure and always youthful looking – now she looked gaunt and strangely greenish of the jowl.

He bowed, and, with ancient cunning, beat her to voice : 'The keys, Mistress, I came to return all the keys.' He held them out.

She took them – he noticed she was trembling.

'How are you, Mistress? Is all well?'

'Yes. Thank you, Surprise. As well as can be.'

'And the ships, Mistress – who sails the ships?'

'Three sold now, Surprise. Only the *Improvement* left.'

'And where is she, Mistress?'

'Leased to Mr Stowe and Mr Wood.'

'She a fine ship, Mistress – don't part with her.'

'Surprise, I'll try – but a woman cannot manage business.'

'But Mistress – Mr Nelmes could manage.'

'Mr Nelmes . . . I was going to say, Surprise, that he is overdue. But you know what that means : Mr Nelmes is lost at sea these many months now.'

'Mr Wood is honest, the Master said, Mistress.'

Silence.

She was still very slim – she didn't look as if she'd borne one child, never mind four.

'Surprise. Aubrey says you've taken – I don't understand, a gun?'

'No, Mistress. I have taken only the things that were mine – that the Master bought on my behalf. But yet I owe him, Mistress, and would now pay you.'

'I expect,' she looked about the garden as if expecting to see something or someone appear from behind a bush or plant. 'I expect the Master would want you to have them, Surprise, for nothing. Indeed, I would we could have kept you by us.'

'I know, Mistress Darrell. Everything must end. The Master paid me well – he paid me for a whole sea trip, and. . . .'

He paused, then spat out : 'It were less than a full day and night – and he paid me the usual for a long sea trip to the West Indies. But my things, Mistress. I owe you more than ten pounds – it an English measure. Meaning a pound and a bit more?'

'A guinea.'

'Aye, aye, Mistress. Two times five guineas British, I owe. I have gold to pay.'

'If you insist, Surprise.'

He was getting out his satchel of gold.

'But I do not know the exchange, Surprise. Besides, why not forget it – we owe you much, Surprise.'

'Please, Mistress. I give my word to pay.'

'Then would you pay Mr Stowe and Mr Wood – ? They would know the measure of gold and keep it safe for me.'

'Aye.'

'Mamma – Surprise has stolen a gun!'

'Mistress. I go now. You need Surprise, send for me by my father – and I always come to do whatever your bidding.'

Aubrey was tugging at the long skirt of her black mourning dress. 'Leave off, Aubrey. Thank you, Surprise.'

He started down the path.

'Surprise!'

'Yes, Mistress.'

'What is it that you have that Aubrey shouts about?'

' 'Tis only a seeing device, Mistress – would you wish me to bring it and show you, Mistress Darrell?' Surprise, you sailing too close to the wind now. . . .

'No. Be well, Surprise – and God bless you.'

He looked at her. It was Captain Darrell's parting. Tears welled in his eyes – he wanted to bid her the same, but it was not fitting. He bowed – this was the lady Beau Nat meant when he prayed for their loved ones on shore, this was the light that lit his stern brown eyes when shore was near and made his nose, the nostrils, shaped as if cut in Vs by a sail-mailmaker, flare, sniffing the breeze before ever home was on the horizon. . . .

He moved quietly down the path and up the long plank to the dock face. He jumped aboard the *Teazer*.

'Come on, August – get the goddamn painters away and the sail up. What the hell you waiting for?'

August looked startled and moved, slowly, to do his bidding.

For a moment, Surprise wished he was a slave; he imagined he *was* a slave: then he'd have to stay and take care of the house of Darrell, Harmony Hall – and they would have to keep him.

Damn her! Damn the white woman – would she had cursed me!

I pay Mr Stowe and Mr Wood.

He put the helm hard over, and then slowly back, the *Teazer*, responding, cleared the dock, and, the breeze catching her, she moved firm and surely, heavy with the cargo.

He had not paid, or given account for the barrels of powder – he flushed with shame and anger.

After a little while on the water, he relaxed: yes, he had. He had figured it all: the powder was paid by the lie; for Captain Darrell had only promised to pay him for the voyage, in his sickness it had passed his mind.

And, he had the swivel guns – the Buccaneers: no man or ship could trifle with his *Bateau* and she be armed with these weapons.

'Hail every ship as if they be your own long lost family,' Beau Nat used to say, laughing, holding his glistening brass voice trumpet in his hand and slapping his high black boots. 'And keep the shot packed tight in your carronades – and ye torches lit.'

VI

It was now September 1842.

'How can Bermuda grow strong and change and grow great,' Senex said, 'when its best sons – its strongest and noblest – leave?'

No one answered him until Surprise said: 'What I want you to tell *me* is, why the *Bateau Bermudien* don't sail right or good?'

It had been a shock past all his worst expectations: he had taken his sail plans to Mr Hunt of Hunt's Island and given all the dimensions of the ship, and told Mr Hunt, the younger (renowned as the finest sailmaker – and not only in Bermuda), that he was carrying out the commission of a fictitious Mr Fowle of Sandys (there being so many Fowles in the parish that Surprise was sure Mr Hunt would not be suspicious) and Mr Hunt had made the sails: a beautiful mainsail all set with reefing lines, four in number, two jibs and a square topsail, and given him the leftover canvas and more besides, and he had paid him, paid him painfully from his now rapidly dwindling gold supply. (And he would not touch Delia's bag of gold: 'That for *your* children – in case something happen to me.' 'No, Surprise – it *my* present to *you*.' 'Child, you don't understand the world: you hear me good: that is your secret treasure. You let no one have that gold. That to save in case Surprise not be around to take care of you and the child. Understand?' 'Yes.')

The *Bateau* was long since launched and rigged – with spar and boom of imported Newfoundland spruce, and bowsprit of cedar lined and protected with bamboo – and all lines and ropes made of the best by the same Mr Hunt in his rope shop, and all treated against weather and rot. And the ratlines and mainstays affixed with bumpers of soft material so that in no wise and in no weather could the lines tear the sails.

Three other good men had come forward, as if from nowhere, the moment it got abroad that the British had purchased, in that year, 1842, both Gates and Boaz Islands (their purpose being to house their convict labour more cheaply ashore).

He could not have calculated that this shock was ahead: his *Bateau Bermudien*, on her first outing, had sailing qualities that could only be described as abysmal.

She would not move through the water (foot) when she was pointed high (was laid close to the wind); she slipped, also, to leeward as if she was greased and not possessed of a keel at all – and, into the rotten bargain, she wouldn't come about any better than a bad handled British jack brig.

Surprise came ashore possessed of an anger that encompassed his father, his friends, even his child-bride – indeed it only stopped a little short of including the minute but seemingly impossibly bright-eyed infant in her arms. He smashed and flayed about and cursed all – including God himself – and only stopped when his eyes came to the little bright eyes, which, seeing his face and totally innocent of his mood, lit up and began a smile that wreathed the whole three-month-old face.

Surprise clucked his tongue at him for only a moment, but a moment long enough for Delia to realise that her man had just, just, retained his sanity, and began again:

'Why? Every man here built and sailed ships – and not one of you can tell me why? What I gotta do? What I gotta do – get a white man to tell me?'

'Surprise?' Delia said.

He didn't answer, but walked about.

She touched him.

'What, woman?'

'Why not you ask King Jack?' The moment it was out she knew it was a mistake.

He raised the back of his hand, looked at her with almost blind rage – and then stopped: he would have actually struck her, she thought, were it not for the child. She walked away.

'Move the mast forward two, three feet,' someone said.

'I'll shove the mast up your arse.'

Senex broke the silence following: 'As to the slipping to leeward – we could add a fin keel, but, as you know, t'will increase your draught – '

'Aye. I know. I thought of that.' Surprise slapped the heel of one hand in the palm of the other. 'What if there was some way we could put it on and take it off – a fin keel, I mean?'

'Impossible,' Senex said.

August, the slow but methodical and imperturbable, said, 'You know how a fish can raise and lower its upper fin – its upper keel, you might say; can we not have something like that, only upside down?'

'Sleep on it,' Surprise said.

'Definitely need some girt weight for ballast,' Senex said. 'You definitely got to have that – and no mistake.'

'I sleep on it,' Surprise said.

Surprise went to bed thinking, to himself, that, for a ship to sail that bad, there must be not one but *two* things wrong with her.

There was the other nagging frustration, too: it was now September, the month when hurricanes and other storms could come up and rage – the best time for departure, June, July and August, had passed.

Despite the risk of storms, they would have to leave soon: there was no question of waiting until the safe month of May. All months ahead were bad, October, November, December, January and February. Of course, they could be lucky and get fair breezes all the way south. They had a thousand miles, he figured, to the real safety of the southern islands. Anegada or Totola and other safe harbours, were exactly one thousand miles due south.

Or they could be unlucky, like so many before them, and just sail out and never be heard of again.

It took a good deal of rum before he fell asleep.

He woke early and the first thing he thought of was his own words: 'I didn't say she was the biggest, I said she was the best – the finest.' He flushed with anger.

What had gone wrong? He looked at the *Bateau* riding at anchor, his precious prow, the cedar cut fine, as sharp as a knife to 'cut to windward'. There was something wrong about the look of her – the heft of her lines by the eye. Something. But what was it?

The Rudd brothers, all former seamen, whose little slipway for fishermen, their livelihood, was soon to be annihilated by British buildings, were staunch additions to the endeavour.

Henry, the eldest, about forty years: quiet, independent – but not to an extreme – was known for two faults, the bottle and women. The women would not be a future problem, for a large, jovial woman named Bernice had latched hold of him. The bottle, Surprise figured, was not the worst fault a man could have – and all got some.

'Move the mast forward, two or three feet.' It was Henry Rudd said that: and it was not a stupid remark. The sail balance was definitely wrong.

Then it came to him – just looking at her. Not the mast, that was too drastic, too complicated – but add to the bowsprit and add another and bigger jib.

That would achieve the same thing: to add to the sails in the bow would move the balance – and he figured Henry Rudd had it the wrong way about: to add sails to the bow would be like moving the mast *aft*.

64

Irving Rudd, some said, was sly and slippery and a chaser and hoarder of gold and silver. He might be that, Surprise thought, but there were other things that Surprise liked about him. He was clever and 'colour-angered', hell-driven by the treatment of whites – and he was slick with tools, a first-class shipwright like Senex, and Senex was not going.

Henry was a good helmsman and an experienced seaman; Irving, the sly, a good shipwright – and then there was Bossie, and Bossie was the opposite of his nickname: a follower, not a leader, and, Surprise knew, a man who laughed at the world and all its trouble.

If there was one type of man a ship needed, it was one who was eternally optimistic, and the *Bateau* had two, Bossie Rudd and August Napier. (Three, Surprise thought, if you counted sweet Delia.)

'Morning!' It was Irving Rudd.

'Morning.'

'You know what's wrong with her?'

'What?'

'One damn thing for sure – that topsail should come off altogether. It's no use and makes her too heavy aloft and makes her lean too easy.'

'I reckon you may have something there. Truth is, with her lines, she must like to sail as upright as possible.'

'That's true and no mistake,' Irving said. 'And what use is a square topsail anyway, except for backing, a square topsail is as useless as horns on a cow, or tits on a bull.'

Surprise mentioned the adding of a big jib.

Irving agreed sagely, smacking his lips.

Surprise smiled. He didn't figure all three Rudds would have thought of it in the passing of seven whale seasons.

But there was something else, too: Senex was right about the fin keel. However, adding a foot to a foot and a half to her draught was bad. If we ever *got* to escape, Surprise thought, we gotta be able to draw less water than most ships as would chase us. . . .

In five days the changes were made: Surprise got Mr Hunt to cut and sew them a big extra jib. Irving added another six and a half feet to the bowsprit and ran a stout line up high on the mast, reaching above the ratlines. Henry and Bossie stripped off the topsail and all to do with it.

E

They had another sea-trial in the Great Sound. The change was astonishing: she performed, in comparison to before, like magic – almost the magic Surprise had expected of his *Bateau Bermudien* all these years.

But she still slipped too much to leeward. Not a great deal, but too much for the perfection he expected.

'It gotta have the fin keel,' Senex said.

'And more weight – ballast.' Irving Rudd scratched his head: he too was balding and the back of his head stuck out uncommonly far.

'Time we got all of us and our stuff on board,' Henry said, 'you gonna have weight enough.'

'Irving is right,' Bossie said. 'Seems to me like she needs weight down low – sort of in her guts.'

'Water kegs will be just that,' Henry said.

'You mean *rum* kegs,' Bossie laughed. 'That the weight you care about.'

Surprise had taken off his green jerkin, had laid it aside and was thinking. August had said a fish's fin – well, that was impossible.

Delia and the child intruded into his thinking: Delia had insisted the boy be called Johnson, and she herself could give no reason, but they agreed. Johnson was a funny name. As it was it made no difference: as soon as the child could focus those bright, burning eyes, everyone called him 'Little Surprise'.

Then it came to him: we gotta be able to lift the keel just like those Netherlander boats he'd seen in Europe. He walked alone some more, picking up driftwood; what if we don't have two outrig keels like they have, but one that fits down through the main keel?

When he told the others, they all protested.

'You talking about cut a hole in a good keel?' Henry said. 'You mean to say you 'spect me to go to sea in a ship that already got a hole cut in her?'

On a high tide they got her beached as far as they could.

'What woman you take, Bossie?' Senex asked.

'Never you mind. Bossie get a woman – you wait and see if he don't.'

They were a man short, but, Surprise figured with the five he had, he was better off than with any other six he could imagine.

Irving had no woman – didn't want one, he said – and neither did August and Domino. But Domino was young: it would be better if there was one more woman.

'What's the matter with you?' Delia said. 'You think there's no women in the West Indies?'

'I wanted us to be sort of complete before we left – a kind of floating village, a tribe. A little country.'

'You make the village when we get there – country, or whatever you want to call it. Let's get there first.'

He reckoned she was right.

Senex and Henry and August and Irving gathered around him. Surprise said: 'This is what I want.' He drew in the sand. 'A cut right through the keel – a cut three feet long. Into this cut must fit – tight but not so tight it can set up solid when long in the water – the fin keel. It must be made of old, aged wood. The fin gotta be a full foot and a half deep. And when it set in place, it got not to leak. When we got to lift it – we got to have a piece to exactly fit in its place, solid. We got to keep caulking and white lead, in a tight bottle, beside it all the time.'

'We could make the whole fin keel top, what-you-call? – counter-sunk,' Senex said. 'Like so – that way it never leak. Leastways, only a little.'

'All right. Let's set-to – every day is precious time wasted. Those Limeys must not come for us.'

Two days later, it was finished. The *Bateau* was back in the water – she leaked, of course, but then, when they set the fin keel in place, and caulked and mopped up and fastened it down good and mopped again, she leaked only a very little.

Delia came over in the dinghy. 'A woman come for you, Surprise?'

'What woman?'

'She say you know her.' She gestured him to come close, and when he did, she whispered: 'She got a withered arm – she got a boy with her. I reckon she's the one from St George's.'

Surprise stood and looked at her. She was a fine-looking, dark-skinned woman, and, were it not for her arm, he thought, any man would fancy her.

'Mister,' she said, 'I owe you plenty. Truth is simple : I know something that which you *must* hear – and, although I owe you, I gotta use my knowledge to bargain with. I got nothing else – me and my boy, we got nothing else.'

'What's the knowledge ?'

'First : if I tell you and it prove your salvation, will you take me and the boy ?'

'Take you *where* ?'

'Where you going.'

'I ain't going no place – save St David's next week, to fish. You mean to St David's ?'

'Man. Don't waste my time. I know what I *see*. We been hiding in the palmettos now for four days : I see this ship and all you have to put in her. I know you going on a long trip – and, since you be who you are, I know you ain't figuring on coming back. I want to go with you – me and my son. And we strong and good workers – never mind what it look like – look at my good arm. You see – it develop like iron. It as good as two arms. And, my boy, he as strong as a man – show him, John, show him what you can lift.'

The boy, who, to Surprise, appeared slow-witted, looked around for something to lift.

'Flex your muscles, boy,' she said, grabbing him, raising his arm. She spun him around. 'And look-it that back – strong. He carry a lot – water, logs, anything. You want a boy to man the pump – he pump all day and all night. His deddy was a sailor – he strong, too. Mr Surprise, you gotta take us. . . .'

'Easy. What this news ?'

'I tell you, you take us ?'

'If the rest of the crew agree and if your news really be important.'

'It as important as *death*. Is life important to you, Mr Surprise ?'

'Yes.'

'Then I tell you : Mr Reid, he knows you are going. The British know you are going. They lie in wait for you – '

'What ?'

'Yes. They wait for you to go a-ways offshore and after nightfall, they capture you.'

'How the hell did Reid know – find out ?'

The woman looked scared. She looked all about.

'How? You expect me to believe you, woman, and you don't tell me how?'

She walked away and signalled Surprise to follow her. She took hold of his arm. 'You save me once, Mr Surprise – though, later, Mr Reid damn near kill me. You want me to show you what he did to me?' She started to raise her long skirts.

'No.'

'Look.'

'No. It not necessary. I can guess.'

She was still raising her skirts.

'No, I say.'

'Then you listen. My name is Jennie – you can trust Jennie as long as she live. You are the big man – the biggest. I stay loyal to you always – if you take me. I be your slave – do anything – you ask, Jennie do it.'

'How did Reid know?'

'One person told. The British have a ship waiting in St George's – and another here in the west at Ireland Island. Both are waiting only a fire, a fire to signal them to sea.'

'What if you lying to me?'

'Jennie not lie. I tell you. You have the British machine thing, Navy thing, they look for. That right?'

'The compass, you mean?'

'Yes. Reid know that – and they catch you with that and being off-shore and they kill you.'

'Maybe. Everybody knows the compass been missing – the British posted a reward for it for many months. Why should I believe you?'

'Then you listen here,' she snapped, now angry. 'You got a flag, too – a special flag. Ain't you?'

'No.'

'Yes you have. And it black. And Mr Reid know. And a black flag is a pirate ship, ain't it? And they charge you as a pirate – '

'But a pirate flag have other things – a skull – '

'No. You know. You a sailor. A pirate flag is black with white on it. And you be charged as a pirate and you die slow.'

Surprise stepped back and turned and looked at the almost still, blue-green water of The Crawl.

After a while, he came back to her, and, this time, he took her good arm and held it. 'You tell no one. You hear?'

'I Jennie. I your slave.'

'Tell no one. We board *now* – you and the boy come now.'

'We come.'

'Load everything. Load everything *now*. Then all gather aboard the *Bateau*,' Surprise said. 'I want a council.'

'The woman come with us?' Bossie asked, smiling.

'Yes.'

'I told you I get a woman, Surprise. What you think of her?'

'He *your* man?' Surprise asked her.

'I never seen him afore in my born days.'

'Bossie told you he got a woman,' Bossie said, laughing a loud peal. 'And you didn't believe him.'

Surprise saw Delia, laughing, and the infant, bewildered, but smiling, too. He, too, smiled.

They were all assembled in the aft of the *Bateau*. All provivions were loaded, every item checked and double-checked. The livestock, chickens and pigs, were lashed in mangrove stick crates on the mid-deck.

'Only one question, now,' Surprise said. 'Who do we elect as leader? Speak?' He looked around.

No one answered.

Bossie then said : 'Henry's the eldest. . . .'

Irving smacked his mouth. 'Sure. Perhaps Henry.'

Another silence.

August looked at Surprise. Domino looked all around. Delia, the child fitting into her hip, cast her eyes on the deck.

'Goddamn, Surprise,' Domino said, 'I say it *your* ship.'

'That's the *truth*,' August said, looking angered and confused.

'Yes, it's my ship,' Surprise said. 'But the owner is not necessarily the master. It's up to everyone to decide who's master.'

'That's true,' Irving said.

Henry looked all about, got to his feet, stretched. 'You fellas talking rubbish. It not only Surprise's ship – it his *everything*. I say Surprise is the leader – and always has been.'

'I want it settled *now*,' Surprise said. 'Now and forever and by everyone.'

'It be anyone but Surprise,' August said, 'and August not going.'

'Shit.' Henry spat over the side. 'Only Surprise can read and write. Only Surprise can be captain and leader. Talk of anyone else is sheer fullish shit.'

All agreed.

'And who be first mate?' Surprise asked. He was thinking: now there can be no argument later – the sea can make fools of men, but now it settled, and from their own mouths.

'*You* say,' Domino said. 'You the captain – it *your* ship.'

'Aye.'

'Aye. Aye.'

'Then we have two first mates,' Surprise said. 'One for each watch. August Napier be the one and Henry Rudd be the other.'

'Aye – that's fair.' Irving looked as if his assent pained him.

Surprise thought quickly. 'And the chief yeoman, the man in charge of the hull of the *Bateau Bermudien*, and all tools and all sails, be Irving Rudd.'

They nodded.

'No man or woman leave this ship from now on without my permission. We sail tonight as soon as it be dark. The British are waiting for us – but we not be where they wait and not go where they look.'

In their after-quarters, Surprise was checking the lashings on the powder kegs. Here, in the captain's cabin they had the greatest protection from salt water – not to mention the greatest protection of cedar wood against British round shot.

Something was wrong with Delia. It had been this way now for many months: she did not have to say or do anything, or act even in any way peculiar, yet he could sense when something made her unhappy or angry.

'What is it, woman?'

'Nothing.'

'I have no time for begging you – what is it?'

'My father. I would I could see my father, to say good-bye

and receive his blessing and let him see his grandson again.'

'The British wait for us in St George's, Delia. I wish I could take you and the boy to see King Jack – but if they take me, you must now know, they will surely kill me.'

'I know. I do not *want* to see my father, Surprise. I do not expect to – but I grieve. . . .'

'I understand. I, too, already grieve for Senex – and I can, at least, bid the poor old one good-bye. What can I do for you, Delia?'

'Nothing. I married you. You come first. We come first. Little Johnson cannot lose *his* father – that be first.' She was weeping. 'But let us go *soon*.'

'It must be dark. Dark or we be discovered. I go now and see my father.'

'Leave him. Surprise, do not put foot on shore again.'

'But why?'

'He knows. . . .'

'Knows what?'

' – '

'What? We have no time – .'

'Knows that Emiline betrayed you – betrayed us all.'

'How he know?'

'Because he is wise. He read your face and the woman, Jennie's. And mine, too, probably.'

'But he cannot *know*. He must not know.'

'Surprise. He is a wise man and he reads faces – he reads the lines of love. He loves you. He loves that woman – or, maybe, he is just trapped by her. But he has lived with her since almost forever – and he knows her. Knows everything.'

'But he *must not know*.'

'He knows. He lie down with that woman every night and he knows. He knows now, everything. I saw it on his face, hours ago.'

'I pray you are wrong.'

'I too. But I am right. She knows too.'

'What the hell does she know? – she the one who told the British.'

'No, my man – listen. She knows that Senex loves you and would that he could be with you. You are a powerful love family, you Billinghursts – '

72

'Le Negre. My name is Le Negre.'
'Whatever you say.'

He went ashore with August. August was to raise an old mast, in the yard, to make it look, later, as if the *Bateau* was still at anchor.

Surprise went up to his father's house : then something about the little wooden structure on its four rounded stone stilts seemed wrong – too silent, almost possessed by silence.

But when he entered the door, the sight shocked him worse than anything he'd ever seen in his life – worse even than the time they placed his little sister in the boiling water, floating with rats' entrails and dead toads, to cure her of lockjaw, and she only five. . . .

Blood. There was blood everywhere. On the furniture, the floor, even spattered on the low palmetto ceiling – worse, it was on Senex.

'What happened, Father?'

The old man sat very still.

'What happened? You hurt? Answer me?'

Senex opened his eyes and said very softly : 'I am all right. I am not hurt. It is time for you to go, my son. You must leave.'

'But what happened?'

'Be still, Surprise, and listen. Bid me good-bye. I now bid you good-bye. I told you afore you are my life – now you must escape or my life be lost. You and the little fella, you are my – what-you-call? – my life after my death. You go.'

'But what's all this? This blood? And you? You not hurt?'

'No. I weak in the heart – and maybe weak in the head. Weak in the spirit. But I be not weak of body yet. I cut her.'

'You kill her?'

'No. Saul did not kill.'

Surprise rushed into the little room, through the canvas that served as door.

Emiline lay on the bed, moaning. She had a garment shoved in her mouth – it was soaked with blood. She lifted her head – the garment, the corner of it hanging from her mouth, dripped blood like a grotesque long tongue. She looked at him. Her eyes flared hatred and fear. Then she put the bed clothes over her head.

Surprise watched her body heave in even rising and falling motions as she moaned. He went out.

Senex looked up at him. The old man, his face looking paralysed in a mask of ancient pain – as if, almost, it was a death mask – except that the eyes moved with a quick and furious yet tranquil light, like an old tortoise's.

'Father.' Surprise was on his knees by the dilapidated wicker chair – white, it was, and with a list, so that, for a moment, he thought of the cabin house of the filthy steamship *Adelaide*.

Surprise kissed the face – kissed him on both cheeks and felt the old man's tears on his mouth.

'Go now, my son. Go.'

Surprise got up and went to the door and turned and looked back.

'She won't die. Emiline won't die, will she?'

'No. But she'll not talk anymore – no, not anymore.'

'Father. . . .'

'I know, my son. Go. Take care of the little boy child.'

'Father, you the best man I ever know – you. . . .'

'Go. I know. You, too. Go.'

Surprise walked down to the shore. The sun was already set. He wiped his face and looked around for August. Surprise, he said to himself, you gotta be a *stone* now. As cool, as cold as a stone. You got to take the ship through the British – take her, guide her as cold and hard as a rock.

You grieve, you grieve later. You grieve now, Surprise, and you be dead: you and your Delia and your child and your *Bateau*. . . .

'The light going.'

Surprise got in the dinghy and climbed to the stern.

'The light going, Surprise.'

'Aye.'

BOOK TWO

I

The wind was out of the south-west, but light and variable. If they sailed north, the sailing would be easy, but they would have to pass the British ship in the Dockyard at Ireland Island. Also, on that course, they would have to contend with dangerous reefs and rocks for ten miles and more.

In many ways, it was the best course (for, even though the night was dark, he and August and the Rudd brothers knew the water well), because, since they were ultimately bound south, it was best if they be seen going north. Or north-west, let the British think they bound for America – or north and then be seen turning east, bound for Africa.

Surprise imagined a British captain might easily see him sail north and know he bound south. Aye, but the British likely guess he sweep east and go south. Best course to sail north and then sweep west towards America – they not think he turn towards the shipping lanes the Royal Navy and British merchantmen take from the Indies to Halifax and Britain.

There was one other way: to go south within the Great Sound, turn west through the tiny gap between the mainland and Sandy's Island. . . .

No. They'd have to raise the little drawbridge and they could be heard and seen, even apprehended. And, although the *Bateau* would just squeeze through with her ten-foot beam, it was now past high water mark, and, even raising the fin keel, they might not get their almost six-foot draught through.

Best to go through Mangrove Bay, cut close round Daniel's Head. . . .

He gave the orders.

'No sails until we are through Somerset Narrows. Two men to each sweep – and muffle the oarlocks.'

'We head south, after Daniel's Head?' Henry asked.

'Yes. We must head to windward all the time. Our advantage against the British is always to windward.'

'You mean – go through that long, narrow Hogfish Cut? – at night?'

'Aye – we have the lighthouse to guide us.'

'And we gonna need it,' Henry said, but went forward to man a sweep.

Two were raising the anchor. Enough noise it made as well.

We get through Hogfish, Surprise thought, we under the guns of Southampton Fort....

The anchor was up. Surprise took the long cedar tiller in his hands. The boy, John, was by his side.

'Pass the word – slow strokes – and then come back to me.'

The boy went forward. Surprise guided them out of The Crawl and did not look back. Against the head wind, slight in the shelter of the land, he steered them south-west and then turned north through Somerset Narrows and headed across Mangrove Bay.

'Boy. Tell them put up the number two jib – the little jib – and keep on the oars.'

The boy, John, looked bewildered.

'Hoist little jib, continue rowing.'

The boy went forward.

Delia came up.

'The child is sleeping.'

'Good. Delia. Do something for me, please. Before the day breaks. Take the black flag and cut the longtail – the white longtail off it. Then cut the black all to pieces – to shreds. We got any blue cloth?'

'None – '

'I was hoping for something light – the colour of Bermuda water.'

'I got my night chemise.'

'Yes – that be perfect. Make as big a flag of it as you can. Then sew the longtail, the white longtail in the upper corner.'

'I can cut it so it big – the chemise is double thickness. I make us a flag.'

'Thank you, Delia.' He was watching forward, closely: he had to clear all the little islands at King's Point, before he could turn west for Daniel's Head. The Head was a mile or so away: from there it was four miles and more to Hogfish Cut, but he hoped they could set more sail for that – decent drawing canvas and cease the tiring sweeps.

Henry's voice kept wafting back to him: 'I-am-rowing,'

the long pause, 'I-am-rowing.' It was a low sound, almost as muffled as the oars.

Every now and then Surprise heard a fish break water: it was a good sign: we surprise a fish, we surprise no one else.

'Boy. Go tell Domino to relieve August and ask August come to me.'

When August came astern, Surprise was easing the helm to sou'-west.

'Haul the big jib, August. Let's try that without the main.'

'Flying jib going up, Captain.'

Surprise waited until the jib was all the way up. Then he eased the helm more to the south. The men on the oars did not have to be told: on the leeward two were hauling in the sheet.

'Boy. Tell them take it in more.'

'Wha'?'

'Tell them : tighten big jib.'

'Yessir.'

August came aft again.

'She's carrying it. Let's put up the main – but, August, stand close. When I say take it down, move fast. We can't race through Hogfish Cut.'

'Aye.'

'And when it's down, you and another standby by the knightheads and watch out and holler for reefs.'

'Aye.'

With the sails now full and the helm giving him a good firm signal and feeling his ship surge gently but powerfully forward, Surprise, in the night season, felt the sweet deep exhilaration of command – to be bound for sea and master of your own ship.

He was glad he had on his green jacket with the brass buttons; he wished he had on a peaked cap, too – maybe he'd get one sometime.

It was a dark night, yet it was possessed of a strange light – so that one could make out more than he had expected.

Then, when they drew even to Wreck Hill – its high rotund hump looming above them – he realised what it was: the light from Gibb's Hill Lighthouse, now just visible in its turning rhythm, had been lighting them even before they could recognise it.

He watched the shore : it was about a full mile and a half now before the Cut narrowed.

He did not need a chart : it was a full four fathoms in the Cut, but only one fathom on either hand, and, scattered on either hand, the heads of reefs, some just below, some actually breaking water even at high tide, no matter now, at half tide. There'd be many breakers – or boilers, as some called them : and that was what they could do to you, break you or boil you.

'Stand by me, boy.'

'I here, sir.'

'When I tell you – go tell them, lower the main. You got that?'

'Lower the mail.'

'Yeah. You tell 'em, lower the mail.'

The faster they were through the Cut, the further they'd be to south and to windward of the guns of Southampton Fort by daybreak. But, too fast through the Cut and they could run aground and be *there* at break of day.

He wondered if the word was actually out to all the forts to fire on the *Bateau Bermudien*. And how could they tell her from other Bermudian sloops? Perhaps they'd wait to see a black flag, and we can escape. Perhaps they'll just fire at any vessel without colours.

He wished he had a whole rack full of flags, the way Captain Darrell had : every flag for signalling and a flag for every country – and then a couple of 'guess who's'. A good 'guess who' could give a ship a few precious moments to windward or leeward for advantage or escape.

'Tell them – take down the main.'

The wind had increased now, and, when the main was off, the ship still deep soughed through the slight chop, itself now rising and falling slightly from the ocean's surge.

'Look alive and skin your eyes,' Surprise called out, his voice, for the first time, loud in the night. He too watched : this was no time to make an error : not in home waters and with a bottom still new from the adze's blade.

'Boy. Come here. Go ask Miss Delia, what hour it is – ? and mark her good.'

80

'Yessir.'

He ain't too dim-witted, Surprise thought – he just looks dim-witted.

'Breaker on the port,' Irving called, and, at the same time :

'Breaker on the starboard quarter – fifty yards.' August called it like the veteran he was.

In a moment, Surprise saw both heads, familiar as road stones, and he eased the *Bateau* a little closer to shore.

They picked their way through, at slow speed, for more than an hour : sometimes it was silent, sometimes a boiler rose up close by, like a ghastly watery hillock, or a great spouting leviathan.

But she was quick on the helm : as quick as a dinghy – and Senex's dinghy, itself, bobbed behind them like a kid following its mother. Or, rather, like a whale followed by a playful baby.

'Boy – tell them to watch for a stake to starboard. Watch for the stake.'

He waited and waited until he thought it impossible that they had not already passed it.

'Stake – fifty yards – I mean *feet*,' Irving yelled.

Surprise sharpened up. 'Take in the jib sheet.'

Henry came aft. 'You're not turning south so soon?'

'I am. We need every minute.'

'It's dangerous.'

'So is British round shot.'

'We'll watch close.'

A little later Delia came up. It was some time before he realised she wanted to show him something.

'What, girl, what?'

'Your flag – it's done.'

'Can't look, Delia. I'll bet it's lovely – but I can't look now. Henry, haul the third jib !' He turned and looked at her.

'See.'

He saw the light blue of it suddenly touched by the ghostly light from Gibb's Hill – the machine cleverness of the British, this girt light that could shine twenty miles and more, never mind the half mile that now separated them. The flag, of pale, pale Bermuda blue and made of the fine thin material of her nightgarment, would, he could see, float and flutter in the slightest breeze.

'Lovely. Ask Domino to sew rope along it good – and some canvas. And to hoist it on the main as soon as first light.'

They were heading due south on a tight reach and Surprise was just thinking: maybe the British see us heading south and think we bound north, when a round shot hit a few hundred yards astern of them (the boom of the firing only then reaching his ear) bounced, and landed abreast but well to port.

Surprise knew that the guns at Southampton Fort were big twenty-four pounders: worse, unlike guns fired from the insecure deck of a ship, these were mounted on the firmest platform, the land itself, and deadly accurate and long ranged. And that bouncing shot meant that the gun was operating at what was, for it, short range.

All sails had been set for some time now. The light had come up fast – a black cloud moving across the eastern horizon and suddenly revealing dawn.

'Henry! Take the helm.'

Surprise got his glass, and, wedging his right calf against the low cedar taffrail, opened the little brass shutters and then looked astern.

He was watching for the smoke puff, trying to see the moment of firing, and he thought: this is the first time a coloured captain looked at the shore of Bermuda through his own spyglass, from his own ship, standing on his own quarterdeck – then he saw a puff.

'Man the sheets!' He spun around. 'Bring her hard on the wind, Henry – tight as she can go.'

He was counting seconds waiting for the shot.

'Hold her steady – there – that's it.'

The spout went up, this time just to port of them – the sons of bitches' heat knew what they were about.

He looked back at the fort. 'Stand by the sheets!'

He tried to snatch glances about the horizon near the mainland, too – looking for the dreaded Royal Navy. If he saw a ship, there was no doubt what their course had to be: steady and sharp to windward, for only to windward could they be sure of outsailing any ship the British had – to leeward or even on a reach, the Royal Navy could overhaul them. In this light wind, or even with a moderate breeze, almost none could touch them to windward – of course, in a heavy blow,

God alone knew how the *Bateau* would sail. Pretty well he felt sure, but heavy weather always favoured a big ship. . . .

He saw the puff.

'Henry, lay her sou'-*east*, and smartly.'

The others quickly let out the sheets to match the helm change; the *Bateau*, loosened off the wind, surged forward.

Surprise counted again: the shot seemed overdue: then it fell, just as he had figured, a hundred and more yards to starboard – just about exactly where they would be had they stayed on the same course.

The British bitches: what if we were a simple fisherman? He looked up at their new and beautiful flag, spanking its blue soft self off the main. How could the British know who they were? How? Must be they just had orders to fire on any cedar sloop.

But he had no time for further reflection: this time not one puff, but one immediately followed by another.

He sweated in an agony of indecision: should he go up to the sou'west again, or head due east? No, let the British guess – hope they'd guess he'd repeat his manœuvre. Yes, he reckoned, he hoped, he was right to fake them and stay on the same course.

'What you want?' Henry shouted. 'What course you want?'

'Steady as you go.' Surprise wondered if the next thing he'd see would be Henry Rudd's head knocked off . . . or-not see, and it be his own.

What had the British done? Likely laid one shot for them to sharpen to the sou'-west and one for them to sail due south – or maybe the bitches outguess him and lay it right on us.

Plosh!

The fourth shot hit a way, way off to the starboard.

That was sou'-west guess, Surprise just thought, and the guess was wrong.

Plosh-sh!

Closer, much closer to starboard – but that was the south guess and both be wrong, you Limey yellow pigs.

'Now, Henry. Lay us due south – due south. A hundred and eighty degrees – '

'But – the Sou'-west Breaker Bar, Surprise – '

'To hell with it!' Surprise said, knowing they were on top of it – halfway through it, and no possible time or way to haul up the fin keel. 'Call out for white water! Look sharp in the bow.'

'Helm – hard a port!' Irving yelled.

Henry obeyed. No one touched a sail – she veered off.

'Helm, hard a starboard!' Irving shouted.

Henry obeyed again and Surprise looked down into the water and saw that they had skirted around a fiery and dripping boiler, as close as any ship could pass a buoy.

'Hold her due south, now, helmsman – that's it. Lay us good – '

The sixth shot fell, dead even with them, but to port again.

Domino came up on the quarter-deck. 'Why don't we shoot back, Surprise?'

'Shut up and man your sheets!'

'Shoot back!'

'Get to hell back to your sheets!'

Domino moved away, jumping the steps in one bound.

Now was the danger – the big danger. They had held this course – except for the evasion of the reef, for longer than any other.

Surprise scanned the shore but could see no puff – maybe it already fire off and I miss it. Our only hope now is to run out of their range – and that last shot did fall as if from a girt height.

Water suddenly cascaded over the stern and instantly drenched them – soaking them to the skin, burning Surprise's eyes. And more too: pieces of wood cascaded down on them, hundreds and seemingly thousands of small pieces of wood, rattled on the decks, stuck in the sails.

Delia screamed below. Henry growled something incomprehensible.

'Hold her steady!' Surprise yelled. 'Steady.'

He ran to the stern rail and looked over and down – the *Bateau Bermudien* was not hit. Relief seemed to flush through his restrained guts and veins – his precious ship was not hit: the rudder was perfect and the longtail carving – all perfect. What was the wood?

Just before he leaped back to stand by the helmsman, he looked at the water astern and then he knew: it was Senex's dinghy: Senex's dinghy had been smashed to smithereens, smashed into oblivion.

84

'The ship is *not* hit!' He yelled so all could hear.

He wiped his eyes, then his glass at both ends. 'Stand by, Henry – stand by for a sharp move.

'Irving – have we gained clear water?'

'More'n three fathoms and deepening.'

'Bring her thirty degrees to *port*. Now!'

Henry obeyed.

The sheets were slackened without need of command.

Plosh!

The eighth shot fell even with the seventh and a little to port of it.

The yellow pigs had guessed him to rights again – but, Surprise smiled with his old sea-worn sardonic grin: they were passing out of range.

'Helm due south.'

'Them Limey bitches have reached the end of their string: they cannot shoot any further.'

The minutes passed – the British fired again: the shot fell behind them, even a little short of the last two.

The wind held steady, if anything it was freshening with the rising sun.

Surprise felt the breeze sweet on his forehead and cheek: he smiled with a deep contentment for he had been in and around boats all his life, and, now, one thing was sure: the *Bateau Bermudien* was the fastest manœuvring craft he'd known or even heard tell of.

They sailed due south all morning and all afternoon and Surprise, constantly scanning the horizon behind them, saw no sail at all.

'That sure a fast way to wreck a good man's work,' Irving said, sweeping up the cedar chips that littered the decks.

'Well, better to hit the dinghy than us,' Henry said.

'Aye,' Surprise said. 'We can build or buy a dinghy – imagine if they'd hit our stern.' But he was remembering the old adage: 'A longboat can do without a ship, but a ship cannot do without a longboat.'

When he got Domino alone he said: 'Don't you ever leave your post again, man – I been a white man and you could be killed for that shit. As to why didn't I fire back – what was

85

coming at us was twenty-four pounds and what we got is *one* pound. You understand?'

'Yes – sorry, Surprise.'

'It all right – and another thing. Say we *had* hit 'em – and killed a British. Killed a British *officer*, say – what you think they do?'

'I dunno.'

'Man – they send every Royal Navy ship from Halifax to South America after us. Yes, sir – they charge us with murder, piracy on the high seas – everything.'

'And, now what they do?'

'Well, now – *now* we got the hope they think maybe they made a mistake. Now they don't even know for sure who we are or where bound.'

Truth was, he'd wanted to fire himself – early he'd thought of it, when leaving the Cut.

That night, still holding due south, Surprise, in their cabin, took his sharp knife and a chisel and, under the ship's name and date and tonnage, he carved carefully in the cedar, one word:

SENEX.

Delia, alone with him save for the child, said nothing. Surprise caught the little boy's bright eyes and smiled – the boy smiled back, and then, as if the smile, the infant ecstasy were too much for him, suddenly turned his little head and buried his face in his mother's bosom. A little sound escaped from him, too – the smallest squeal of contentment soughing over into rapture.

Surprise sighed and, moving, put his arm around Delia.

'They can't catch us?'

'No – we are safe. Safe for a while, anyway. To catch us, I figure they'd have to come upon us – and, even if they did, the *Bateau Bermudien* could sail in circles and still keep ahead of them.'

Surprise, three times a day, walked to the bow, threw over some orange peel, and, pacing, followed even with it as the ship passed – when it reached level with the small quarter-deck, he stopped. That way he gauged their speed.

They had two days and two nights good sailing and then the wind died to a whisper and then to nothing. The halyards slapped against the rolling spar, the sheets lolled aimlessly back and forth.

'Pull that rope out of water!'

The heat was oppressive.

Around nightfall, a tiny breeze got up, just enough to give them steerage way.

'Whale! Whale!' Bossie shouted, pointing to starboard.

They came up on it slowly. It did not, strangely, seem to be moving at all. Surprise thought it must be a girt leviathan asleep on the deep.

Then, in the failing light, he made out the shape – a ship, a ship, dismasted and so much awash as she appeared to be floating slightly under the water.

He thought he could see a name on her stern. He got his glass but he saw, through it, even less well than with his eye.

'It be a ship.'

'A ship!'

'Aye – a dead ship on the water.'

'A bad sign.'

Now Surprise could make out her name: in white it was. 'A ship found abandoned is a *good* omen, mates. A good omen indeed.'

The words he'd read were: *GERM*, Rhode Island.

'See if you can put a rope around her, August. A rope any place – maybe around the bowsprit. Ain't that a bowsprit, yonder?'

'Aye. Aye, Surprise, it is.'

'Get a lantern – we get a rope on her and tow her through the night. Tomorrow – who knows, maybe the deep will yield us something good.'

August was bracing himself ready to board her.

'Maybe dead men!' Irving shouted. 'Maybe dead men on her. Trapped below – I say, let's get clear of her.'

'And I say, get a hold of her. Rope her. Take her in tow. August – watch how you go. T'will be slippery and you liable to have her sink under your feet – you hear?'

'All right, Surprise. Bring her up to starboard – easy. Maybe I not have to jump aboard.'

August managed to get a loop of rope part over an anchor on her deck and part over one knighthead – they passed the taut line astern.

'She ride there easy, all right. Less'n the wind gets up. Don't look like it will though, August.'

'What her name, Surprise? She have writing on her – what it say?' Irving asked.

'It say *Blossom*, it say. She an American ship.'

'I say, let's cut her away.'

'Might be gold on her, Irving.'

'More likely bad spirits and dead people.'

'Belay that shit – *you* a seaman, a Bermudian seafaring man. You sound like a woman – a woman from St George's.'

Surprise and Henry and Domino watched through the night : she was a big ship and if she sank, they must cut her away smartly, before she towed them under. Surprise kept trying to get Domino to sleep a bit on deck, but he was too excited. The wind remained slack and the *Bateau* rode heavy tethered to her great, monstrous sea anchor.

He, Surprise, took a seaman's rest : sleeping a few moments standing here, sleeping a few moments sitting there : waking to the slightest sound or breath of wind.

The morning dawned promising another still, hot day – but the air seemed strangely crisp for September.

They hauled the two craft together, side by side. The *Germ*, all but the broken rails and gunwales submerged, was a half as long again as the *Bateau*.

Surprise stripped off his jerkin and his shirt and got ready to board her.

'Take a line and fasten it to your waist,' August said.

Surprise did so.

Irving looked suspiciously at the great waterlogged hulk. 'She been rotting around the sea for years.'

'No,' Surprise said. 'Look there – broken wood, only just discoloured : I reckon just a few months.'

'She could sink a vessel running into her – she could have sunk us,' Henry said.

'What her name again, Surprise?'

Surprise made ready to jump. 'Her name is *Bud*.' He jumped.

'Last night you said *Blossom*.'

Surprise was on her deck, sloshing through the water, about six to twelve inches deep, going towards her hatchway.

The hatchway was closed and tight and he could not move it. He tried feeling beneath it and then ducking under the water: he could neither feel nor see anything holding the hatchway closed from the outside.

It did not escape his mind that, if the hatch was secured from the inside, then some remains of human life must still be there.

'Throw down the axe.'

'It be dead in there – I *know* it,' Irving said.

'Uh-huh,' Bossie laughed, 'and if Surprise finds *gold*, what you going say – ? You going say I-told-you-so – where's mine? S'pose that what you going to say.'

They passed over the axe with rope on its handle.

'You want me come aboard?' August shouted.

'No, me!' Domino said.

'I be all right.' Surprise started to pry at the hatchway into what must have been her officers' or captain's quarters. He paused. 'No, come to think on it – August, come down, will you?'

He waited on the deck which was in the shadow of the *Bateau*: he wished now they'd hauled her the other side, so that they had more light.

By the looks of her, he'd guess she was a schooner – but all her rigging was gone save the stubs of two masts, part chopped, part splintered broken. What had brought her to grief? She was old, but not too old – perhaps a great, great storm, maybe a waterspout had sucked them up, he could not tell?

Perhaps there were many men trapped below – water-soaked and rotten and falling apart. He looked around for fish, for sharks. It was the thought of a shark swimming right out of the ship that had made him call for August.

But he knew he was going to try to look through her. Say

89

she did have gold? Even an instrument, a nautical instrument would be good. Even a few flags.

Maybe a cannon. It could be. Or just a nice big roll of canvas – good for patching and covering a hole in their ship, should it ever happen.

For himself, he like to find a captain's hat – a fine Yankee cap. For Delia, maybe some new dresses, likely too big, but she could cut 'em down.

'August. You watch. I pry.'

'Right, Surprise. I gotta say it exciting, but I less'n half like it.'

'Aye.' He wedged the axe head in the top of the hatch – it wouldn't move. Next, working underwater, with only his head out, he tried smashing the exposed hinge pins. The water severely cushioned the blows.

'Give it me,' August said quietly.

He pushed the axe in, halfway down and in the middle. The doors sprung apart and opened a little.

Surprise jumped back. Then, nothing appearing, moved forward again and pulled them open.

Sometimes, with the rising and falling of the ocean swell, the *Germ*'s quarter-deck was free of water, at others, it was a foot awash. With each movement of the swell she gave out deadened thumps and creaks.

Surprise had the doors wide open and was bending to look inside – suddenly he leapt back and a sound escaped him.

A box of reddish mahogany, floating like a cheeky toy boat with only a slight list, came out to meet them.

August picked it up. 'Why lookie here.' He hefted it and then passed it to Surprise.

'Light – and locked too.' Surprise shook it. Something slight but heavy rattled inside.

He figured they could close the doors, return to the *Bateau*, open it, examine the contents and then return. But time was precious: they needed to get all they could and get clear.

'I pass this aboard,' he shouted. 'But no one is to open anything until August and I return. Understood?'

'Aye,' said Henry. 'Pass it up and easy. I get a basket for whatever else you find.'

They opened the hatchway again.

90

'You or me, Captain?'
' 'Tis pitiful dark in there.'
'Aye.'
'I go.' Surprise held his nose, blew air from his mouth and went under.

August looked after him but could see nothing. He watched and watched. Then he looked up and shrugged, as if embarrassed, toward his companions.

Surprise broke surface, gasping. He had in his hand a piece of rotten leather – the handle of a trunk, perhaps.

'It a girt cabin,' he gasped. 'No sign of any bodies – but I did bump something bad, later I figured it was only bedding.'

Henry lowered over a basket.

'I go.' August doubled over and flip-dived down.

'I don't know what we get from her – maybe nothing else,' Surprise said to his companions.

Delia called from the rail. 'Why you not let Domino dive – he young and used to it, Surprise. Deddy always say he a born diving fool!'

'Aye – perhaps.'

What August had in his left hand decided them all towards serious salvage: three English silver shillings.

They examined them and then put them in the basket.

'It a cabin for four men,' August said. 'The captain, I reckon, and three others – maybe his family. Maybe officers.'

'Any bodies – man, tell me,' Irving yelled.

'No. No bodies.'

Surprise did not like diving, nor going into dark places under water. He wanted, too, to see what was in the so perfect mahogany box.

'Close the hatches again.'

He and August took the shillings and went back aboard the *Bateau*.

The box was exquisitely made: even when they knocked the pins out of the hinges it would not open. From the heft of it they could tell no water had got in.

'Two wide chisels and snap the lock,' Irving said. 'That way the box not be harmed, only the lock tongues broke.'

'Maybe we should look for the key,' Delia said.

'Girl – that long gone.'

Irving's tool soon sprang open the box. So cleverly made was it (with an interlocking thin lead-tipped wooden washer) that the green baize inside was not even stained or damp.

There were two silver watches in it, each wrapped in a purple velvet jacket.

'They must have belonged to someone rich,' Irving said, touching the filigree on the back of one.

'They ship's watches,' Henry said.

Surprise took the key from the velvet and wound one gently. He listened. Nothing. He shook it. It ticked and ticked and ticked. He smiled. 'They be not watches, but chromometers – for navigation. This, shipmates, is a good *good* omen indeed.'

The other item in the box was a leather-bound book. Surprise took it up.

'Henry. Take a good look all around the ocean. Keep a watch. A lookout. Better post two – and I read out to all what here. Then we see what else we can get up from this good luck ship.'

'Bossie, watch with me – you yonder, me this way.'

Surprise licked the thumb he only recently so carefully dried.

'She a schooner,' Surprise said. 'Name of – , name of *Bud*.'

'You say *Blossom* last night.'

'Well, I make a mistake. She name of *Bud*, from Providence, Rhode Island. This the log of Captain – wait a minute – Madden.' He turned the many pages and read the last entry. ' ". . . hove down on beam ends, Captain Madden and cook washed overboard. Foremast cut away and mainmast went with it. . . . Righted . . . full of water. Have been on wreck subsis – subsist on nothing but water these many days . . . mate, two seamen and a coloured man. . . . All now resigned to death. . . ." That the last.' He turned back.

'Look like she be six days out of Montego Bay when it happen. She were bound for Charleston – '

'What her cargo?'

'Don't say – no, here. Lumber – and part in ballast. No wonder she float. The lumber. What you see, Henry?'

Henry Rudd was half up the ratlines. 'Nothing. Clear still water from horizon to horizon.'

Surprise got up. 'John – take these to my cabin and lay them down gentle – you hear?'

'Yessir.'

'Put them on a bunk, so they can't fall and break.' He stretched impatiently. 'Mates. We don't know what we got here – nothing any good in the hold. But the cabin : we should get all we can from the cabin. I say we let Domino dive and see what he can bring up – him and anyone else as wants, working one down, one up. I say we give it until noon and then haul arse out of here.'

All agreed.

'That give us three full hours. We can't waste any more. We getting to the Indies – we better put water between us and the Royal Navy.'

'T'ain't no breeze worth a fart, anyway,' said Bossie.

Surprise licked his forefinger and held it aloft. 'No. There ain't. But it might rise with the sun. Tell you, let's haul ourselves around to the other side of the wreck – that way Domino get light in that cabin.'

They did so.

Domino set to diving with Bossie helping.

Surprise had the jib hauled and furled and pegged with the special cedar pegs Senex had made – one hard jerk on a sheet and the sail would fly free. He had the mainsail kept half-hauled in readiness and he himself, at eleven o'clock, climbed almost to the top of the spar and swept the horizon until his eyes spotted with his concentration – trying to make his eyes sweep deep to the very edge, and beyond for the telltale sign of a spar or a pennant.

Bernice hauled on board the basket after almost every dive Domino made. Bossie brought up little, for Domino could stay down three times as long : Domino the strong and young and fearless – fearless, as Surprise felt, almost to foolhardiness.

At noontime they had on the deck a pile of English shillings and sixpences. Strange, Surprise thought, all the coin English.

They kept counting it. And by noon, the breathtaking count was over one thousand shillings and almost as many sixpences.

It was becoming so vast a find that Surprise became worried and called all hands to eat and talk.

Jennie, her one arm, just as she promised, as good as anyone's two, had cooked – and the cedar wood they carried for burning gave almost no smoke at all.

'We're all rich,' Irving said. 'Damn if we ain't.'

Surprise let them talk. He finished his plate and wiped it with his bread and then handed it to Jennie.

'We gotta get it all,' Henry said. 'Let's stay till nightfall.'

'I agree to that,' Surprise said. 'And I feel we should divide it all even amongst us – '

'You talking about women too?' Bernice said.

'You are with me, woman, so shut up.'

'I say we should keep all the money for the whole lot of us – for the whole venture,' Surprise said. 'But, say anyone want to leave the venture at any port or place – then he entitled to his share.'

'What about women?'

'I want nothing,' Jennie said. 'I stay with Surprise.'

'Is it really ours, legal like?' Bossie asked.

'Aye. All found at sea and abandoned – even the ship, belongs to the finders.'

'What her name – really? You say *Blossom* and you say *Bud*?'

'It's the same thing, in it? She's a flower to us.' Surprise smiled. 'But I say we keep the whole moneys to pay for our whole venture – but anyone want to leave, they entitled to a sixth of what's left.'

'And women – you act like we don't exist?'

Surprise was angry. 'We don't have time for arguing. Only Jennie is unattached – she entitled to a half share, I reckon. As for you, Bernice? You want me to count you *and* Delia and Jennie and divide it in ninths? Divide it nine times instead of six?'

'I say, to hell we do,' Henry said. 'We divide it in sixths like Surprise say. And I say, let's get back to getting *all* that's left. What the hell's the use of squabbling afore we even got the coin on our deck. Hell, there might be *gold* down there. I say, let's set to.'

'Agreed.' Surprise took a drink of water. 'Who can spell Domino with diving and who to watch with me?'

'I dive,' Delia said. 'Jennie, you take the boy – '

'No – '

'Stop, Surprise. You don't know, man. I can dive as good as Domino. You want the best divers, here we are. Me and Domino.'

Bernice said : 'Why you not let me take the little boy?'

'You can take him,' Delia said. 'He likes you. But you holler at me if'n he's hungry. When he gets hungry, he like his Deddy – he can't wait.'

By sundown, they had gleaned a deal of junk they threw over the side, over two thousand sixpences nd two thousand three hundred and seven shillings.

'Sure is a lot of money,' Irving said.

Domino and Delia also brought up a spyglass – water-filled but unbroken – and a quadrant.

With this last, Surprise quite forgot the money. It was perfect, and, a more simple instrument than a sextant, he had far greater hopes of being able to master its hidden scientific secrets.

He took it to his cabin, dried it, oiled it and fussed over it.

The others were awed by his silence, his withdrawal, his knowledge.

'That man can read anything,' Bossie said.

'Aye,' said Henry. 'If a man can read the stars – well, that man can *really* read.'

'That what he read with that funny theeng?' Bernice asked.

'Aye. He read the stars.'

'Don't see what good no stars are to us,' Bernice said. 'We gotta worry about what's down here – not what's up in no sky.'

'Then it's a damn good thing you ain't master of this ship, woman. For if you were, we all be surely lost – lost forever in the cradle of deep goddamn woman ignorance.'

'To hell with you, man. I had my way, I take my silver and go to hell back to Bermuda and live me a life of easement.' Bernice, the baby in her arms, went into peals of laughter. The baby was about to cry, but she noticed it, and rocked him and cooed at him and he, quick as ever, smiled.

Surprise was at the rail: 'Can you find any flags? Is there a flag rack in that cabin?'

'I try.' Delia, clad in nothing but her undergarments – and laughing at the fun of it all – went under again, like a boy or a mermaid.

'What about cannon?' Surprise asked Domino. 'We could certainly use a six pounder – or a pair of fours.'

'I looked, Captain. Nothing. She have no gunports at all –
only painted white squares.'

Delia came up empty handed.

'Let's stop.'

'I go down one more time,' Domino said.

The wind, freshening a bit, had begun to flap the loose
pieces of furled sail.

Domino was gone until they feared he'd split his lungs.
He came up at last, holding above him another box – also
mahogany – but longer and flatter.

'There's nothing else.'

'All right – we must sail. It time to set sail. Domino, take
that loose piece of timber there and fasten it upright – here,
throw him spikes and a hammer. Fasten it as a warning to
other ships.

'Can't we sink her?' Domino called out.

Henry laughed. 'How do think you sink a load of lumber,
boy?'

They cast her loose, set all sails and headed due south.

The box contained a pair of flintlock pistols, very wet and
rusted.

'I clean 'em up good,' Irving said.

'Yes. And you'd better load them and mount them by the
forward hatchway, so that they can be grabbed easy as you
rush on deck.'

'Look – it got a shot mould and all.'

'We got lead?' Domino asked.

'Man, of course we got lead.'

Before nightfall, all gathered close by the helm for dinner.
Bossie alone was on watch forward. Everyone was in good
spirits, and, before long, Surprise said:

'If we can find the *right* island, one that can succour us in
food and water, we can start our own new colony. But I tell
you this: we gotta hope the British don't come for us.'

'We can forget all the Bahamas,' Henry said. 'The British
patrol there thick and even the Bermudian whites got close
relatives there. Same in the Turks Island and the Caicos –
Bermudians there and come and go.'

'What about the black island – Hispaniola or San Domingo
– whatever it is?' August said.

'All right if you speak French or Spanish,' Henry said. 'I don't. I been to Port-au-Prince – and it one spooky bad place. I tell you I don't want to go again.'

'Then what about San Domingo?' August asked.

'Spanish. Bad as Cuba,' Henry said. 'I don't know about anyone else, but Henry Rudd ain't going to no place as got mad Spanish.'

'I agree with that,' Surprise said. 'Truth is we want an island with no one on it – and where the British won't molest us.'

'We find an out of way place,' Irving said, 'how they find us?'

'The British are funny – sometimes they never give up. And no one ever licked the British save George Washington and Thomas Jefferson – and that fight ain't necessarily settled yet.'

'But those Yankee white people ain't going to be any help to us.' Henry swallowed his last morsel and began to get out his pipe.

'They is and they ain't,' Surprise said. 'See, I heard of a funny thing. A funny document thing. It called the Monroe Document. It all signed and written up by President James Monroe. Long time ago, too : early twenties, round about the founding of that Liberty place.'

'In Africa?' Henry said. 'Yeah, I heard.'

'Well, this Monroe Document say that no English or Europe government or army can interfere with no little countries – 'cept and if they do, the United States attack the big people and defend the little.'

'That so?' Henry said sceptically.

'Aye.' Surprise stood up. 'It's so, I figure, if we can find an island and make it *our* country – we can write to the United States President and tell him we are there and want protection if attacked.'

'This President Monroe take *our* side – against white English?'

'He already *fight* the English, Henry. He and Jefferson was the ones fight the Second War – in 1812. And they lick 'em, too. Leastwhys, they lick 'em at sea.'

'Now you know,' Henry said. 'Nobody can lick the Limey *army* – why the Limey army, in Bermuda alone, is as many as the grains of sand on a beach at low tide – nobody can lick that.'

'Maybe not,' Surprise said. 'But the United States lick 'em at sea. They had nerve enough to stand up to 'em, I figure we can, too.'

'I don't want to *lay down* for them,' Bernice laughed. 'Never mind stand up to them.'

'Ease, woman, ease.'

'How can we get a letter to this President – tain't like he in St George's and us on St David's?'

'No. But, maybe we can hail some Yankee ship sometime – if we get our island, our new colony – and send the letter that way.'

'Huh,' Irving said. 'More'n likely the British take the Yankee ship, read our letter and come cut our arses.' He laughed.

'We see,' Henry said. 'We gotta watch this weather. It that time all right, Surprise. It the time for *anything* – '

'Wisht I was at home,' young John said.

'Boy. You better thank Gawd you ain't. Home is where we is going – home is right here and right *now*. You hear? You'd better get used to it.'

III

The wind held steady out of the sou'-west, day after day.

Surprise threw over his orange peels – or sometimes a bit of wood – and guessed his speed.

Sometimes he took out the quadrant and took sights of stars at night – but he knew no pattern to them and knew not how to calculate their angle and height and transfer it to a chart. Indeed, he knew only how to find the Polar Star, and he knew he could steer, roughly, by that, if he had to.

Least, he had the compass, and, steering due south by that was far more accurate than steering by the Pole Star.

Sometimes, to impress his followers, he got out his sextant and looked through its spy glass at the horizon. He knew it was also to measure the angle of the sun and stars and that in some way it worked with clocks (and he had all three clocks going now: his old one and the two new silver ones – all keeping time, and the new ones kept together and his ran fast) but he didn't know how to put the puzzle together. Besides, his sextant was missing the arm thing that swung from the top and crossed up and down the gradation thing, in an arc, below. The others didn't know that.

But, looking at his charts, he could figure they had to cover exactly one thousand miles *due* south, to come to the Virgin Islands. Barring storms to take them off course, they might make it.

He kept a daily addition in the log book of the *Germ* – and Irving had fixed the box so that it again closed good. After writing in it, he put the watches and the log book in the box and tied it tight with twine.

His figuring was: Day One and night: eighty-five miles; Day Two and night: a hundred and twenty-five miles; Day Three: nought; night thirty-five miles; Day Four: seventy-five miles and night; Day Five. . . . He did all his figuring, first, in single strokes (|||||) plus one, make a gate (♯♯), and then he counted them all up for each day.

By the end of the ninth day, the wind still holding moderate to fresh from the sou'-west, and allowing for its veering and sometimes putting them on a quicker reach and sometimes a fast broad reach, he added up carefully again and again, and came up with nine hundred and fifty miles.

He set a double watch in the bow by the knightheads.

'Keep a sharp look out,' he ordered, 'for Anegada Island be before us – and we safe there – for it only black people. But watch sharp – for Anegada be but very flat and you cannot see her long afore you run upon her.'

He thought, if they had drifted at all eastish, they'd spot Sombrero. And if westish, the Spanish big island, Porto Rico. And if they spotted those high hills, they'd steer clear and to the east.

He just wished and needed to make a landfall across this big, big patch of ocean. For he could figure their position pretty good and exact if he could see two points of land and recognise them from the charts or from his past memories. He knew how to take a bearing on a mountain, say, or a beacon and read its angle towards them on the compass; and then, finding a second bearing, read that angle and draw the angles on his chart – and where they crossed was where the *Bateau Bermudien* would be.

Beau Nat had shown him that and good : and how to take a third bearing to be sure.

But it was this big, big crossing of the pitiless sea – and it giving no signs, only wave after wave and countless wave. So they were heading south and he was guessing nine hundred and fifty miles. But what was missing was Beau Nat's magic books of countless numbers and dates – and what was missing most was the magic of the sextant and the clocks.

'Sixty-four degrees and forty minutes west,' Captain Darrell would say : 'And thirty-two degrees and twenty minutes north. There we be.'

And Captain Darrell be in a vicious temper if he go *two* days without a 'sight' on a star or sun. And now they be nine days without the magic of the sextant.

The burden was, Surprise discovered, that he could tell no one. No one. He needed them to believe in his leadership, his magic or they would not follow him through any perils that lay ahead. And perils there were bound to be : even a raw cabin boy knew of perils that happen on the ocean – never mind what *he* knew.

He wished he had Senex with him – without Emiline. He could confide in Senex and Senex might have some wise counsel. . . .

Surprise figured he could do without any counsel – just as long as he could tell someone, share the burden of this loneliness.

Tonight Bossie was one on watch and Bossie was sharp-eyed all right, but – when Surprise was about to leave to go and add his figures again, and he, Surprise, was thinking : what if we smash tonight, in dead dark, upon a reef and cut us open; what do I do, and us with no dinghy? – Bossie had said : 'I bet you I the first person in this ship see the first virgin on the islands – I bet you *that*, Domino.'

And I, Surprise thought, I alone am responsible for ten souls this night – and one of them be a virgin indeed. What if little Surprise drown this night? What if the light go out in those infant eyes – and it be my fault, my miscalculation, my ignorance?

He would he could be alone and weep for he knew that the light *was* in those eyes now, and, though little Surprise be

100

his, it was not in his power to put the light back in those eyes, if it go out.

God of ocean and sky, he prayed, God of all vastness and light and darkness, guide this little ship and this man and have mercy on the virgin life here entrusted.

God of Senex and all my fathers, God of Darrells and all white and all Africans, protect us and make this thy servant wiser than he is. . . .

Irving came and said: 'There be no bottom at twenty fathoms, Surprise.'

'Aye. Try it in an hour and every hour – for land is near and shoal water too. Have no fear – but keep swinging your lead and your eyes sharp.'

Past midnight, Henry on the wheel said: 'The sky's scudding up – and, funny theeng – seems to be moving from sou'-east, yet the wind be sou'-west.'

Surprise took the lantern and looked over the side at the water. He looked to see if it be milky, indicating shoals and high winds far off disturbing the bottom; but he saw only the black blue of deep ocean.

He lay down and slept and dreamed a blood-soaked dream: Emiline had cut his father's bowels open and was eating his entrails. . . .

A shipboard bang almost woke him. Then he dreamed that little Surprise was washed overboard and he could not get the *Bateau* to come about to pick him up. The child was overboard and the ship would not answer the helm, would not come about. . . .

By first light, Surprise was on deck and what he saw, was, he figured, part of the cause of his dreams. The *Bateau* was taking green water over the leeward rail and the deck was near all dark with wet, and spray was whipping back and wetting the mainsail – which, he instantly noticed, had been reefed in.

He went to the tiller.

'I take her, Henry. Take off all but the second jib and tell them to look sharp for'ard. Raise the other watch.'

'I reefed twice – but did not want to wake you, man.'

'Thank you.'

'What you figure coming, Surprise?'

'Don't look good – let's hope for a landfall.' He smiled. 'She sure sails sweet and deep.'

'Aye.'

By noon, they were on the opposite tack, still holding south, but the wind was high from the south-east and rising all the time.

Surprise made his calculations: the ship was now hitting her maximum through the water. They had already passed the thousand miles south where they should see land.

At two o'clock he had them take off the main entirely and put up the larger jib and take off the smaller. If it got rougher near nightfall, he'd hove-to and put out Senex's sea anchor.

Trouble was, it was sticky – hot, and the wind, even discounting the whipping spray, was soggy feeling: he tried to wish it not so, but knew a storm was coming. And another thing he knew: there's damn few little storms in September, only big ones. Below, he found his shark oil barometer showing milky.

And the worst sign of all: he, Surprise, felt depressed and heavy and he noticed that everyone else seemed miserable, too. All had the pre-hurricane heavies.

By nightfall it was blowing a whole and howling gale from sou'-east by east. They got all the canvas off and the sea-anchor over and then the rain came. It hit the deck like someone was throwing it in buckets from the masthead; it whipped, with the tops of waves, in their faces. Their bodies, whatever their clothing, were long since soaked.

He'd told Jennie at four o'clock to douse her fire and at five minutes after four a wave doused it. Now it was past seven of the evening and the light had a ghastly purple tinge to it – he'd seen it before.

It was so damned *stupid*, he thought: we were right about to make the Virgin Islands and now this girt gale is blowing us half to hell.

It was just like Captain Darrell said: all hurricanes come from the south-east. It was funny, like the south-east was the home of hurricanes.

Well, the wind was carrying them clear of land – if his

102

figuring be right – and there was nothing now to do but lash the helm and see how the *Bateau* ride.

The sea anchor, forward, held her like a tethered horse, and she did dip her bow in pitiful deep already. Well, that was the price you paid for a sharpish ship to cut to windward.

If it got real bad, he could consider putting the sea anchor over the stern but that was dangerous.

'Lash everything down tight. Check the livestock. Leave no jib canvas on at all but the little one and that down and lashed tight.'

He went forward in the failing light and stood with his arm around the tall spar, which, aloft, pitched wildly deep back, and even wilder deep forward – and she did rotate, too, and swing perilous to the port, then astern, then to starboard, then down, down.

He himself hauled down the pennant – heaven knew they had no need to be told the direction of the wind.

By eight he logged that it was blowing upwards of fifty knots – for that be when the sea be strangely flattened at the tops of waves, and so stinging the eyes as to make all seeing difficult.

He checked that all was lashed down in their cabin, reassured Delia – who laughed a lot with excitement and only looked worried when she looked at the child.

He went forward and checked his ship in every way. The keel was leaking but very slightly; the pump was operative, good, but not yet needed. She was making a little water in the bow, from where the knightheads came through the deck – but it didn't look to be serious.

At twelve he changed the watches on deck from two to three men each – which would mean four hours on, and four off for all – and logged that the wind be nearing hurricane strength and definitely a severe storm.

He tried to get some sleep, but, around three a great crash brought him on deck and he found August wrestling with the boom that had busted loose and was bidding fair to bust the tiller and the taffrails both.

They secured it.

At first light, he noticed that the *Bateau*, as she pitched forward into the sea, not only buried her prow but buried it deep – worse, she went down and in like she was never coming

103

up. Then she did shake – much like a wet dog – and, though you thought she was never going to rise, but pitch sheer to the bottom, yet did she rise, shaking the giant seas off her and shedding them astern in a foaming black and green and white cascade.

'I want that jib hauled – two men on the halyard and two on the sheet.'

As to seeing land, he couldn't see beyond the second giant wave : and the waves looked like the great hills of the Azorees – or maybe Porto Rico.

When they got the jib up he was on the loosened tiller and he sent the boy and told them to get the anchor in.

The weight of the sea anchor, together with her sharpish properties of the bow, was just too much, he figured – he'd rather keep the bow into the wind by a bit of sail and the helm.

Bring her up, let her tack over, bring her up. It would be a tiring business afore long.

Irving came near.

'Man, give me a small piece of mainsail up – just a shirt full, mind. Enough to give us some balance.'

'You might be better let it blow us by the stern, Surprise.'

'We might come to that yet.'

Truth was, with a storm, like everything else at sea, it was a lot of guessing : was the storm long and big and deep afore you or behind you?

If was afore, then sail into it, or at least, fight a bit against its force and let it blow by. If behind, then try to run with it, run away from it, or run off to one side – if you could guess which side to run.

No one could, he reckoned, save the oldest and wisest sea dogs. He knew a fella, once, a Red Indian, old as death, who could read a storm's depth – or said he could. And he, Surprise, had even once been in the middle of a storm and it be *no* storm at all – as quiet as a marsh and the frogs croaking – but the storm raging all around like a maddened giant clock and they be riding on the still centre of the hands.

They got the sea anchor in and lashed and damn near lost the boy, John, overboard.

'August. You tell Domino, he be responsible for that boy. You tell him, that black boy go over the side and I throw him after.'

'Aye, Aye.'

The spray stung his bald head and, the next time he went below, he'd get his woollen cap – the one with the rope choker on it.

Surprise fought the storm – letting the jib and piece of main fill, letting them carry her forward to steerage and then bring her about, and repeating it all, until noon. Then he gave the helm over to Henry – who was looking greenish about the gills, that purple green that only a coloured man looks. Strange, it was the tinge, he thought, of the purple of a hurricane's light.

What could he do at nightfall?

What reckoning could he log now? What rate of drift? And into what caverns of rock were these caverns of seas carrying them?

That night, he found, to his delighted relief, that even in pitch blackness, so sensitive was the *Bateau Bermudien*'s helm, that he could feel her up, and over, and feel her fill again.

He wrestled her all night, trusting no other. He noticed he seemed to have the strength of two men – it was the excitement and exhilaration that the furious weather communicated, he figured. As if the lightning and fury in the storm somehow got into the marrow of his bones.

At morning, when he found Delia, she burst into tears – during the night the baby had sprung loose from her for a moment, and was, she said, bashed blue with bruises.

But, bracing himself against all roll and pitches, he examined the child and found nothing broken. Indeed the boy laughed at the tickling.

'We wrap him good and tight all over – leaving only space to breathe and tie him in the bunk with you.'

'What when he dirty hisself?'

'Let him – won't hurt him none – might cushion him a bit.'

'And me – what me – ?'

He gestured at the lids of their so carefully made and fitted heads – water was bouncing even up to them, and spreading on the inner deck. 'I gotta lash them down – you gotta go, go anywhere. What it matter?'

She smiled and held on to him : 'Nothing matters 'cept we live.'

'We live, girl. This a good ship, you know. This no goddamn rowboat – this the pride of Bermuda.'

He went on deck.

August came up : 'All the animals but the sow be drowned.'

'No wonder. Throw them over and take the pig below.'

'I did.'

'Tell everyone they must make earth, make dirt every day. Anyone get bound up must take salts – worst thing in a storm is to have bound-up bowels.'

They rode the storm thus for four days and three long nights. Surprise had the little jib moved aft, so that she was fastened to the bow of the ship herself, ignoring the bowsprit. It helped a bit.

Long since they secured the main – and got it below deck.

Surprise logged nothing : it was too rough to write and he was afraid he'd wreck the box, the log and the watches. What was there to log : that it was the worst storm captain or crew had ever known? That it was blowing past all knowledge, past all measure?

The last measure was 'hurricane force' and that be when men can only crawl on their bellies; and this? It was as if wind and spray would tear the very stubble from their shaved faces and leave raw flesh.

On the fifth day, around three of the afternoon, the starboard stays and ratlines sheered off at the deck. Bossie, trying to grapple with them, was badly cut about the face and left shoulder –

And then the spar cracked louder than the hell of the storm and Surprise knew there was no course left but to : 'Cut her down! Cut down the spar! Henry, August. Get everything you got and cut her down!'

The boy John, he'd bound, the day before, below – for safety at first, now it was for pumping. And all women too took turn.

The spar would not let go, would not come to the deck where Surprise hoped to secure it – for, to lose such a treasured piece of spruce, would be loss indeed.

But she would not come down – and, the foremost stay

106

being fastened to the long bowsprit, where they could in no way reach it, there seemed nothing they could do.

Then the whole spar collapsed outward into the sea to starboard and Surprise left the helm and himself grabbed the axe and struck blow after furious blow at the splintered but still holding, tenacious, spruce wood.

She'd pull them over, lay them on their beam ends, or worse, capsize her altogether.

Even if he got her loose, Surprise knew, the spar could be smashed into and through the hull and hole them bad.

But at last the spar fell over the side – all hands heaving – and the ship seemed to right herself from her perilous list to starboard: and, at any moment, he feared she'd take a big wave flat against her side, it being into the wind now, or almost. A ship broached was more helpless than a horse fallen in the shafts.

'Get the sea anchor over the *stern*,' he yelled. 'The *stern*.' And ran for it himself and found Bossie there and Irving too, and, all bloodied they struggled with the canvas and coils of rope up the deck and back to the quarter-deck, where, the steps gone God knew where, they chambered up against the heave and spray and tangle and all manner of slip and sea.

Wherever you grabbed your hand was torn as if all matter of steel or split and splintered wood were attracted to it by magic.

But they got the sea anchor over and lashed it first to part of the taffrail and then forward to the main stern cleat, and, just as they did, the taffrail was whipped away by the sea anchor rope, splintered, gone, like sage bush sticks in furious fire. But she held on the main cleat.

He grabbed August, and, holding him, shouted in his ear: 'Get every piece of rope – every piece on the ship – and trail it astern. You hear? We got to break the seas, behind, up – afore they break and broach the stern to pieces. Get everything over.'

He went and double-lashed the helm amidships, only half daring to hope that his beautiful rudder, Senex's masterpiece, would not be smashed.

On the sixth day, the wind died a good deal but the sea still raged as if tormented into perpetual wrestling agony –

as if it, the sea, fought for its survival, its supremacy over wind.

'The spar and rigging,' Irving yelled, coming in the after cabin (where all was in ordered disarray – the top of the adult head nailed across a broken after port). 'They're ahead of us – they're held by the forestay. All's held, Surprise. All's trailing in front of us. She dies some more, we can save a good deal, maybe.'

At dawn, on the seventh day, they were at work, trying to put things in some way shipshape (trying with Surprise's guidance to rig a jury rig, to give them some form of self direction) when Bossie, his head and shoulder bandaged and purple-brown with dried blood, cried out, 'Ship – ship ahead. Ship on the starboard bow!'

'Where?'

'There – and a big bascombe she be, too.'

The ship was coming up on them slowly : she was a brig with no sail on but a small spanker aft and a patched little jib for'ard.

Irving came and stood by him. 'Man, it be a good thing you moved that sea anchor aft – not for'ard – or else we'd be stove in for sure – '

Surprise looked at him and drew in his breath. 'Chief Yeoman. You get below and find dry powder – *dry*, you hear?'

'Aye.'

'And you load first one and then the other Buccaneer – keep 'em hidden below but ready. Have the shot rammed home good. Take two with you.'

'Aye.'

'August. You load the pistols, you hear. Dry powder – but keep all weapons below deck.'

August's sad, patient face came closer to him. 'Captain. Ain't much we can do – not with us dead on the water.'

'First Mate – I tell you, Surprise not be dead until he starts to *stink*. You hear?'

'Aye. I go.'

The brig was moving very slowly. Gradually Surprise could make out the flag : Stars and Stripes.

He breathed no sigh of relief : British captains flew the

colours of whatever nation they guessed the ship was that they were approaching.

Surprise figured it best to show no flag at all – he didn't even know if their blue flag was still in existence.

He shouted to the hatchway: 'You ready with those Buccaneers?'

'Not yet.'

'If you have to, you going to have to fire one by tying it to the ship – only one gunlock is left.'

'We fire it holding it if we have to,' Bossie shouted.

'And you be blasted overboard and the precious guns too.'

There was no answer.

The hail came across the restless ocean with surprising clarity: '*Nancy* of Boston. What ship are you?'

Surprise cupped his hands and, without hesitation, said: 'Sloop *Bateau Bermudien* from Barbuda.' The name was an island he'd only seen on the charts – it came into his head without conscious thought.

'Be ye pirates,' the voice came back, 'and I will blast ye to kingdom come.'

Two of the brig's four gunports flapped open and two fat-nosed guns were run out. Fore and aft, Surprise counted three swivel guns manned and aimed.

'Women and children on board. Been in storm for six days. Lost rigging, ship's boat, all livestock. Have no reckoning.' He went to the hatch.

'Delia, get up here with the child.

'Have you any reckoning?' Surprise hailed again. 'Any reckoning at all?'

Delia came on deck and Bernice came up from the forward hatch too. 'You women walk – parade around.'

'What place ye from?'

'Barbuda Island.'

'Ye a long way from home. Our reckoning at first light, seventy-five point twenty degrees west and sixteen point thirty north.'

Surprise sang it again inside his head: making the number indelible so that he could work it out on his chart.

'Be ye Christian folk?'

109

'Aye. Christian and God-fearing too, Captain.'

'Ye need water?'

'No. Need no water. But would be glad to buy some salts – salts for the bowels.'

The brig was pulling by them. The hail came back like the faint call of seabirds in a fog.

'. . . too rough for long boat . . . come about . . . throw aboard. . . .'

'What he say?' August called from below.

'It all right. He a decent merchantman from Boston,' Surprise said. 'He throw us some salts for the bowels.'

Next to the salts, Surprise wanted to see exactly where they were: he couldn't wait to see it clearly. By the sound of it, he guessed they must be in the Windward Passage, and that sure was blown to hell and gone.

The Yankee ship was a ways off, coming about.

Years before, after his first voyage to sea, as a boy, he'd come back and told his father that he'd weathered through the Windward Passage, heading for home, from Kingston, with Captain Darrell. It was in January. The seas were monstrous high and near tore them apart; ever since then, when he dreamed of himself drowning at sea, it was always in the Windward Passage.

Captain Darrell didn't mind. 'Better here than the Florida Straits.' And Surprise came to understand when he could read the charts: the Florida Straits were all strewn with rocks and reefs and islands. . . .

A Yankee seaman in the heaving bow of the *Nancy*, just aft of her beautiful high-painted figurehead, threw a jar that Domino caught without moving.

The captain came in view, red-faced, on his quarter-deck. He had a brass voice trumpet. 'Ye be runaway slaves?'

'No.'

'I guess ye be.'

'Freemen all.'

'Ye keep clear of the north of us. Spanish privateers and all manner of pirates.'

'Sire – is your reckoning to be depended on?'

'With your life, man.'

'Thank you, sire.'

110

'I'll not log I've seen ye.'

Surprise hesitated and then hailed. 'Have you seen any British – any Royal Navy ships?'

'Aye. But not for days. Recommend you head for a deserted harbour – '

'What money for the salts?'

'None. And God be with you.'

The Yankee brig, in passing, was giving them the first quiet water they'd known since almost past memory.

'*Bateau*, what other help you need?'

'None, thank you, sire.'

'What strength wind you hit?'

'Hurricane force for six days – '

'What your last bearing?'

Surprise hesitated, then spat his only sure knowledge. 'Sixty-four degrees west. Just north of Anegada.'

'You been in hell's tempest indeed. We've had none such. Two days out of Santiago, bound for Barraquilla.'

'God speed you, sire – and many thanks.'

'God speed you – 'tis a keen sloop you have – if you can keep her afloat.'

'Aye.'

Surprise got out the chart. He believed the Yankee captain. Christian Yankees make few mistakes.

Their position seemed impossible: just south of the eastern tip of Jamaica. Over two hundred and fifty miles south of where he had figured: for he had figured them north and east of the Windward Passage and they were two hundred miles *south* of the southernmost water of that passage.

'Everyone who has bound-up bowels, take salts – but use it sparingly – *conserve*. Conserve everything at sea.'

He walked the deck, little steps for a little deck, and came to the decision: they'd head for one of the deserted coves on the north shore of Jamaica. There they could make repairs and get themselves seaworthy again. This rolling around in the vast ocean must stop as soon as possible.

He consulted his chart again. About one hundred miles nor'-west by north and they should be able, the day being clear, to see the peaks of the Blue Mountains.

Careful sailing by day and careful by night, or maybe be

hove-to at night, and they could slip around the point and towards Port Antonio.

Beyond Morant Point the coast was deserted mostly – there to find a safe harbour and do repairs.

They rigged the broken boom as a jury mast, mounted between the knightheads. They used the littlest jib for'ard and the large jib as a saggy mainsail.

These sails gave them way, and, the wind now moderate out of the sou'-sou'-east, they held course to clear the eastern tip of Jamaica.

They towed the partially shattered mast, alongside and astern of them.

Surprise already began to think of repairs: exactly what and how.

Irving said: 'Given a little while in still waters, I reckon I can re-step that mast good. We just going to lose eight or ten feet of it, is all.'

'Chief Yeoman: think on this: how you going to rig the mast on a girt hinge so that in a big blow we can take it down? How you going to rig it on deck so we don't lose eight to ten feet at all?'

'Deck-stepped mast is not as strong as keel-stepped mast.'

'True – but it need no extra strength if we can take it down.'

'We take down the mast, what we sail with?'

'Raise the boom – as a jury-rig – every time we hit really heavy weather.'

'Could be.'

'Aye, Chief Yeoman. Could be.'

IV

They were weathering north of Jamaica, along that island's northern shore. August was at the helm and young Domino in the bow.

Surprise threw over chips of wood and walked the length of the ship. Then, when looking at the fecund green shore,

112

and thinking, as he so often had before, how pitiful slow a ship always appears to move when in sight of land – whereas, at sea, you have only the close-to ocean to measure by and you seem to be flying through that, it came to him.

We doing about four knots plus now – with only a jury-rig. I made a mistake. A girt terrible mistake : when I say we been doing one hundred miles, we been doing at least a hundred and thirty miles.

On shore there was, now that they'd skirted the tiny seaport of Morant Point, no sign of life save the very occasional wisps of smoke : wild people, most probably, Surprise thought, and coloured and no trouble.

He went below and rolled out the chart again.

There was no doubt of it : in his miscalculation they must have been a long way south when the hurricane struck.

His first emotion was anger at his inability to calculate their speed correctly – fury, fury with himself for endangering his ship and all the lives. . . .

Then he broke out in both a sweat and a laugh – only the sweat, as he looked at what they'd sailed through, came first, and the laugh afterwards. Somehow they'd sailed *through* the great arc of islands into the main Caribbean Sea. It was impossible, almost entirely impossible, that they hadn't struck. . . .

As the old folks say, the Lord had had them by the hand. He laughed again – must be the Lord, for it sure weren't Surprise Le Negre.

Before sunset, the day after the day they were hailed by the *Nancy*, Surprise spent a long time watching the shore through his spyglass.

They were well east of Port Antonio and there was a perfect harbour : by the look of it, almost a circle of rocks and land protecting a little cove with a sandy beach peeping through.

There was only one thing wrong : although all the land appeared deserted, about a mile and a half back, he'd seen, high on a high promontory, what looked like a watchtower – or, hopefully, the ruin of one.

He looked again at the shore and then gave the order.

'Tight furl all canvas. We ride the sea anchor tonight.'

'By the stern?' August asked.

'No, mate – by the bow.'

In the morning they inched towards the shore with only the little jib.

Surprise had both Buccaneers mounted and ready on the quarter-deck, one in its lock, the other tied with rope.

To Delia it was the most beautiful, the most enchanted place she'd ever seen. All of them were disproportionately happy to be in still water and within reach of land.

But this cove was more than that. It was sheltered almost entirely with only the narrowest entrance that was due north. On either side of the entrance were high black rocks, the shoulders of which gently sloped off in a rich profusion of greens and wild flowers – she'd never, not even in Bermuda, seen such flaming colours.

The water was absolutely clear and sandy-bottomed, like Bermuda.

But in this cove, the circle of beach was not coral coloured as at home, but as white as whitewash. And, to her, an unbelievable creation of nature: a clear rushing of water flowed, seemingly down from the hills, into the cove, through the trees, spilling right through the sand, into the blue water.

She asked nothing, for Surprise was watchful and as worried looking as a tom cat on a Saturday night.

But when they beached the ship (it took a long while: for they grounded in the middle of the cove and had to fuss and raise the 'fin keel' which took more'n three hours), and when it seemed reasonable, she took the child and walked ashore.

The cove water was warm, as warm as Bermuda and warmer, and the sand very fine and hottish – but this bubbling water, that seemed to laugh all the time, was piercing cold and lovely, and, impossibly enough, it was not salt. She tasted it: it was fresh water. Like someone had made a hole in a water tank at home and it all come pouring out.

At home, at this rate, you'd lose a year's supply of water in a minute. Here there was no end to it: water, fresh, clear water, pouring, pouring, pouring forever.

She set Johnson in it and he squealed with shock, at first, at the cold, then laughed and they played in it together.

Surprise had men on watch, armed on the *Bateau*, and he

had gone off for a third time on an armed patrol, but Delia felt that she was in heaven. At least – at the very least – in a beautiful dream that would soon end and she'd wake up and find herself being wracked and banged about in the confined and painful and evil-smelling cabin.

But she did not wake up. This cove was her dream-home, ('dream-home' being, to St David's Islanders, the ultimate-most destiny – that place, imagined by many in the sweet heat of youth, but seldom ever glimpsed at in life), she began to think. Then she became quite aware that this time, this place and this time, was to be very, very short in duration. This cove was her dream-home, her dream place: it would not last long, and yet, she knew, all her life she would measure from this time: all before and all after.

The baby wrestled gently and flapped in her arms, resting his bare bottom on her thigh, they both being bathed in the beautiful and abundant water. The sun was warm and sweet, the wind gentle. . . .

She walked, with the baby on her left hip. She picked great flowers of red and purple she'd never seen before. In the trees – some of them big, big trees, like cedars only pale, pale green of leaf – she saw giant birds moving. They cawed and jumped and flew and lighted on branches: great birds of green and sometimes red and always flashed with yellow. What place was this but paradise?

She wandered about in a heaven of herself and her baby. Fleetingly she thought she'd like to share it with Surprise: then she realised she didn't want to share it with anybody. She wanted only that it last a few, few more precious moments.

And, in a few moments he came up to her and said: 'Get back to the ship, girl. There's something bad about this place. Something *evil*.'

Not wanting to talk, she heard her own voice as if from another, from out the bright and pale trees: 'Is it not every-thing we need?'

'It is – but it scares me. If it be so perfect, why not there be others find it and already live here? Live here for a long time. Something is wrong.'

'Nothing is wrong for the present, Surprise. Be still.'

'You get back to the *Bateau*: I cannot be still.'

It was, she thought, a painful marvel to discover that she

115

had lived fifteen long years – and, in all that time, the more did she discover that she, and everybody else, she guessed, was, in this world, absolutely alone. There was no sharing of the real her with anybody – certainly not if one discounted the moments of making love with her man – but wasn't she, really, even *more* alone in that ecstasy?

She decided that life was painful and beautiful. The beautiful made painful by its fleetingness and her aloneness – and the painful, like when Johnson was born, made beautiful by his, Johnson's, utterly alone first cry. . . . But, then, after that, she and her baby were together and that was more deep beauty than she'd ever, afore, in her wildest hopes, imagined possible. . . .

Surprise had scouted the cove three times, in three directions.

It was, obviously, what they wanted : shelter, abundant water, fruit on the trees (and, probably livestock to be bought or bartered, if they could find a settlement) and hard wood for repairs.

'I found a tough, dead tree – looks like mahogany,' Irving said. 'I figure I can make it work for almost everything. Mahogany almost as good as cedar.'

'The ship must come first,' Surprise said. 'You take August too to work on it. How many days it take you?'

'Five,' Irving said. 'At least five.'

'Too long – fix the mast and rigging right away. Forget all else till that be done. How long?'

'Gotta take two or three days.'

'It has to be finished in two days – by the second nightfall. The way we are now, we are trapped.'

'Fact-of-the-matter,' Bernice said, 'I don't believe I *ever* going to leave. This land ain't rocking and what ain't rocking is heaven to me.'

'Shut up, woman,' Henry said. 'Go help Jennie gather wood.'

'And wood that doesn't give off much smoke,' Surprise said. 'What wood is that?'

'Dry wood – you know. Dead wood. Nothing green. No leaves. Ask Jennie.'

'I go too.' The boy John looked very happy to be on land.

'No, boy. You stay. I have special work for you.' Surprise

116

had the *Bateau* beached and secured, the tide was going out.

'Defence of us and the ship be first. One Buccaneer, the one in the good pivot, stay on the ship. Bossie, you take the other, and with the boy, you rig it – as hidden as you can on that high rock.' He pointed to the mouth of the cove. 'And you keep watch – four hours. Then I send relief.

'But all mind this: I found an iron pot on that high rock. It be grown over with weeds – but I figure it been used by people before us and not too long ago. I figure it a lantern. Maybe settlers, maybe escaped slaves – don't know. But we must watch carefully.'

August and Henry were looking at him: he guessed they knew that what he feared and what was most likely was that the people were buccaneers – and not Bermuda style buccaneers, but real pirates. Probably English or Irish or Spanish – and they could return.

'Everybody listen: it be absolutely essential that, if any people come, it be *they* be surprised by us and not us by them.

'Henry – you and I be the other watch.'

Bossie laughed (his wounds from the storm were not yet healed): 'Why you two men on one watch and just me and the boy – ?'

'Because, I got other plans – Henry and me also have scouting to do: one here on watch, one scouting.'

'And what about Domino – he only have to catch fish, because he your family?' Bossie, laughing again.

'No. He has special scouting to do – and you be glad it ain't you. Or you want to climb a mountain and go through a strange jungle?'

'Easy, Captain – not me,' Bossie said.

'But you and the boy *can* fish – while you watch.'

Surprise had figured a way to keep Delia and the child close. 'Delia. You to refill all our water kegs – every one. And get the sow on land, but tie her good. Then do whatever you can to resupply the ship and then get the other women to help you clean her up.'

'That all?' She laughed and slapped Bossie playfully.

'Go now, Bossie. Take only an already part-used keg of powder. Four shot and the Buccaneer.'

117

Bossie went off to the boat with John.

'Henry – take one of the pistols and leave one on board by the for'ard hatchway as before. You or I have the other with us. We go, first one to the east and then one to the west. You first – with the pistol. Take a pocketful of coins – the littlest silver ones – they look like more. Try and see what friends you can make : see what chickens or such you can buy. But be very *friendly* to all. Keep the gun hidden.

'And, Domino – that applies to you, too – be friendly. But try to find out from all you meet – but being circumspect, not direct – where is the British and how many and how armed? As much as you can.

'Domino,' Surprise drew in the sand. 'We here – it be here I saw the tower. I want to know if it be armed and who by? If be empty, how long? Then I want you to scout to the south – make a sweep and report back. But take only two days – you must be back before the second nightfall. If you not, we come look for you.

'But, have a care, lad. If we can't find you after two days and the ship be ready, we are sailing. You understand? The whole party cannot be risked for one man. So, get back in two days.'

'All right. Domino won't get lost – what you think I am, a stupid fowl or goat?'

'No. But have a care. And Domino : this bush is *rough* – not like Bermuda. You a tough strong man, that why I send you. But, use your head. For example : don't try to cut through the jungle. See – to climb that hill, what you do?'

'Just start out walking and climb it.'

'No. You follow this stream as far as you can. Then follow whatever path you can – but all the time, watch and walk careful.'

'What I have for a weapon?'

'You take one axe – that's all we have.'

'No gun?'

'No gun. All guns must be close to the ship – to protect the ship. Without the ship, we are all lost.'

Surprise looked at their faces. 'Anything else you want to know?'

No answer.

'All right, Domino. Take a water bottle and the axe – and your shoes, mind. And go.'

'What's worrying you?' Henry Rudd asked when all had gone. They could hear Irving and August's tools already chopping away.

'You go, first. To the east. Try to find people. Livestock – and news.'

'Yeah, man. But what's worrying you?'

'I don't rightly know. I don't like this place. Something's wrong.'

'It got everything. . . .'

'That's why I ask, why no one here?'

'Maybe it was once a sugar plantation – sugar finished long ago and all people gone.'

'Could be. Well, let's get moving. Get back afore dark. That be the rule : each one of us save Domino, be back at dark.'

Surprise scouted more around the cove. It was peculiar the way the coconut trees grew only in a slim ring around the white sand that circled the water's edge.

There was sand and moisture further inland, why only the ring? Had the coconuts washed there from the sea? Had this once been planted as a coconut plantation, and later all but the ring of trees cut down by pirates? For what? Fires, he guessed.

He came up behind Bossie and the boy. Bossie was trying to build what he must have hoped would eventually be a gun carriage. It looked like a child's first attempt at building a boat.

'No, Bossie. Do it easy. Look. Tie it to this tree. Tree is sturdy and you can hide behind it. That easier.'

Bossie smiled, embarrassed.

'You see any boat coming. Send John to warn us. Any boat get close – wait and see who they are. If they be pirates – you try to hit 'em with that Buccaneer gun. You hit 'em long-ways – right up, say, a long boat – and you have five pebbles in that gun – you hit 'em that way and you kill five, maybe six. Then reload.'

'How I know if they be pirates?'

'Well, I hope I be here to tell you. If I not – well, you can smell 'em.'

'Smell 'em?'

'Certainly. They smell like they never wash and eat bad and drink rum, you shoot first.'

'All right.'

'Apart from that – you can *see* them. You see an old officer in the stern of a longboat, it probably a trader. You see a young white officer in a uniform – probably British Navy – and in that case, come get me or Henry or August.

'But you see there be no officer. You see the men look like maybe they could kill your mother or their own – just for fun. You know the kind?'

'Maybe I do, maybe I don't.'

'Well, you see the mother-killing, sister-raping look – you just *guess* you see it and I be not here, you shoot to kill.'

'All right, Captain.'

They sat around the fire, eating. Jennie had caught two parrots and they tasted good and Surprise knew she watched him eat with delight that she pleased him.

Henry had returned having found nothing but another inlet that proved deep and time-consuming to try to skirt. No sign of life on the other bank at all. He had seen only one giant iron pot – much overgrown. He said it was a whaling pot. Surprise hoped it was.

'I say let's stay here forever,' Bernice said. 'This is as sweet a place as ever I see.'

It was what Surprise feared: that they all want to stay. It was a beautiful spot – but, from inland, utterly indefensible. Doubtless there were British inland; certainly there was a great British garrison at Kingston. . . .

The child seemed to do a lot of crying: he made no more noise, Surprise guessed, than the rest of the party, but the shrillness of it made him nervous.

'He all right?'

Delia's big eyes looked up at him, reading his face with her usual youthfulness and good spirits. 'He all right. He miss the rocking of the sea, I 'spose. Damn if I do.'

'Sleep on the ship.'

'No, Surprise. Let me sleep on the ground – please.'

'It dangerous – you and the boy.'

'Please. I watch – I sleep light. Please, just for one night. I sick of that stinking boat.'

'All right.' There would be more talk of staying, he knew that. But this was not the place to start a new life: not only indefensible, but there was no way of making a livelihood here. At least, there was none that he could see now.

Best just get the ship fixed and worry about all else later.

'How you making out?' he asked Irving and August.

'You talk of a hinge mast,' Irving said. 'We figure' – he held up two fingers, 'this way – two staunch uprights of mahogany. One pin through the mast – after we get her all clean and cut and shipshape. Then, when the mast raised – pull taut against the head stay, like so – and slip in another pin.'

'What you make the pins of?'

'Off-cut spruce.'

'Better it be iron – better still bronze.'

Irving smacked his mouth. 'I saw some bronze – just like we need – on that schooner – that *Bud*.'

'Forget it – what we got?'

'One piece of bronze left over from the keel, Surprise.' August's dark and heavy creased face hardly ever changed expression – you wondered where all the creases came from. He wasn't old, either – a little older than he, Surprise, about thirty-five. 'Senex put it aboard.'

'Good,' said Surprise. 'One piece of bronze be better than none. You make the hinge piece bronze, eh, and the holding pin spruce?'

'Aye. That be best.'

Henry was sucking his pipe. 'I reckon I could stay here forever.'

'At dawn, I leave for the west. Henry, you be in command.' Surprise spoke low so that the women wouldn't hear. 'If pirates come by – scare them off. Kill many, if you have to. But make plenty of noise – like we are many.'

He lay down beside Delia, nestling his body against her. In the light of the half-moon, he could see little Johnson, nuzzled against her other side. The child had his nose flattened, with his mouth, too, into her underarm – it was a wonder he could breathe. But he was. Surprise gently put his hand on the little back. He could feel the steady breathing.

121

He kissed Delia's shoulder. She made a little movement in sleep.

Surprise lay his head down. Instantly it came to him what had been nagging in his mind, not properly realised before: the flat open piece of ribbon-like long grass that skirted the cove, inland – it was a road. Or it once had been. The British army could march up it three abreast, if they wanted – certainly two abreast.

Just let us get the mast fixed, stepped, and get the hell out of here. Haul arse. He wondered how Domino was faring: probably lying alone, scared in the dark of the bush. But, perhaps he'd found the watchtower empty and was sleeping there, in comparative clear – free of overgrowth and thus unafraid. He wished he'd given the boy some tips about sleeping in the bush and you scared: like, how it was better to get a little sleep up in a tree and be unafraid, than try to get a lot on the ground, and you be scared. . . .

In the morning, after eating some wild fruit, Surprise took the pistol, a pocketful of sixpences, and, heading up to the disused road, turned right on it and headed west. He moved at a jog-trot – for speed – but taking small paces for safety and to make as little sound as possible.

When he was a boy, he'd jog-trot all day when he had to. And he had to quite often: his job had once been to jog beside Captain Darrell's horse (and he, Darrell, pretty young then, too – thirty or so, younger than he was now) wherever Beau Nat went. Sometimes he'd jog from Salt Kettle to Hamilton and from Hamilton to St George's and back all in a day. He didn't mind: he liked proving his body in those days, testing his strength and endurance. Both seeming then, unfathomable: now he knew he was bigger and stronger, but he knew the exact fathom depth of both his strength and his endurance.

He kept his eyes keen and his ears keened: this was no goddamn time to be winged by no Carib arrow from some fullish young buck as would like to tote him home as a trophy or for dinner.

After Surprise had left, Delia set her mind as to how she could best comfort little Johnson. She decided to try to make the contraption for her baby that she had long thought about. He

122

liked best (was happiest and most content) to lie on the warmth of her chest: he was like a little chameleon warm and still in the sun. Trick was to construct a thing as would hold him in that position and she not be lying but standing and walking around. Little babies crave to be held all the time, the old folks said; true, but how to hold them body-close so that they can sleep and yet have one's own arms free?

The shape of a square topsail such as on King Jack's craft, gave her an idea. That shape, tied at the top around her neck, and, at the bottom, around her waist: the whole to be made of broad-weaved cloth so as not to be too hot.

She found a piece of sackcloth and tried her idea right away. It was hard to get little Johnson into a comfortable and secure position. Then she found that, if she began from a lying position, and fastened the sackcloth secure – his legs out above the cloth going around her waist and his head out at the top – it worked best.

After an hour or more's experiment – stopping once to nurse him back to sleep and, again, as always, marvelling at the power of his sucking and at the strength of the tiny muscles in his cheeks and jaw – she got what she wanted. It was simple, really – a sack to hold him secure and warm and safe – and she found that, thus held, he slept and paid no mind to noise nor jostlings that would, and she be only holding him as before, have awakened him.

With a smile for herself alone she called it Johnson's womb-sail.

Surprise figured he must have run about four miles, when he stopped short: there was a thatch cabin, with smoke.

He hid in the bushes to catch his breath and wait for his rushing heart to calm down.

Funny, there was a dog wandering outside the hut, but though it should have both smelled and heard him by now, it made no bark nor even indication of awareness of a stranger's presence.

He moved through the bush, skirting the hut. There were other huts beyond. About seven. A little village. There seemed to be few people.

He crept closer. The people he did see were sort of strange-looking, at first he thought they were Carib Indians. Then he

123

guessed they were a mixture of Indian, Negro and white. But they all seemed old-looking – or was it just sickly?

He watched for a long time, trying to take good stock but being sure he was not discovered. The worst thing, he thought, would be to startle them.

He saw a few skinny fowls wandering about – but, even they, by the way they pecked the ground, seemed sickly. As if they were tired. Past the huts, a small growth of scrubby corn – all weed choked.

He waited more than an hour but saw only six people – five women and one old man. There must be more. Maybe the young men were out fishing or hunting. He decided that now was a good time to make known his presence.

If it was his village, he thought, and a stranger came, first thing he'd want to know was that the stranger was like him – human. Perhaps he should sing. No, better to whistle, low and cheerful – surely that was as harmless and human as one could be.

He stepped quietly out of the bush, stood upright in the path, pushed the flint-lock well down inside his trousers, put his hands quietly on his hips and sauntered forward, whistling.

He came very close before the first woman noticed. She jumped and called out to someone in a hut.

Surprise just kept walking slowly towards them whistling. When he got about fifteen feet away he stopped.

He smiled at the woman. She did not react at all. He whistled again – a tuneless whistle, such as any boy, he thought, anywhere, might make. She was joined by another woman, also old-looking.

He smiled again. 'Hallo.'

The first woman broke into a smile and bowed. ' 'Allo.'

A second man came shuffling out of the hut.

'Hallo. Good day,' Surprise said.

' 'Allo.' The man instantly threw himself on his knees. ' 'Allo. Good friend. Rice. Rice, good friend.'

'Me friend.' Surprise held out his hand with four sixpences in it. 'Me – friend.' He moved towards them.

The women drew back. The man made as if to throw himself prostrate on the ground.

'Easy. Friend just want chicken.' He held his ground.

No response.

'Friend.' He pointed at himself. 'Chicken.' He pointed at the chickens wandering about.

The second woman walked over, stealthily, to a chicken, picked it up, wrung its neck and brought it forward.

After many patient attempts, Surprise got them to accept the four sixpences. Then he explained that he wanted live chickens in a pen. 'Coop' was a word they understood.

At last they brought a chicken coop – exactly like a Bermudian one, only not made out of mangrove sticks.

Another word kept recurring: 'Rice.' It took Surprise a long while to discover that this was not food – like the Trinidadians and others eat – but a man.

The man was less timid than the others, he was toothless, and, like the rest of them, covered in sores. Surprise threw a sixpence on the ground. The man picked it up.

'Rice. Good friend.'

Surprise threw another.

After a long while he got them to put five chickens in the coop. They made to get more – but he could only see three more and he didn't want to take all their chickens.

'Meat?'

They looked blank. He sure didn't want them to touch him: he was worried, already, lest his party catch something from these sickly people.

'Goat?'

'No goat. Gone,' the first woman said.

The sores on her neck, above her ragged smock, looked like small snakes beneath the skin.

The man was on his knees again. 'Take.'

Surprise had been ashore in a lot of places, but he'd never seen such a people. All had hollow eye sockets, bloodshot eyes – and every chest was caved-in looking.

'British. You see British?' He imitated a soldier – marching, saluting, shouldering an imaginary musket.

'Rice. Friend Rice. Take.'

It was useless. Better to take the chickens.

'Pig.' He said in a last half-desperate attempt.

'Rice.' The first woman said with what might have been a trace of venom – he couldn't tell.

He counted out ten shillings: twenty whole sixpences. It

was about twice what they'd cost in St George's market. Then laid them on the ground.

He picked up the coop and started off. After a while he turned back. They hadn't moved. He walked on again.

Turning once more, he saw them grabbing up the sixpences like chickens. They saw him and stopped still. Then the man went on his knees again.

Surprise shouldered the coop and jogged back up the road.

He gave the chickens over to Jennie. 'Keep them cooped up and see if they'll lay.'

'All right, Captain. We got some corn left. I feed them up.'

'Don't let anyone eat any – save the dead one. You cook that tonight.'

'Jennie cook good for all.'

Surprise told Henry his news. Then he washed in the stream in the cove – first getting his soap from the *Bateau*.

It was very refreshing washing in the fresh water. Then he shaved his face and head, using his pocket mirror.

'I don't like the sound of this Rice,' Henry said, sitting on the bank with the pistol.

'Me either. Henry, I reckon it a British overseer of some sort. Worst, a pirate. Maybe the head of a band who sometimes come to this cove.'

'Aye. That's what I guess. I guess a band of pirates. This their home base.'

'Well, by the growth on their pot – out there – they been gone about two months, at least. It all depend what Domino find.'

Henry went, again, to take his turn watching at the cove entrance. Surprise turned to help Irving and August.

'As soon as the mast is even halfway ready,' he told them, 'I want the *Bateau* afloat and kept afloat. 'Tis deep over there to the east of the entrance. The fin keel must be put back and caulked good, and fastened good. We must keep her ready to move at all times.'

That evening the *Bateau* was floating, at low tide, east of the big rocks, hidden from the sea. Surprise moved the whole party there, too.

126

'All fires be in the shelter of this rock,' he told the women. 'We must not be seen from the sea.'

'How about from there?' Bernice pointed inland.

'We have to take a chance on that – from what I've seen, we've got little to fear. But everyone watch out, as before.'

After eating that evening, Surprise got out his charts.

'This place is beautiful,' he said so all could hear – yet keeping his voice conversational. 'It has much. But it has two big things wrong – danger from there,' he gestured out to sea, 'and from there.' He gestured inland. 'Also, it has no place where we can see all who approach from a distance. No place where we, as small people, can defend ourselves against a large.'

Surprise was only planting seeds in their minds. He knew perfectly well what he wanted: he wanted a little island. A place whose confines he could see and feel – like Bermuda, like a ship.

This being a mere landing party on a great mass of land, gave him the crawlies. It was like being fleas landed on a lying down great cow – we land on a part of her belly, and other fleas already all over her and know her well and come and throw us off, or eat us up.

Much better, he thought, to be fleas on a little animal. He had in mind, as best, an animal shaped like a hat. Fleas could survive on the slopes of a hat.

He kept looking at the chart. 'There got to be a place for us.' There was Dominica – too big and British there. St Kitts, British again. Antigua – about as bad as Bermuda, though he knew the Royal Navy had moved their big force away from Antigua – English Harbour, where Admiral Nelson once was long ago.

'Most likely place is Nevis – but we need a Nevis without people.'

'You talking to yourself?' Bernice asked.

'Yes and no.'

'You already said it.' Bossie was lying, tired, full-length on the ground.

'Said what?'

'You already said the island with no people – said it days ago.'

127

'What one?'

'Barbuda.'

'You know it?'

'Sure I know it. Me and Henry both. We been there. No people.'

'When were you there?'

'Four or five years since. We was there looking for salt with Captain Comstock.'

'He stay? Did Comstock settle any people on Barbuda?'

'No. It no good for people.'

'Why?'

'Good for salt. Good for coconuts maybe – no good for people.'

'*Why?*'

'Simple, Surprise. It got no goddamn water, that's all.'

Surprise felt his stomach shrink as if he had been standing on a high cliff and he suddenly looked down and was falling. He tried to hide it. 'You sure no people stay?'

'Now, Surprise. How can any people stay – I told you, it got no water. Now, salt can survive without water and a coconut tree and maybe a sea-bird and other such – but not human beings. You know that. No water, no people.'

'Aye. But let's think on it. Says a high hill on it – says so right here.' He jabbed his finger on the chart.

'Yeah. I go relieve Henry – '

'Has it got a high hill?'

'No, not a high one – only a little hill.'

'It got trees?'

'Shit, man. Yes, it got little trees – but *no water*. Don't you hear good?'

'Go relieve Henry then. I go scout inland for Domino – whilst there's still light.'

Surprise put the charts, carefully rolled, back in his captain's cabin. He hardly recognised it; Delia had cleaned it as shiny as the best parlour at home.

Only the head seat, still nailed over one port, was out of place. It'd have to stay that way till he could get to it – he didn't even remember if they'd shipped any spare glass. Maybe he'd have to makeshift with wood.

V

The next evening Domino came back. His legs and arms and face were lacerated with cuts and covered with bumps and welts.

'Surprise, I see a ship – miles off, but coming this way. A big ship.'

'How many miles?'

'Maybe four, maybe six?'

'You all right?'

'Man, this is just from the *bushes*. Man, this island is for *animals*, not people.'

'How many masts? How big a ship?'

'Two – maybe three. Ten sails at least. I figure it a girt ship – like fifty men could climb out of her.'

'Where?'

Surprise got his glass and went, hurriedly, with Domino, to the rock at the cove entrance.

At first he could see no sail at all. 'And the tower, what about it?' He saw her : royals or skysails visible – and not two masts, but three. A ship. A real ship.

'Tower was scary.'

'Any people?'

'No. No people. But smell of people. Smell of old shit. Not animal shit, Surprise. You know how people shit smell – it different.'

'How old?'

'I don't know – but it still stink, so it can't be long.'

'People shit can smell for a year or more.'

'No, Surprise. This not a year, I don't think.'

'See any sign of British – soldiers or sailors?'

'None. But – but many miles inland – maybe nine or ten. On an inland hill I found a village. No people. Scary. They was there but they weren't.'

'How so?'

'Can't say. I just felt they was looking at me. And I was right in the open – and they was there only minutes before.'

'You *see* them?'

'No. But, the fires was burning. I stayed a bit – but I tell you a fact-truth, Surprise. I felt them looking at me from the bushes. I was scared, so I ran off.'

I

129

'Uh-huh.' By the way the ship was laying, she was heading twenty or so miles to windward of them – which would be, Surprise thought, exactly the course he would lay for this cove if he was the captain and figured the wind might head him or even just slacken with the setting sun and the tide.

'You think I was a coward? Do you, Surprise?'

'No. I think you were a brave man, Domino. What's more, you were a smart one – and that's even better.'

'Oh.' Domino, embarrassed, broke a small branch off the closest tree. 'Oh, thank ye, Surprise.'

'My pleasure.'

'What's coming?' It was Irving.

Surprise gave him the glass. 'What do you think?'

Irving took a long while, then got the focus. 'A big bascombe and no mistake.'

'Aye. But what she doing?'

'Laying for Port Antonio, I 'spect.'

Surprise laughed. 'You 'spect or you hope?'

'Hope is more like.'

'Aye. Let's load the *Bateau*.'

'But I got more taffrails to fix – and the steps to make and all sorts.'

'You got the mast stepped and ready, ain't you? And the keel fixed?'

'Yes.'

'And the new gunlock for the Buccaneer?'

'Yes – but I got all sorts to do.'

'Irving, sometimes you're like an old woman. You can do them at sea. Come on. Let's make ready. Domino, watch here. I send relief in a little while. And holler out if she comes close and shortens sail.'

'Aye, Surprise. I don't like her.'

'Well, she ain't here yet, lad. And, even if she comes, she don't know we are here. Least, not if you are sure that tower was empty.'

'No one – I told you.'

'All right. You did well. You one hell of a good seaman – a landsman, too.'

The fire was doused. The mast stepped and the mainsail hauled out on the boom and all ready to hoist. The air being

130

light, Surprise had two jibs hauled and furled with Senex's cedar pins.

He went to the furthest inland part of the cove and looked back : no, the approaching ship could in no way see the *Bateau*'s spar – indeed, she might have been made just to fit behind that guard rock at the cove mouth. For she showed not at all above the rock, against the sky, yet, were she not so sharply raked astern, she would just show.

Delia came up. 'I can't find the sow – she broken the rope.'

'Oh, Goddammit, girl. You've got to.'

'The child's got to eat, too.'

'We *got* to have that sow, is all.'

'If Johnson don't eat, he holler. If those men come from that ship they hear him. Johnson gotta eat.'

'All right.'

Jennie went to look for the sow.

Surprise laid his plans. The hope was the ship keep going by. But, if the ship sent a boat that night (that ship could in no way get in the cove at any water) then they would have to be ever mindful that the moon, soon to rise behind them, would outline them against the sky, or even the distant foliage.

A longboat, he figured, would come in the cove. The Buccaneer gun on the rock must fire first, as the boat passed close. August would be best : August was a good gun layer – Bossie was an unknown quantity, but, to Surprise's mind, definitely not a quick and independent thinker like August. Besides, he still frail. . . .

August fire first : closing off the longboat's escape. Then the boat would rush forward – some dead, he hoped – in confusion.

Passing into the cove, Bossie must fire one pistol from the west – drawing their attention to where the boat wasn't.

The *Bateau Bermudien* must be lying to the east – but stern first, to give her and her people the most protection and to allow the second Buccaneer to fire.

That Buccaneer be his, Surprise. And he have Irving to load.

Domino to help August on the rock.

Henry and young John be on the east shore with the second pistol. They be the reserve to throw in where needed. Also,

131

they be good and ready to start hauling the bow of the *Bateau* around.

For, Surprise figured, if they could win the battle against the longboat, the *Bateau* must sneak out of the cove, and, the wind being westerly, must turn west (although their ultimate destination was east) because, their only hope of escaping that ship, if she pursue them, was to windward, where she, being all square-rigged, save for spanker and jibs, could not sail. . . .

The *Bateau* was turned. All was ready – Jennie even arrived with the sow, and they were aboard.

August was at the rock with the Buccaneer (loaded with five stones and more stones, powder and shot ready) and Domino with him.

Bossie was on the west bank with his pistol.

The sun had set and the light was going with it fast. Surprise was wondering how long it would be before the moon came up. . . .

'Surprise.' It was Domino. 'The big ship is dropped anchor and she a pirate, August say, for sure.'

'How far off ?'

'Only a few cables – maybe a quarter a mile.'

'All right – go back. Right away. I follow you.'

When Surprise got to the rock it was too dark to use his glass – but he saw two things. The first pleased him : the ship was at least six hundred yards off. The second shook him : they were lowering not one longboat but two. And, by the look of them, there were twenty men in each.

'How many men ?' August asked.

'Can't see. Maybe a lot. Bad thing is two longboats.'

Surprise sat and watched and watched. It was a question whether to let both boats in the cove and really fight them there, or to let only one in – and leave the other outside. Outside, August and Domino, at best, could only get in one good shot at the second boat – then that crew would likely be all over them.

Both longboats in the cove would mean, he thought, certain defeat, unless they had both Buccaneer guns inside the cove. . . .

132

There was not time to make a minutely thought-out decision.

'You fire – waiting for point-blank range – on the first boat *when* it entering the cove. Then stop the other if you can.'

His eyes were flashing in the half-darkness. August felt scared, but he figured Surprise could probably kill the pirates with his bare hands if he had to.

'Don't let that second boat enter.'

'Aye, aye, Captain.'

'But, August – the other part is hard. You gotta get this Buccaneer back to the ship after you fired on the second boat.'

Domino looked cool in his excitement. . . . 'You understand, Domino?'

'Aye. I help August load – then I fight.'

'Yeah. Well, you'd better get back to the ship, too.'

'I got my axe – and this, too. My sword.'

Surprise saw that he had a machete. 'Where you get that?'

'In the bush village.'

'All right. It all depends on cool heads – you follow August, Domino. You hear?'

'Aye, Surprise.'

When Surprise took his last look back, the first longboat was moving steadily towards the cove.

There was no time to tell anyone but Irving.

'It's two boats – maybe forty men.'

'God Almighty,' Irving gasped.

Surprise liked Irving but he felt that the man lacked a certain desperation that was now absolutely necessary.

'Irving. We got to fire this Buccaneer not twice – but three times into that first boat. You hear?'

'Aye.'

'Then we got to load it *again* – you hear?'

'Aye.'

'Irving. You know what happen if these pirates take *you* alive?'

'They rape the women,' Irving said, sagely. 'That for certain.'

'Irving. They are going to *rape you.*'

'No!'

'Yes, Irving. It ceremonial to them. They going to *rape you.*'

'No!'

'Yes. That's what they like best. Then they going to hang you up by your balls and lower you to the sharks.'

Silence.

Surprise whispered. 'How many times you going to reload this gun?'

'Three.'

'Aye – and more, if need be.'

They waited for only minutes, but each second registered in their bowels and in each anus.

The air was now almost still. First they heard muffled voices. Then the clear creak of oarlocks and splash of oar.

Surprise actually saw the bow of the first longboat appear within the cove – and registered that its gunwale rope was rotten, before August's Buccaneer blasted the night with a flash of light and thunder that reverberated in the rock mouth and echoed into the cove among the coconut trees.

Shouts filled the silence that appeared to follow.

The longboat was three-quarters in the cove proper. It was time for Bossie to fire.

Past time.

Surprise and Irving lay low, still – waiting for Bossie's bullet to fly overhead if he missed.

Surprise got up and aimed his Buccaneer. He was trying for three men – but knew, by the way the longboat was facing, he could only get two.

Henry actually fired from the east and knocked a man over – Surprise changed his aim.

The Buccaneer roared, spewed yellow-white fire and blinded them both.

Irving was ramming, loading powder, ramming, loading pebbles. Working like a scared monkey grown more arms than an octopus.

Sounds came from the ocean. August's Buccaneer crashed again in the night, but Surprise could not now see it.

Then he could see the whole longboat – men were pouring over its side. Several were amidships, two stood in the stern. Surprise levelled on the men amidships, then changed his

134

mind and blasted, almost point-blank now, at the two astern, assuming them to be leaders.

He saw one smashed overboard in the light of the gun's blast, and, simultaneously, the side of the other's head blown away, as raw as an orange cut in half by a knife.

'Load again.' He turned. 'Get the ship around, men.' It was, he realised, without thinking, the sight of the women working on deck – Bernice, Jennie and Delia – with knives in their teeth, that triggered his play-acting that he commanded a large band.

'Get the ship around, *men*. First mate, Rudd – get the ship around.' His voice, to his amazement, imitating a British officer.

'Men : fire on all you see. Get aboard. Get that longboat in tow.'

He layed his Buccaneer to fire again – but all the pirates were gone.

The ship was moving around. He couldn't see Henry. He heard a pistol fire close behind him. Heard other sounds of firing again from outside the cove.

Then Bossie was swimming to their stern with his pistol out of water in one hand.

'Get her round and then haul a jib,' he whispered to Irving. Irving leapt.

Surprise gave a lung-bursting yell. 'Lieutenant Napier – get your men aboard this ship !' His command filled the cove, and might, he instantaneously reflected, have scared him, had he been. . . .

There were two men climbing over the rail – he nearly fired, but one was John. He whipped out the cedar tiller and smashed the other's skull to pulp as if it were a paw-paw.

'Get that longboat's rope and tie it to our stern.'

He looked for the other pirate boat, hoping to get a Buccaneer shot right down it – for their stern had now drifted, or been pushed, so that it was facing the cove's mouth.

He saw only a figure on top of the rock – August struggling with the Buccaneer.

'Napier – get down !'

'The gun – ?'

'Throw it, man !'

August heaved the sixty-inch-long Buccaneer and it landed,

135

holing the deck and falling back and smashing part of the taffrail Irving had only just fixed.

'Jump!' he ordered and turned back and put the tiller back in the rudder and flung it over; eased it back and flung it again.

'Sweeps! Man the sweeps.'

Again he was at his Buccaneer but again there was no target.

The *Bateau*'s bow was coming around and he was filled with frustration because there was nothing he could do – even orders were pointless – yet he must remain on the quarter-deck, the one person to give command, to consolidate efforts if consolidation was needed.

'Haul the ship out of the cove. All hands. Haul the ship out of the cove.'

He was giving commands to console himself, he knew, yet he also knew that if any man looked to the quarter-deck and saw him *not* be there – that man might be disheartened and hesitate, and hesitation was, this night, death to all.

Bernice and Jennie had the far sweep out and were pulling. Bossie had the pirate's longboat secured astern.

No John. Where was John?

He heard a halyard squealing and could see two on it – Irving and someone.

August and Delia struggled with the other sweep.

The *Bateau* came bow around and faced the mouth of the cove.

Surprise swung his helm amidships. 'Give a girt haul on the sweeps and then ship 'em!'

Then he was fending the ship off the rocks – off and through the cove mouth.

He made to strangle someone who jumped off the rock on him: he got the man's adam's apple between his two thumbs and he was going to crack it –

It was Henry Rudd.

'Shit,' said Henry, and shook himself and grabbed his own neck.

'You all right?' Surprise didn't wait – he was trying to push the ship and count heads, too. Bossie and Irving and Henry and the women probably all right – August aboard.

John perhaps all right. Domino missing.

136

They were clearing the cove's mouth, a bit of moon was behind them, but not much. They were moving and he was doing, damn near, damn all.

'Henry Rudd. Re-load that pistol.'

'It loaded Captain. They all dead or gone.'

'We steer west.' He put the helm over and she was hardly moving, then she all but stopped.

He realised Irving had the main half up. The wind had changed entirely.

He put the helm hard over the other way. He was about to shout that they would now head east – he wanted to in case Domino needed to hear. But he realised that the ship would hear him, too.

There she was, riding at anchor with a small light in the bow and a big lantern in the stern. He measured the distance – figured he had a one in three chance of hitting her a blast across her quarter-deck and decided against it.

'Pass the word. Where is Domino?'

After a long while August came up and said.

'Cut in close, Surprise. Domino should be on the shore.'

'Where?'

Surprise eased the helm over, the sails were filling with a phantom wind now coming out of the north-east.

'If we don't see him soon,' Surprise said, feeling the boat surge forward with the wind, 'we gonna leave him.'

'You can't leave him,' August yelled. 'He the one as saved us *all*.'

'Then you sing out for him. Skin your eyes.' The shore and rocks loomed close and then above them.

'All listen! I am going to circle the ship once – man the jib sheets! Watch the boom.'

He eased the helm to port and the bow came to seaward, seeming to all but graze the rocks. . . .

'Bossie – re-load that pistol. Henry Rudd, bring your pistol.'

The *Bateau Bermudien* swung out to sea in a tight circle – obeying the helm keenly, yet something seemed sluggish astern, as if she were dragging not an anchor but several fish pots. . . .

Surprise grabbed a pistol and shoved it in his belt.

'Henry Rudd – take the helm. Tight circle now,' he whispered. 'Bring her in close – I jump ashore, you do another circle – but wider – and I be back. If not – set sail for Barbuda'.

'Surprise!' It was Bossie. 'The longboat astern act funny – like she made of iron, or sinking.'

'Haul her in on a close rope then – give me that pistol.' Surprise went to the stern rail, hauled on the longboat's painter with all his strength – the longboat would not move any closer until Bossie pulled with all his strength, too.

Surprise, as the longboat ranged up towards the *Bateau*'s stern, leapt into her. In the moonlight – now coming out from behind some cloud – he saw something enormous and strangely bright lying in the longboat, underneath the thwarts.

As he scrambled aft, he paused and felt down. It was something metal and gigantic – then, trying to heft it, and, at the same time feeling the longboat's behaviour, he knew what it was : a cannon.

'Haul that painter tight!'

As the cove's mouth loomed up again he quite expected to see ten pirates, pistols and swords drawn, waiting for him.

He saw no one. Only the rocks and the dark trees beyond.

Past the mouth he leapt ashore, stumbled and fell. He got up gingerly, and checked one pistol to make sure it had powder in the pan.

'Domino,' he called. No answer. That pistol was all right – except the flint felt askew.

'Domino.' He looked into the dark ahead, seeing nothing, feeling the other pistol with his fingers.

'Domino!'

Something smashed him to the ground. He vaguely thought it was Domino, then he knew, by the smell and the girt weight, it wasn't.

He couldn't move – one hand was caught inside his waistband, on the pistol's flint and mechanism.

He saw a flash – an arced flash – and ducked his head towards the trees as much as he could (which wasn't much since this girt body was all over him) and a sword smashed on the rocks, and Surprise, tipping the muzzle of the trapped pistol upwards, fired it through his trousers.

A low, long gasp followed, and, wondering quite where it came from – perhaps himself – Surprise heard the weight say : 'You barstard – you done me. . . .'

138

He flung the weight off and leapt towards the trees, from where, he realised, he could see better – at least towards the sea.

He moved until he felt bushes and then turned. The *Bateau* was swinging out to sea in a perfect arc – phosphorescence licking her sharp bow and licking, too, the longboat astern.

Then he saw a body lying almost at his feet – he knew it was Domino by the compactness of the physique, the body could have been Delia's.

He felt his way towards it, the moon dimming again behind the clouds that skimmed over the distant peaks of the mountains.

His fingers felt wetness and warmth. Felt more – a great gash and hole where the shoulder tendon should be. Domino couldn't be long dead, he thought.

'Rice has me captive,' Domino said.

Surprise jumped back and aside and pulled his loaded pistol. Silence.

He could see no one – just Domino's body, dark, still, vague, on the rocks.

'Where is he?'

'Captain Rice has me.'

'How many men he have?' Surprise could see, out of the corner of his eye, the *Bateau*, more than half through her circle.

'Domino. How many?'

Domino said something: Surprise went closer to him. Leaned his ear over.

'How many?'

'Only Rice – others all run.'

'Rice is dead.' Surprise hoped his guess was right. He bent over, pushed his pistol inside his trousers, and started to lift Domino.

'Ayeeeeh!' Domino screamed in pain.

'You've two choices. I leave you or you suffer – which?' He lifted again.

Domino screamed again, piercing the night. Without hesitation Surprise hit him an uppercut.

'You all right?' Domino made no sound. Surprise hauled both Domino's arms as high as he could, bent low, turned and got the limp body more than half on his shoulder. He didn't want to give the jerk that would settle Domino's weight – a deal lighter than most men's – in the right place. But, trying to move and seeing the ship coming on fast, he had to.

He staggered towards the shore, slipping, groaning.

The *Bateau* had gone by, there was no time for anything else – and, Surprise, seeing the longboat arc awkwardly closer, seeing it actually touch, for a bang moment, the shore, let himself and Domino fall into it.

'Steer east by south,' Surprise said.

'What?' It was Delia bathing his face.

'Steer east by south.'

'Easy, man, easy. We been steering south-east for three days.'

'Where I been? Who is steering? Where's the ship?'

'Easy, man. Easy. You lost a lot of blood.'

'Where I been?'

'You hear me all right, Surprise?'

'Yes.'

'Who am I?'

'You Delia, of course.'

'Well, I just checking. You been talking crazy and fullish for three days.'

'Who steering?'

'August steering – and Henry, too.'

'Where they steering *to*?'

'Steering for the Virgin Islands – steering for Barbuda.'

'Who say Barbuda?'

'Easy, man, easy. Barbuda what we agree on – what we all feel where you want to sail.'

'Who agree?'

'Everybody – every *man* – to the last one – and every woman – save Bernice, who want to go home to Bermuda and Domino, who too sick to know what he want – until yesterday. Now he want to go to Barbuda, too.'

Delia paused in her stroking of his face with the wet cloth. Surprise had gone again – or, perhaps, she hoped, he was just sleeping.

Jennie came in. 'I kill another fowl – let's see if we can get the blood down him.'

'He been awake – and making sense.'

'Good. Get blood in him. Blood makes blood, that's what the old folks say – and the old folks is generally right.'

Surprise came to again. Jennie was there. She was dozing, the light from the port making her dark chiselled face reflect steely blue.

'I been dreaming of salt.'

'Captain. Who am I?'

'You – you are Jennie and you look just beautiful – beautiful in the light.'

'You want water, Captain?'

'Aye. Want water bad. I dream of salt.'

She gave him a cup. 'Funny you dream of salt, man. The others been talking of salt.'

He drank. 'Jennie, how old are you?'

'Sometimes very old, Captain.'

'How many years?'

'Don't rightly know – but I born in two, then – .' She made a zero with her fingers. 'Don't know how old I am – but Mistress Reid she write down the day the mare dropped a foal – and the day I born. Everything in one book and mine say two, then – '

'Then you are twenty-two.'

'Maybe.'

'How come you only twenty-two and you have a big son like John?'

'He born when I very young. Very little.'

'Who his father?'

'A man.'

'Was it Mr Reid?'

'No. Not Master Reid. John's father a black man. Master Reid do lot of bad things to Jennie, but not that – '

'Get me my jacket.'

'No, Captain.'

'Do as I say.'

She turned and reached for it. She helped him out of the bunk and out on to the deck.

Henry came up.

'Man, you look bad.'

'What course you sailing?'

'South-east now for three days, three nights and a half day.'

'Then sharpen up. Henry, hear me good: sharpen up to east by north every day and ease off by night. Watch for land. You see land, you get me on deck – however sick I am.'

'Aye, Captain.'

'Watch wide-eyed. There are islands all to the north and east.'

'We know.'

'You know the current carrying you both north and west?'

'No.'

'Take me below.'

Henry got him back in his bunk. Delia helped and fussed and made him comfortable.

'Henry, what's this talk of salt?'

'Nothing. We all figure you must want to try Barbuda. There we might be able to harvest salt – that's what we all figure you figure.'

'Aye. I dreamed of it.' He smiled at Delia. He would not tell his other dream. He'd dreamed and dreamed that the child, little Johnson, little Surprise, of the startled eyes, had died. The dream was unbearable, and, waking, often, until now, he believed it reality.

'How is everyone?'

'All good – save Domino,' Henry said. 'But he better.'

Irving came in. 'How ye be, Surprise?'

'Better. I dream of salt.'

'Aye. Henry and August say you say we go to Barbuda and find water and harvest salt. That what Henry say.'

'I rest now.'

The next day he was up on deck again.

'That one helluva girt longboat – more like a ship.'

'Aye,' August said. 'You know what she have *in* her, Surprise. You couldn't guess what we find.'

'A brass cannon.'

'How you know?'

'I know everything.' Surprise smiled.

August laughed. 'Man, go long.'

'Where the cannon?'

'Below.'

'How you haul her out? You stop the ship?'

'No. We put on all the jibs and let down the main and keep under way. Then we haul the cannon out of the longboat – cradled in the main sheets – by the main halyard.'

'Lucky you not break the halyard.'

'Man, you so right. You know why?

'Why?'

'It be *three* cannon.'

'*No*. Not three big cannon in that one longboat.'

'No, Surprise. The brass one and then two smaller iron ones.'

'I look later. They all below – the cannons?'

He knew the answer before it was spoken for the *Bateau* was sailing heavyish for'ard. Funny, he thought, she seems to like it.

'How she sailing?'

'Just as sweet as ever. Maybe sweeter – you see the main?'

Surprise looked aloft. 'What the hell is that? Who rig the ship like a damn dinghy?'

'Irving. He added to the main. He make the main so she haul *all* the way to the top of the spar.' August's face creased even more than usual. 'You not be angry – he mean well, Surprise. Fact of the matter, I be damned if she don't sail good – even better *on* the wind.'

'That so?'

He repeated his order of the previous day: 'Sharpen up by day, ease off by night.'

The day after that he had a look at the cannon.

The two iron ones, about five feet long, were the usual sort of six pounders. These were made in Philadelphia. Much as he liked Yankees he didn't like Yankee guns – comes to killing and mechanisms, everything British is best.

The brass cannon was strange. By the mouth of her she wouldn't take more than a nine pound shot – but her length. Very long. Must be nine feet and the usual nine pounder was about six feet.

The markings on her were strange: a crown, but not British words. He guessed she was Dutch – and a damn fine piece, too.

Far too big for the *Bateau*. He reckoned if they ever fired her on the *Bateau* they'd all end up overboard. Not to mention the fact that to mount her, topsides, would make the ship top-heavy as all hell.

For the first time, he was feeling hungry.

Later he took the helm. She felt very good. Fast and gentle on the tiller – but not too gentle, they being on a broadish reach. 'Bossie. Hoist the pennant.'

In a few minutes the long pennant was curling and weaving like a tender weightless snake.

'Bossie. Hoist the flag, too!'

'Where it to?'

'Ask Delia.'

Irving was busy repairing the taffrails. Surprise noticed he'd already cut clean and replaced the piece of damaged deck from where August threw the muzzle of the Buccaneer.

Bossie came up with the flag.

'Irving Rudd – Chief Yeoman.' Surprise felt happy to see the pale blue of their flag with the beautiful longtail on it. 'Lower the main a piece and rig the flag.'

'Aye, Captain.'

'And Chief Yeoman. Another thing. Your new rigging of the main be good – but you ever make a major change on my ship without my consent again and I throw you to hell overboard.'

'Surprise – you sick and near death – how could I ask you?'

'That's what I mean : it a good thing I was.'

Domino came on deck, limping but smiling. 'When we get to Barbuda, Surprise?'

'Tomorrow we spot St Kitts, maybe. Tomorrow you see Mount Misery – if'n these fellas ain't been steering fullish crazy.'

VI

On the morning of the seventh day out of Jamaica, Surprise was on deck.

'Land – to port.' It was Bossie, three-quarters up the stays.

Surprise had his glass to starboard and there he saw what he didn't want to : another island.

144

'Stand by to come about.'

They started the tiresome tack to the north to clear St Kitts.

'Why we not go through the islands – there was water?' Domino asked. 'Barbuda beyond, ain't it?'

'You been reading my charts?'

'Aye, Surprise.'

'Then you read closer. The channel between St Kitts and Nevis is called The Narrows. It filled with reefs and hidden rocks. Only a local pilot could get through.'

'Oh.'

'You see that mountain: that Mount Misery herself. Four thousand feet of misery. Anytime you see her, be warned. She ain't named for nothing.'

'It's got clouds on top – like the mountains in Jamaica.'

'Only it ain't like Jamaica. These clouds aren't real clouds like those of the Blue Mountains. These clouds are tears.'

'Why so?'

Henry said: 'It's supposed to be the dead. Tears of the dead. The British and the French killed all the Caribs – all of them.'

'And anytime you see Mount Misery, watch out for rocks. We got to pass to the north of St Kitts. South we perish.'

'How many Caribs they kill?'

Surprise said: 'You know the British. Thousands. All of them, anyway. And St Kitts, man, and Nevis – the British kill thousands of African slaves. Thousands and thousands. And when Abolition come – the British leave them to starve.'

'I don't want to go there.'

'We ain't.'

'How far to Barbuda, Surprise?'

'A full day's sail, now.'

'How come there's no people from St Kitts went to Barbuda, Surprise?'

'That's the problem, lad – '

'It sure and rightly is, Domino. It the problem.' Bossie put the second spyglass in its rack inside the aft cabin. 'The problem is, how do a man live without water. And the answer is, he don't.'

In three hours they came about again and laid east by north for Barbuda. Nearly everyone was on deck, watching St Kitts, to the south, and the pale purplish mount of St Eustatius to the north.

'You know, Surprise. We could've captured that ship of Captain Rice.'

'Yeah. How so?'

'It only have five men on her. He told me. I sure would have liked to have captured it – that pirate ship.'

'What happened between you and that second longboat?'

'I smashed 'em,' Domino said, cradling his own smashed arm and shoulder.

'He sure and rightly did,' August said. 'He have a axe in one hand and his machete in the other and he walk on the water and cut them all down – and hole the longboat too.'

'You did real good, Domino.'

'Without you, Surprise, I'd be dead.'

'Without the Lord have us by the hand – we be all dead.'

'I say aye to that.' Bossie laughed.

'Only thing I wish is I didn't lose my sword – I'd as soon go back to the cove and get it.'

'Never mind that – you all keep a sharp eye. Could be British.'

'Bossie, you sure this Barbuda exists?'

'Aye.'

'Says so on the chart, too – but I believe it when I see it.'

'It there all right.'

'Well, as long as we can't see Mount Misery by nightfall, I be happy. That mountain gives me the crawlies inside my back. Only one place worse.'

'Where that?' Henry asked.

'It the Misteriosa Bank. There the sand rises up out of the waves and snags a ship.'

'Aye, I heard.'

'And the Misteriosa Bank moves – the chart say it be one place – and you strike afoul of it another.'

'Aye. I heard tell of that, too.'

BOOK THREE

I

At eight the next morning, the *Bateau Bermudien* was sailing, circumnavigating the island of Barbuda.

By the heft of her, Surprise thought, she was just right. In his mind he was already calling her New Bermuda.

To begin with she had a fine protective ring of reefs and shoal water around her. To continue she had a more than halfway good anchorage – a lagoon, sheltered by land on three sides, especially to the north – and the only exposed side was west (but a coral reef there affording considerable protection); and if it blew hard from the west, there was the beach handy to run the ship almost high and dry.

The island was shaped something like a crescent moon – with the lowest land, good for salt, to the extreme south. Then scrub trees gradually getting more lush until, in the middle of the island, they were halfway decent timber trees.

But, best of all, the hill. It wasn't a hill, really, it was a precipitous hillock : must be nigh on two hundred feet high. A natural fort. A natural observation place.

'Three men,' he blurted out, not really meaning to speak his thoughts aloud, 'could hold that hill against an army.'

'Could and they have water,' Henry said. 'A little water to go with the guns and the powder.'

'He mean water to go with the rum,' Bossie said. 'The rum and the women and *then* the guns and the powder.'

'Oh, shut up.'

'Least, it all mean the same thing – water.'

'And there – that be good land for growing, I bet.' Surprise pointed.

'Don't give us any of that shit,' August spat. 'You know damn well we all seafaring men – and farming is a disgrace. Farming is a disgrace to a seafaring man.'

'It no disgrace to me,' Jennie said. 'I be a farmer's daughter.'

'And salt,' Surprise said. 'Salt harvest is a disgrace?'

'Hell no – a sailor live by salt, you know that.'

'Aye – I just wondering how fussy you want to be.'

'That level piece to the south is a natural for salt beds, all right,' Henry said. 'A natural. Captain Comstock said so hisself.'

'He also said, Henry – you remember? There is no damn water.'

'If I find water, then, you be happy?'

'Surprise – if you find water where no man has – I not only be happy – I not be thirsty.'

They took the *Bateau* into the bay gently, using first two jibs, then only one.

The tide was low, well past mid-water, and Surprise noticed two strips of rock, with a channel running between, to the beach.

'Sing out, Chief Yeoman.'

'By the shallow – less two. Less two. You going touch any time.'

'Drop the anchor.'

'Drop anchor.'

Surprise surveyed the island like a happy madman. In the first day he walked clear around it at the water's edge and climbed the hillock from two different directions.

But he could communicate his enthusiasm only to Domino, to Jennie and to John. He hadn't expected any enthusiasm from the Rudds: but August's quiet indifference, his nonchalant scepticism, maddened him.

As for Delia, her seemingly uncaring wandering by the sea-shore with her child – as if waiting for him to give up and leave – drove him, by evening, to fury.

During the evening meal he began to pin Henry and Bossie down about the water.

'Where did Comstock look for water?'

'Everywhere.' Bossie.

'Shit. He could not look everywhere?'

'He *dig* lots of places – we did.' Henry.

'Where. Exactly where?'

'By the foot of the hill.'

'Of course, that the most obvious.' Surprise drew a map of the island in the sand. 'Now, this the hill – where he dig?'

'Here – and here.'

'And here too.' Bossie.

'He dig here in the middle of the island?'

'Yes. Two places.'

'You know exactly where the holes are?'

'Could be.' Bossie.

'No could-be's. Yes or no?'

'Yes – mostly.' Henry.

Surprise walked up the beach by himself.

He looked up at the hillock, his mountain.

It looked, in all truth, like the head of a man's cock. Pity it didn't piss out the top.

On the leeward side, of course, a few trees grew – some almost to the top. One tenacious tree, bigger than the others, grew only about twenty-five feet from the top. Maybe water there.

Around the west of the hill, and stretching in a curving crescent, there was a strange crevasse – as if the whole structure of it had broke, broken as the hill grew taller above. Trees grew in some profusion in the sheltered south-western and southern part of this crevasse – two different strips of green trees seemed to meet and then come together and the green continue down the hill until it met the heavier green of the larger, lusher trees around the bottom.

Where was water?

The sea, pale, sandy-bottomed and blue-green (and the beautiful sky, blue and touched here and there with fluffy clouds – and to the west, all yellow and green and then red with the sunset), seemed to mock him. It was all as beautiful as Bermuda: even more beautiful and it had no people.

If there had been no one with him, Surprise knew – if there had been no one watching him – he would have kneeled down and asked the God of the sea and the sky (God being, to him, all things more powerful than him – and that be many) to give him a sign.

Then he thought that if he did not kneel down – and right now – that God of cold and heat and hurricane, that God of water, would never give him a sign.

I make a deal: I meet you halfway, he said – and straight-away walked into the water.

God, God, he thought. How can there *not* be a God when I got this pain from longing in my chest? This deep pain, this deep longing.

He walked in deep. He didn't look down to see where his

feet trod. Let them fall on sea egg spike or the fire of red sponge or shaft of coral itself.

He walked slowly on and on until it was near dark and the water near to his mouth.

He turned and looked at his hill again. If the powers of earth and heaven put the trees – against nature – where the water was not, at the base of the hill where the white man searched, then he, Surprise Le Negre, would search where the trees were not : at the top of the crevasse.

When he got back to the fire, his anger had abated – but he would speak to no one.

After drinking some water from the cask cup he withdrew a long way and lay down by himself.

If they are going to follow me, he thought, then they must see I can stand alone.

When full darkness came, there being no moon, he could not sleep, but thought of his mother.

He could not remember her except as warmth; as an odour, sort of, of warmth. Yet he had been five years old, he knew – from what others had told him – when she died. A child of five should be able to remember much.

She was, he knew, a strong woman in will as well as body. Some had called her 'Doctor', for she knew all manner of cures. She would work for no white person; indeed she stayed, mostly, on the boat with his father.

She was a great beauty, he'd heard, too. Proud of head and firm of body – he knew the style, for he had known her brother, a man who looked, until he moved, as if he was cast of bronze.

It flashed through his mind that maybe he looked a little like that himself. He hoped he did – but he doubted it, for his uncle was a powerful beautiful person to behold.

He was asleep when someone touched him. And, although he had a mind, immediately, to pretend he thought it was Delia, he knew it was Jennie.

She said not a word. He said nothing either. But from the way she moved in the actions of earth and love, he knew she was not after the mere fleeting satisfaction of his manhood against her womanhood. No, like he being after the water from the hill, she was after the water of life – and it aroused him to the core of his earthly being and manhood. (And,

152

although he said nothing, his fingers detected welts on her buttocks – too deep for a whip, it must have been a hot iron.)

Delia felt the child, blindly, happily, nuzzling to nurse her breast. Comfort to her and to him.

She knew Surprise wanted to be alone and she grieved for him in his sorrow.

She thought of her own father and then of Senex. Senex had said to her after the child was born, just a day or so after: 'A mad British soldier killed her, you know.' Peculiarly, she not only knew that he was speaking of Surprise's mother – but she knew that she had somehow known it before. 'Just a crazy fella who was drunk and went fullish. Found her alone swimming and killed her. Funny thing, it was daytime. If it had 'a been night I could understand. But it was daytime.

'I am over it now. It be almost thirty years – but he not be over it. So, take care, little one: when he remember, he need you, but you need to take care, too – I say all this because I not forgive myself if any harm come to you and me not tell you. . . .'

Delia wondered, on the beach at Barbuda – on that dark night – if she should go to him. But she had an inkling she had ought better not – what if he be remembering his mother's death this night and kill her? He wouldn't do that, she reckoned – but, in a mad dream, he might roll on the child.

Just before she fell asleep she thought of home, of Bermuda. Of cassava pie and King Jack with his 'no toes belly'.

At the break of light, Surprise took young John and, with an axe and a shovel – they lacked a pick of any kind, and the rock would ruin an adze forever – went to dig water from the mountain.

Surprise passed a hole, at the bottom of the hill, that he could tell was man-made.

They walked through the trees and began to climb. The trees became thinner but Surprise kept along the line of them, upward and to the west.

They climbed all the way around the crevasse, higher and higher and then just horizontal. There, suddenly, the trees stopped and the crevasse continued on and then up, harshly up, in a barren and wretchedly dry little hump all its own.

153

Just to the left of this hump, to the west, Surprise saw a particularly dry-looking bright streak of golden yellow sandy clay.

He stopped. He was thirsty already. They had not brought water.

He raised his hands – one containing the axe and one the shovel – wide and stretched and looked up at the sky and a grimace and a yawn came over him.

Then he began digging. He cut, first, a square of two feet, with the axe. Then he dug with the shovel.

He dug about three feet down, and though the land formed a natural platform, he knew he'd have to make it wider if he was going to go deeper.

He cut the opening to about four feet – and, with the shovelling out, the natural platform enlarged.

When he'd dug this new width four feet or so deep, he came out.

'I dig, Captain?'

'Aye, John. You dig – keep the sides straight and neat.'

John dug with the slow, methodical and unrelenting tenacity of a middle-aged labourer: as if he'd dug all his life and knew he had a whole lifetime ahead to pace himself to keep on digging.

Surprise wondered if young John simply inherited this attitude, this ancient manual patience. A tree was a few paces off. Surprise wandered there and broke off a twig – the leaves were floppy and heavy, as if they themselves were full of water. Yet they were not, indeed he bit them and they were dry and bitter.

He wandered back towards the hole, with the twig in one hand.

The shovel came up, dumped, went down, cut and scooped, came up again.

He stood looking right in. 'I dig now.' He moved the twig from his right to his left hand – in preparation to chucking it aside – but, the moment, the instant, the twig was connecting both hands, it seemed to be pulled, downwards.

The twig fell on John's head. He came out.

Surprise began digging again. The hole was up to his chest.

He dug all morning. The hole was over his head.

'Master – let me work.'

'In a little while.'

The shovel seemed to touch a place that was a little damp – at least not barren dry sand and clay – and then, the next shovel piercing and it was really wet.

Surprise tidied the whole digging so that it was square and shipshape at the bottom. Then he took a mighty heft down with the shovel, jumped one foot on its shoulder, and lifted out a square sod.

Before he got the sod out of the hole, his feet were wet.

When he looked down, he was standing in water.

John let out a yipping sound like a small dog chasing something.

'Shut up, boy! Let me taste it.' He kneeled down and scooped up a hand of sandy water. It was fresh.

Next time he cupped his hand, the sand had settled some and the water was flowing clear. It was tangy tasting, but be damned if it was brackish.

He climbed out, suddenly utterly tired – even depressed.

'Can I taste it, Captain?'

'Aye, lad.'

The boy jumped down and drank and splashed it all over himself.

'Come on.'

Surprise climbed wearily down the hill. The boy was behind him. He was glad of that, for, like the mountain, he was shedding water.

When they reached the camp, the others gathered around – save Irving, who was working on the *Bateau Bermudien*.

'You find water?'

Surprise nodded. He sat down heavily. Delia came and sat beside him and put her arm around him.

'The Captain,' John squealed to his mother and the others. 'He just jump in this hole and the water squirt out.'

When the excitement died down, Henry said, 'It going to last, Surprise?'

'Can't tell yet, can we?'

'I go look.'

Bossie was already scrambling up the hillside.

In the afternoon, Surprise wandered, cautiously, into the wooded area of the island. He came upon pigeons, guinea fowl and a larger, shy bird he hoped was wild duck. Best of all : he heard the grunts and found the tracks and then saw wild pigs. These last seemed an almost more important omen and portent than the water : for he knew from Senex that what the first shipwrecked settlers on old Bermuda found, and what did most sustain them, was pigs.

He got back and told the others.

Bossie said : 'I *knew* they was there – but the water, that something else – Now you *know* water don't grow at the top of no heel, but it does.'

II

In the months that followed the water did not lessen. Neither did it increase. Whatever they took out of it, two feet of water remained, always, in the bottom. Irving built a stout cover over it; and a rig and a rope for the bucket.

Surprise insisted that they build a fort and lookout first. They objected.

'Let's find out if we can harvest good salt first.'

'No. No fort, no colony. No New Bermuda. British take us by surprise and we are finished. We build just a rough fort and a lookout to begin with. Later we make it strong.'

His idea of a rough fort turned out to be a circular redoubt, at the very top of the hill, with dug-out, sheltered, deep and water-protected shelves for powder and shot. Worse, he insisted that the brass nine pounder be hauled to the top.

Six men could not lift it – at least, they barely could. It had to be hauled by block and tackle. They drove in a great spike twenty-five feet up the hill, hauled the brass cannon to it; secured the cannon, uplifted the spike and drove it in twenty-five above; rigged the cannon again, hauled it and repeated the process till they reached the redoubt.

'Beautiful. Now we make a gun carriage.'

'Stop that shit, Surprise. We need hardwood.'

'We got just enough on the *Bateau*. When we finished this we go for more hardwood – and other things.'

'All right.'

'And also, we must fashion six nine-pounder size shot out of rock.'

'You a madman.'

'Then I, Surprise, do it.'

Their first shelter was a longhouse at the base of the hill – but to the west and in the lee. Only the six uprights were of wood – the rest was of palm, coconut and shrub.

Surprise and Delia slept, usually, on the *Bateau* – once, when Surprise had attempted to go without her to another island for supplies, she had flown into a fury.

'You think I'm an old woman who just want to live here and work and work to death? I want to see people – to *be* seen. To talk. To live.'

It was decided that their best chance for a town that could supply all their needs was the French island of Guadeloupe.

'I don't want to go no place that speaks French,' Henry said.

'Then you suggest we go to Antigua and pull the British lion's tail?' Irving said.

'I don't like coloured people who talk French. They all voodoo people – ugly, crazy.'

Henry agreed to stay behind as Governor and be in charge of the work to complete the salt beds.

'We got to spread the news in French ports that we got salt – right?' Surprise said.

'Yes.'

'The Dutch at Saba and St Eustatius know us now – but they can't give us tools and medicine and shot. . . .'

August said: 'Aye. It's the Yankee ships we need – and Yankee ships visit French ports.'

Surprise figured to sail very wide of Antigua and circle around to Guadeloupe. That way their chances of bumping into the Royal Navy were slim.

Fortunately, the *Bateau*, from any distance, looked like a typical inter-island sloop or fisherman. It was only when up close that it could be noticed that she was bigger and far finer, and something enough out of the ordinary to excite interest. And Surprise aimed to keep it that way: never let the British Navy get close enough to them to get interested.

Another trip to another island would do Delia good, Surprise figured. She was already big with child, and so was Jennie – though Jennie was that kind of large woman who carried a child without it being obvious, at least, for a while.

They decided to try the northern town of Port Louis, and, after skirting Antigua, they went there. But it was a scrubby, small place that had no merchandise they wanted, save only fish-hooks and line and some tools. No one in Port Louis had even heard of matches.

'Strikes me,' said Domino, 'that the West Indies is downright backward.'

They had a choice now between Pointe-à-Pitre to the south-east, or the capital, Basse Terre.

Both Surprise and Irving wanted to avoid the capital – but Delia was strangely insistent that they were wasting their time anywhere else.

'And another thing, Surprise. I think you should anchor offshore and go on land pretending you be the agent – or mate – of a white man. Why invite curiosity?'

They eased gently into the harbour of Basse Terre under a full-reefed main and a single jib. There were on board, only Surprise, Delia and the child, Irving and Domino. Surprise had known all along that to leave New Bermuda for several days was essential but also essentially dangerous. For, in leaving, they must divide their tiny force – worse, in the division, both groups were weak.

On the *Bateau* he and Irving and Domino could sail but they could barely fight, if they had to. On land, Henry, Bossie, August, Jennie and young John were only slightly better off.

Basse Terre was both a smaller harbour and a smaller place than they expected.

They anchored away from most of the shipping (even from the derelicts – for there were many derelict and semi-derelict craft there) and out of the channel.

Surprise and Domino went ashore first in the longboat.

Before he left, Surprise had said to Irving. 'Got a big problem you may be able to figure. The *Bateau* need a surprise.

158

Need a big weapon. This I think of – one of the six pounders to be mounted – '

'Man, you mount one and she have a perilous list. You mount two – and she not be able to carry much – '

'I figure all that. I figure one. One six pounder to fire out the stern.'

'Then you have no cabin.'

'Aye. But just say – just say, Irving, we could move that six pounder in and out. Say we could roll it from the very bow of the cabin to a stern port. Bang! There be a surprise for any ship.'

'Impossible.'

'You figure. You a smart shipwright. I can't figure it – but I figured you just might.'

They had no flag showing on the *Bateau*. They were attempting to look as inconspicuous as possible.

'What would you do if you saw the British coming right now?' Surprise asked Domino.

'I ease gently back to the ship. Why you always asking that question?' Domino was rowing the longboat. Surprise sculling and steering.

'Because, any time I be not around – I want you to be always thinking. Always ready.'

'Man, I'm always ready.' The morning sun was very hot – even spring months, like April, were hot down here. 'Surprise – when we ashore, can I have some money?'

'Sure.'

'I mean – of my own.'

'What for?'

'To spend.'

'I suppose. How much?'

'Don't know. But some of my share.'

'How much?'

'I did a lot of diving – and I done a lot of fighting.'

'How much?'

'A hundred shillings.'

'Shit, man. You better wait.'

'Wait – what for? You said before we all entitled to a sixth – '

'Wait and talk it over with Delia and Irving.'

'You the captain, what *you* say?'

'I say wait and talk it over. I give you ten sixpences now.'

Domino looked sullen.

When Surprise got back to the *Bateau* he had news for them – and Delia had news for him, too.

'It nearly all coloured people,' he said. 'Coloured merchants – or part-coloured. Even a coloured policeman. White men, too – but all Frenchmen.'

'I seen an old friend, Surprise.'

'Who?'

'A ship called the *Thos Jefferson.*'

'*Thomas Jefferson* – where?'

'O'er yonder.'

'Well, I'll be. . . .'

'You think it the same captain?'

'Same ship,' Surprise said. 'That sure.'

'You better go over and talk to the captain.'

'Why?'

'Maybe he take your letter to the President man.'

'Girl, you think way ahead of me.'

'Where Domino?'

'He on shore. Delia, your brother wants one hundred shillings. What you and Irving think of that?'

They talked of it and decided, in Irving's words, 'to think it over.' The original agreement had been to divide money only if a person wanted to quit the venture.

'There's many ships – and some from the Bahamas.'

'I figured that,' Irving said. 'Any from Bermuda?'

'No. Not that I see. And the British absolutely *hated* here. Delia, I go on shore again – you come. They don't speak English good, or don't want to.'

'All right.'

'Shipping man say they *always* need salt – both delivered here and at Pointe-à-Pitre. And they have ships as would get it from us – at Barbuda. Pointe-à-Pitre is *twice* as big as here, girl – I told you we should've gone.'

'Uh-huh. And if we had, we not see the *Thos Jefferson.*'

'You right.'

'You go over now?'

'Yes – but you come, too. Maybe Captain like to see you and the little fella.'

'Yes,' she said, smiling.

Captain Macdonald of the *Thomas Jefferson*, New York, recognised them but could not place them.

They asked permission to come aboard, which was readily granted.

'What's the little fella named?'

The little fella, shy of no one, and just learning to walk, staggered forward. Captain Macdonald caught him.

'He named Johnson.'

'Johnson Le Negre.'

'You know my name then?'

'What name? You named Captain Macdonald.'

'Captain *Johnson* Macdonald.'

Delia kept silent. Maybe, she thought, it was where she'd got the name – but she had not done it consciously.

Surprise asked to see the captain alone. They walked to the opposite side of the ship. Surprise had figured out an order of information and question, answer and counter-question. He'd say they'd run away: if the captain was sympathetic he'd tell him where from, not where to. If the captain proved old-fashioned, he'd ask him a question about navigation.

Captain Macdonald either saw through the subterfuge or was simply a very open man. He said: 'You can relax, sailor. I'm not a curious man, at all. But if you're curious, you can know that I'm a Massachusetts man, born and bred – and we don't hold still for slavery.' He looked around the sky – as if checking the weather. 'No, I'm agin it – and my mother before me was agin it. She was damn near a charter founder of the railway.'

Surprise didn't quite understand, yet he understood that Captain Macdonald was a generous, easy man and that he liked him, Surprise, and Delia and the child.

'That our sloop,' Surprise said, pointing.

Captain Macdonald took a careful look at the *Bateau* through his glass. After a long while he said: 'She's of unusual beauty. And I'll warrant she sails like a gull.'

'Like a longtail, Captain, sire. See the longtail on her stern? She sail just like one – skimming the water like an arrow.'

'She's *yours* – *belongs* to you?'

'Aye, Captain.'

'No. How so?'

'I and my father, we built her – that's how, Captain.'

The captain looked her over again. 'Well, I never did see a sweeter looking filly – she looks more like a yacht than anything else.'

'Captain Macdonald. I would ask you a deep question?'

'Ask away, laddie.'

Being called 'lad' or anything like it, had always infuriated Surprise. Strangely, from this old man, it felt warming, soothing – almost a caress.

'We have settled on the uninhabited island of Barbuda. We call it New Bermuda. We are just a small band of Negro settlers. We were born under the British flag – but we want to be an independent place.'

'You from Bermuda – of course. I remember now. Your wedding day. Why, your wife is even prettier than afore – oh, aye, you must be proud of her – and the little lad.'

'Thank you, sire. I am. But the question is, if we found a republic, would the President of the United States protect us?'

'Why? How?'

'Under the Monroe Document.'

The captain thought and paced away and came back. 'Possible, laddie. Possible, but not probable.'

'I had thought, sire, that if I wrote a letter to your President – President William Harrison.' Surprise was proud that he knew the right name. 'And told him that we exist as a free people. As a Republic – that he would protect us from the British.'

'He might and he might not. Depends on the Congress –'

'What's that?'

'The elected representatives of the people.'

'Oh.'

'Depends too on who Barbuda belongs to.'

'To *us* – we found it empty.'

'Perhaps it does, perhaps it does not.'

'If I wrote to your President, Captain, and he *knew* of us. If he only gave *promise* to protect us – this I could throw at the British if they come to capture us. Such a promise – and

162

it be written down – be more powerful against them than shot and powder.'

'Aye. But Barbuda be British, I think.'

'Uninhabited, Captain – we found it just as one find a floating abandoned ship.'

'Oh, aye.'

'If I wrote such a letter, Captain – is possible you would give it to President Harrison?'

'I can send it to the President, yes. I think you'd better write to President Tyler, though – President Harrison died.'

'Oh – sorry – I not very educated, Captain.'

'You seem *very* educated. How could you know? President Harrison died suddenly. Look, I'll write it down for you – 'tis a funny name. You write the letter and I'll take it for ye, to New York.'

'We'd be very grateful.'

'And how are you going to make a living on your island – Mister – oh, yes, Monsieur Le Negre?'

Surprise was flustered with happiness. No white man had ever afforded him such a title.

'Salt – and we will fish and we have some wild fruit, and fowl and pigs.'

'I tell you, laddie. There's one plant you should have. The Jamaican breadfruit – in bad times that plant alone, and no other plant, can keep people alive.'

'Sire, it's a pity we didn't know that last year – we could have got some.'

'But you have salt?'

'Should soon have plenty of the finest.'

Captain Macdonald said: 'Then you've a good start. All British ports have been too often closed to American ships – we don't like it. I'll come for salt at Barbuda next trip – and I'll tell others.'

'That, Captain, is all good news indeed.'

'And if the British come against you, laddie – you'll be powerless. What can you do?'

'I've never fired on the British yet, Captain. And we are all good clean living free people. No one of us is wanted – ' Surprise stopped short: the last fact, he realised, was hardly true. Both he and Jennie were, doubtless, wanted.

'Not one of us has ever committed any crime.'

163

'I wouldn't give a *damn* if you'd all committed crimes against the British. What I want to know is, how can you fight them off, if they come? You've no armament.'

'Captain Macdonald, the *Bateau Bermudien* mounts two long swivel guns, Buccaneers – and she can outsail any ship – to windward she can.'

'Oh, aye. I don't doubt it by the lines of her.'

'And, on New Bermuda, we have a fort with three cannon.'

'Ye do? Well, that's a bit more like.'

'Only one trouble. I've no real shot for the cannon.'

'What size do ye need?'

'Nine pound balls and six pound balls.'

'They cost a pretty penny, laddie.'

'We've money, sire. Silver coin. British silver coin – and uncut. All good coin.'

'Well, you away and write your letter. We'll see what shot we can find. How about twenty-four of each weight?'

Surprise walked a moment himself. Events were muddling his mind : good fortune confused him.

'I need more six pound shot than nine.'

'Aye. We'll remember that.'

The captain walked back with him to where Delia was at the gangway.

'Pretty little Mistress Le Negre, you were well met when you find this husband.'

'Thank you, Captain.' Delia looked from one to the other. 'And well met when we found you and your stout ship.'

'Lassie – do you know about trees?'

'Trees?'

'Aye – about how to plant and care for them.'

'No. But I can learn.'

'Well, come back tomorrow. Your man's coming back with a letter. You come too and I'll give you a breadfruit tree – a wee one. No. I'll give ye two, if you'll nurture and care for them well, mind. I'll not give ye a one, unless you'll nurture them – and understand they're more valuable than gold and silver.'

'Yes. . . .'

'I'm taking some to New York. Though there we can only

keep them alive in special houses – they can't stand the cold or frost.'

Surprise studied the name Captain Macdonald had written down for him : John Tyler.

Earlier, he'd gone ashore, found Domino, come back with him, and, in his excitement, agreed to give Domino his one hundred shillings.

Domino had immediately wanted to go ashore again. 'Irving, you take him. And Domino, she be a good woman – why not bring her back?'

'Who said I have a woman, Surprise?'

'You think I've never been a sailor in a port before? She a good woman, you bring her back. We need new citizens – new little citizens.' Surprise laughed.

'You be careful, Domino. You be careful, you St David's hot-head,' Delia shouted after him. 'You hear me?'

John Tyler, President of the United States. Surprise wrote very carefully on a piece of the fine paper he cut from the log of the *Germ*. He knew the President would be a busy man, so he kept it short. And, the elected President of the people who had elected George Washington and Thomas Jefferson and James Monroe, would be wise, quick and decent – he'd tell the simple truth.

He simply asked protection under the Monroe Document, for the eleven souls who had settled the island – then, remembering the unborn children, he made the number, thirteen. Thirteen souls who need protection against foreign European powers, particularly the British.

He dated it, appropriately enough, he thought, 13 April 1843, and he signed his name with a craftsman's care: *'Surprise Le Negre*. Elected by the people, President of New Bermuda, formerly known as Barbuda.'

Then he thought that was too uppity sounding. He cut out a new piece of paper and wrote it all again, titling himself, 'Leader of New Bermuda'.

Irving was pleased with all he heard. Particularly when Surprise and Delia came back, the next day, with twenty-four nine pound shot and forty-eight six pound shot.

165

It took a powerful amount of hauling to get them aboard and below.

'How much he want, Surprise? How much?'

'Two hundred and fifty shillings, he say.'

'Man. That a lot.'

'Irving. I had expected he'd say over five hundred shillings.'

'Oh. I thought less.'

Captain Macdonald had read the letter in his cabin with Surprise. He approved of it – made a couple of corrections, with Surprise's consent – and sealed it in an envelope, which he had Surprise address in his hand: The President of the United States of America, Washington.

The captain spent a deal of time explaining, about the little breadfruit trees, to Delia. He spent a deal of time, too, touching and playing with little Johnson – who he called, 'My bonnie brown boy.'

He bade them farewell and pressed a brown paper wrapped package in Surprise's hand.

'You'll come and see us soon, now, Captain Johnson Macdonald,' Delia shouted, smiling from the longboat.

'Aye, lassie. I will. As long as ye look like sunlight on the water, I'll come. When *you* get old – to blazes with ye, I'll not come.'

Surprise, rowing back, felt his chest fill with a happiness that choked him, almost as if he were drowning.

He tried to tell Delia. 'I never think it possible – you know – in one life, that I know three such men as Captain Darrell, Captain Macdonald and Senex, my father. . . .'

After a while, she said: 'And King Jack – what about *my* father?'

'Oh, him too, of course.'

'You don't have to lie to me, Surprise, sailorman. I know you don't mean my father.'

Surprise wished he was alone. For if he was alone, he could weep with happiness. It was a pitiful thing, he thought, how little each of us can share of our feelings with another.

Domino did not return. They waited two days. Irving went ashore to look for him – Delia insisted she go too.

Surprise stayed on his ship with only little Johnson. He had the boy in his cabin, playing on the red cedar desk. The boy held tight, and shoved constantly, in and out of his mouth the present that Captain Macdonald had given him : a silver spoon, on which was engraved the word : *Johnson*. The engraving was worn, as was the spoon, and Surprise and Delia guessed it was the captain's own childhood spoon.

In the package, wrapped around the spoon, was a brand new flag, the Stars and Stripes of America, and the note : 'Fly this if you have to – and some of ourselves will be with you in spirit, if not with powder. All the best, J. Macdonald.'

Surprise had his hand resting on the flag as he sat at his chart table.

He wept and said : 'Little fella, do you know that to match all the evil, all the thousands of dogs and swine of this world, there are a tiny few big good men. Do you know?'

The boy paid him no mind at all – but made sucking sounds on the spoon and reached a tiny hand for a strip of light, which came through a port and shone on the deck, trying to pick it up.

On the third day, Surprise took Delia ashore, and, spreading a few silver shillings in the tavern he thought most likely, found the girl Domino had been with.

Surprise was hot and angry and despite Delia's presence he gripped the girl by the wrist : 'Tell me where the man Domino is – or I'll wring your neck?'

She spluttered something incomprehensible to either of them.

An older woman came over. She spoke English. After a while it became all too clear.

Nothing had been done to Domino, he had gone with other sailors in another ship. Yes, the girl said through the woman, the Bahamas sailors.

Outside Delia said : 'He wouldn't go. He wouldn't leave without telling me.'

'Stop it, girl. He went with the Bahamians. He got homesick, I suppose. He got a ride to Nassau most likely. From there he can be in Bermuda in a couple of months – '

'Why wouldn't he tell us?'

'I don't know. But he gone.'

167

She knew Surprise was right. Indeed, she was relieved he wasn't angry.

'It were no good for a young blood like Domino – not raking salt, a job as can break the spirit of all but the most patient – and no girls. That's why I hoped he find a woman here.'

III

Back at New Bermuda, Surprise worked, as always, as if possessed, to complete his fortifications.

Irving worked on the *Bateau* rigging the complicated carriage for the six pounder.

'Paint that damn thing,' Surprise said good humouredly. 'I not want a rusty piece of old iron in my beautiful cabin.'

They had brought back from their trip, not only fish-hooks, lines, lead and matches, but rum, sugar, flour, lard and other foodstuffs. They also had a wide range of tools for their salt industry, for house building – and charcoal and a bellows, and a quantity of iron, strips, wire and squares. Irving had carefully purchased timber – most of it inexpensive but good, coming from old ships.

They also bought six yards of pale blue silk for a flag for the redoubt, four goats, two dozen tame fowls, a rooster – and, to their minds, the most essential medicine : salts for the bowels.

Delia planted, in the most sheltered spot, her breadfruits, and watered them three times a day as Captain Macdonald had advised.

Before two months were up, in June 1843, she got Jennie and Surprise alone on the *Bateau Bermudien* (she and Jennie now both being eight months pregnant) and levelled her intense brown eyes on them like two cocked and loaded swivel guns.

'I know damn well what's up and who put it there. You bursting with child and it Surprise's child.' She raged on for a long time and ended, against their silence and immobility, pounding on Surprise's chest. '*You damn well not have two women* – you choose. Her or me – and the one you not want is going to *DIE!*'

Surprise was gathering his emotional fibre to answer her – but feeling weak of both mind and body. It was Jennie who answered.

Her voice was quiet, respectful, dignified and heavy with the power of a quite different certitude :

'I do not want your man. I want no man, no husband. You are Delia, Captain Surprise's wife – I am only his servant, his slave. The day I come to him, I say I be his slave and I mean it. Nothing else. You, being Captain's wife, are my mistress – '

'But you having his child – '

'Yes. But you listen to Jennie. Jennie have no time for nonsense. Jennie is old – not in years, but in all she seen. You not seen the evil in this world that Jennie see – and I thankful you have not – '

'But you take my man.'

'No. I not take him. Nor want him. I just a slave woman. You listen. You have a kind mother and father with a house and happiness. I have nothing. Me born to the house of Master Reid. He evil man – like he call himself, a horse doctor. Jennie no bigger than your boy and he start beating Jennie for laughter and burning her – you listen.'

'–'

'Jennie seen everything. Master Reid, he a man who like to tie horses' heads to cedar trees – and, he a doctor, cut them – cut with knives. But he like to hear them in pain. He like to make Jennie watch.

'Jennie's mother he whip and work till she die. Then he bury her – first chopping her legs off so she fit in the small hole he have dug. You seen nothing that Jennie see. Evil everywhere on that master's property.

'Jennie a little girl and Master Reid made a field man take her – "rape" is word he say, laughing. It happen in a barn and Master Reid watch. He look – for fun. It daytime fun.

'You see this arm? More fun – horse doctor. Horse doctor make Jennie get with child with a man Jennie hate – '

'You mean – him – Mr Reid. Don't you?'

'No. Delia – leave her be. Leave her talk.'

'*You, shut up.*'

'You listen to Jennie. It not Reid. It a big black man who

169

all know is crazy – half-witted. How you like to be mated
with a man all know is half-witted? Then Jennie have John
and he a good boy and Jennie take care of him and run away.
I run away two times. Master Reid catch us and beat me and
burn me bad.'

'I know. Surprise told me.'

'When Master Reid say he burn marks on John too – I not
run any more for many years. Then I run all the way to
Captain Surprise of the Western Isles for his protection. For
him to take away. If Jennie get away, Jennie stay his slave.

'You see what Jennie known? I have no time for nonsense.
You Captain Surprise's woman – wife. Jennie only want,
before she die, to bear one child by a good man – by a man
she want. To have a child she want and choose – that's all.'

Delia turned and looked out of the cabin porthole. Her
body still heaved in the great breaths of her anger. She made
great effort, it seemed, to control herself – then she turned
back to them.

'And you, Surprise – what you want when this happen?'

'Nothing. Peace, I suppose.'

She went as if to strike him. Jennie came between them.

'Captain Surprise not come to me, girl. I come to him in
darkness. Where you been in life if you can blame a *man* for
that? A woman come to *any* man in darkness and give herself
– that *her* – that her doing. There no blame to the man. Any
man just act natural, or he be dead.'

Delia, for more than an hour, kept repeating her accusa-
tions – but what became clear, to Surprise, and he felt her
anger was justified, was that she had to live with the others
of the island and they all knew, or would know, the child was
Surprise's.

'Look at Johnson,' she said when Jennie had gone. 'Look
at him, he the image of you. Her child be the image of you,
too. Besides – they all *know*, Jennie not go near Bossie nor
no one else.'

'I am sorry.'

'*You* are sorry.'

'Yes, girl. I am. Because I see no solution. There are some
things for which there are no solution. That is life. I understand I have wronged you – but there is nothing I can do to
right it.'

170

'Nothing?'

'Nothing. Delia, you have your choice. Either to accept it. Live with it. Wait and let your anger heal – accept me again, for I love you.'

'You love me?'

'Yes. And, if you don't believe it – you have the other choice.'

'What the hell's that?'

'To go on in bitterness. To nurse the bitterness to you – nurse it until it become an old toad of pain. Until the bitterness possess you. Until it eat you up.'

'I have Johnson. Him I love. You have wronged me.'

'Yes. I have wronged you. But, now, you must not let bitterness wrong yourself.'

She turned and left the cabin.

He sat down at his chart table. The cabin was still in disarray and full of wood chips and sawdust from Irving's work on the sliding carriage for the six pounder – the *Bateau's* surprise.

Again he wished he had Senex to talk to. It's funny, he thought – I am a pretty old man myself now, thirty-five years. My bones pain me, often, with aged shooting pains – yet I still wish for the help and wisdom and tenderness of my father.

He got up and ran his fingers in the carved name on the bulkhead: SENEX.

Delia bore another son. Bernice was to be the midwife, but it was a hard birth, and, after many hours, Delia herself screamed for Jennie.

Surprise sat a little away in an agony of male frustration. He would have liked to have got drunk as Henry and Bossie and August were – but he dared not, lest there be the slightest thing he be needed for.

'You damn fool,' he heard Jennie say, 'it coming by the arse.'

'How you know?'

'Damn fool – get away. I feel it. Easy now, girl. Breathe deep and easy. Jennie help you.'

The boy she called Jack. He was small and, unlike Johnson, stayed very pale-skinned long after birth, and was to

171

remain almost mulatto coloured. A real St David's Island child.

Jennie, as Surprise prayed for, had a girl child.

She wanted to call the child Bermuda.

Surprise wasted not a minute. He took August aside and said: 'You must tell her, August. You *know*, that name is accursed for a child. No child ever survive who called Bermuda – not from the first child, the old folk say, born on the island. It a cursed name.'

'I tell her.'

Jennie called her child, Marie.

Delia would have little to do with him, though she was civil in front of the little colony.

Surprise busied himself with work. In the redoubt at the top of the hill, surmounted now by a flagpole from which fluttered their enormous blue silk flag, he designed for every possible occurence he could imagine.

First he had a ten-foot trench dug inside the fort – it was to remain open, he ordered, and the loose sandy soil to remain beside it, ready for any further orders.

With August, he fashioned three dummy cannon of wood and painted them black. Mounted on the redoubt, it appeared they had five cannon where there were only two.

The cannon on the *Bateau* was finished, practised, improved, practised. All the men knew how to work it. (Though only Surprise and August knew really how to lay, aim, the weapon – and only Surprise knew quite how limited its range was, for the windage was considerable, and the design of the barrel itself made the amount of charge it could withstand dubious.)

All knew, too, how to work the salt beds. To flood, to wait for the drying, to rake without mixing any sand with the salt, but leave a base of salt beneath. To stack the salt in piles and then to protect them from the rain, but not to protect them so well that air did not keep the new salt dry.

In their salt endeavour, the shape of the southern part of the island, and the trade winds, greatly aided them.

172

'You'd work ten years at home in Bermuda and not get a stock like this – or lose it all in a downpour.'

One man always had to be on watch. Domino's absence did not make life easy. But John was proving himself a fine worker.

On a stormy day in November 1843 – the clouds scudding low and dark, obscuring the sun to yellow blackness and making even early afternoon feel like sunset time – Bossie came skidding down from the redoubt.

Bossie, Surprise was just thinking, always is the one who sees something : this time, it be the British. The Royal Navy coming for sure.

But it was not so. It was a small open boat, and, through the spyglass on the redoubt, Surprise took measure of its tattered sails and rigging and then of the people in her.

'They all dead – or got bad sickness.'

But the open boat came on, steadily towards New Bermuda. Someone was steering her and steering her well enough to make putting out towards them, in the *Bateau,* against a head-wind, pointless.

The brass nine pounder was charged and ready. Surprise had one pistol, Henry another. Bossie manned a Buccaneer on the *Bateau.*

But as the boat drew closer the arms seemed pointless. The people in the boat were all coloured and all looking near death.

Finally, unarmed, Surprise and his men took the longboat out a little way to meet them.

'Fella steering with a oar,' Irving said. 'Don't we know him?'

'Looks like – what's-'is-name from The Flatts,' Henry said.

'Uh-hum. That's right – it is,' Bossie said. 'That's what's-'is-name from The Flatts and no mistake.'

'Who the hell is what's-'is-name?' Surprise said.

'You know – um-mum, what's-'is-name – '

'I don't know, that a fact, truth.'

'Saltus – is his name.' Henry.

'Aye. Ned Saltus, a carpenter fella.'

The boat was an open Bermuda dinghy. There were seven people on board – two dead, five living.

The smell of the dinghy was fit to turn back, as Bossie said, a dumb mule.

All on the boat were suffering severely from exposure and lack of water and food.

'Don't give them much water – on the inside. You all hear? Pour it on 'em on the outside – but don't give 'em more'n a half a cup of water an hour to drink.'

They drew the dinghy to the water's edge : it was of very heavy construction, of about fifteen feet, built as a fishing boat to withstand the usual bashing occasioned by fishing through the reefs on Bermuda's southern shore.

The man, Ned Saltus, his mouth open, split and horribly dry, choked on his first cup of water. 'You, Surprise?'

'Aye.'

'It took a long time to get to you.'

'Where from? How many days?'

'We put out from Hungry Bay, Paget. Nine of us. Thirty-one days out.'

Surprise noticed that they had cut the days of their voyage, in notches, on the boat's gunwale. He felt them. The other prominent thing was the water casks – he tapped them, all empty – carefully strapped under every thwart.

'You come straight here?' Nine souls, he was thinking, be too many for a vessel of this size.

'Yes – we settlers. We come to join your colony.'

The others were feeding them water, bathing their bodies.

'Get 'em on shore and in the shade – but easy,' Surprise said, 'You hit a bad storm?' he asked Saltus.

'Yeah. Turned us right over – exactly twenty days out, it did. All clung to boat. Lost two drowned. We righted her.'

Surprise tapped the dinghy's side. The casks must have kept her afloat.

'Two dead,' Saltus said.

'We bury them. You really came *straight* here?'

'The Lord sure had *them* by the hand,' Bossie chuckled. Then helped a woman out on to the sand.

'We see islands. The Virgins – then Anguilla, which I know. We not stop anywhere for fear of giving us away. After Anguilla – I steer straight here.'

'How you know which way, man, no compass?'

174

Saltus looked at Surprise with tired, bloodshot eyes. 'I do a lot of guessing. And I can read the stars.'

'You been to sea afore?'

'Course, man. I be Captain Seon's ship's carpenter for thirty-five years. I can navigate by the stars. And tell time, too.'

'You tell time, *the hour*, by stars? – man, go long.'

Saltus nodded with heavy tiredness. 'It be clear nights – I always know what time it is. Always.'

Surprise had heard of men who *claimed* they could tell everything by the stars : up until now he'd not believed it : now he believed Saltus, the man had no need of compass or clock. That was real *scientific* knowledge, and, compared with this knowledge, his, Surprise's powers seemed dim indeed.

'A man that can read the stars,' Henry said, 'that man can *really* read.'

Surprise went to lift Saltus out. He cried out in pain.

They rigged a stretcher out of bamboo poles and got them all into the longhouse.

'I clean out dinghy, Captain,' John said.

'Tell you what, John. You just swamp her and let the sea clean her out. Take out the casks – then anchor her good, then swamp her.'

Surprise went to see about digging the graves. August was already at it.

As Surprise suspected, Ned Saltus had heard of their settlement of Barbuda from 'a young fella come back to St David's'.

'Who else knew?'

'Not many. We only know because my wife from St David's.'

Ned's wife was one of the dead. The other was her brother, a fisherman from Paget, whose boat it was.

'Why you leave?' Surprise asked. He figured that if anyone on Bermuda knew, now all knew – he'd had ample proof of that truth.

'Sick of freedom that ain't freedom.'

Surprise thought : shit, our whole colony given away – and for what, an old man (old, even if he was clever) and four sick people.

Ned Saltus was fifty-two. The three women were his three

175

daughters – pity, Surprise thought, Domino missed them, though they were a sorry sight.

The other man was young, but so suffering from exposure – the reddened eyes and turned-down lower lids, – the open, gasping mouth and open sores – that he resembled a boiled lobster.

'How old he?'

'Fifteen.'

'That more like it, if he live.'

Surprise called a meeting. Henry, Bossie, Irving, August. Delia and Bernice came. Jennie was tending the sick. John standing his normal turn on watch.

There was much talk. After a while Surprise cut it short.

'There only be two questions: why did they come? and when is the British coming for us all?'

'They say they sick of no freedom.'

'I don't believe that *all*. Henry, you know Ned Saltus well?'

'Pretty good – Bossie knows him better.'

'All right. Bossie, you find out all you can about why. We got to know everything – that way we may know when to expect the British.'

'All right.'

'In the meantime, we must have two on watch all the time. And all guns kept loaded.'

Through all November no ship came. A Guadeloupe schooner came for salt in December.

Feb 1844 Surprise kept up the double watches. By February 1844, they had sold two more loads of salt – another boat from Guadeloupe and a very small sloop from St Eustatius.

The daughters of Ned Saltus were not bad looking, Surprise thought, but his hope of their mating up with anyone appeared pretty unlikely. The Rudd brothers seemed to have a deep, if unspoken, distaste for marriage – Henry's relationship with Bernice being typical: they spent their Sundays alone in a remote part of the island where Henry had built a shack past the salt beds. There they drank rum and did, anyone getting close knew, a lot of laughing. Bernice was a sensuous woman, with a provocative swinging way of walking – but she had eyes

176

for Henry only. However, whenever she chided Henry, his stock reply was : 'You can leave. I ain't keeping you.'

So it was with the Rudds. Surprise thought Irving and Bossie might take up with the girls – but he knew they wouldn't be tied to them. The Saltus girls, on the other hand, were Christians : no matrimony, no nothing else.

He was thinking on this enigma, one day, as he worked salt, when August, of all people, came and announced that 'they' were calling a meeting.

'They' turned out to be virtually everyone but himself.

Ned Saltus was willing and useful : he was building a new longhouse and two separate houses besides. He was a skilled carpenter – more happy working on land, he said, than at sea, though he'd spent most of his adult life as a seaman. That was not uncommon, yet there was a something about Saltus that made Surprise suspicious – he couldn't quite pin it down.

The young man, George, was a stone mason. His profession was useless to them. Neither did he learn other jobs easily : Surprise and Irving, hauling the *Bateau* over by her spar, had put him to scraping off barnacles and weeds. After half a day, they gave up on him : he was chewing into the good cedar with the scraper. He seemed good only for salt – and not too enthusiastic about that. Fortunately he caught on to the workings of guns – otherwise, Surprise felt, he'd as leave use the boy for bait. The boy also had eyes for the youngest Saltus girl – but she couldn't stand him. This one hell of a way to build a new colony, Surprise thought, no one want to breed.

'They,' as it turned out, voiced by Ned Saltus, wanted to know if it was truly a republic.

'Then we have a right to have a vote whether it be one watchman or two?'

'Of course,' Surprise said. 'But this be a dangerous time – and we best needs have two.'

'Two men doing nothing while others work – ain't necessary,' Ned said.

Surprise couldn't understand it : Saltus have something to hide, he the one should be most afraid of the British.

They voted, and only August, Delia and Jennie voted with Surprise.

'Anyone who can work or watch is entitled to a vote,' Surprise said.

M
177

They agreed.

That netted him only John. Five votes to nine.

Surprise was hurt. He thought, looking at the Saltus girls, of saying women had no right to vote – then he realised that wouldn't help him.

Next they called for a vote for a leader.

Surprise got up and left the meeting.

Delia found him working on the *Bateau*.

'Well?'

'Henry is voted Governor.'

'Well, I'll be . . . *Governor!* Sounds like *old* Bermuda.'

'But you are voted in charge of defence – the fort and the *Bateau*.'

'Oh yes.'

'And it voted to divide up all the money taken from the American schooner.'

'Amongst all?'

'No. Amongst those who were there.'

'Damned fullishness.'

'And all the money that be taken for salt : that be divided amongst all.'

'Damned fullishness.'

Surprise remained outwardly good-natured. Inwardly he was pained and angry. He now wore his green jerkin, with the brass buttons, at all times.

'You the one as wanted a republic – each person one vote,' Delia had said.

He supposed she was right. The trouble with a republic, Surprise decided, was that the majority ruled – and the majority of people were not only not wise, they were damn fools.

In March 1844, young John gave the alarm. 'Ship coming. Big ship coming.'

Surprise got to the top of the hill, to the redoubt, a while after several others – he had been away down by the salt beds.

'It come for salt, I bet.'

'Sure. She French.'

'No – maybe she American.'

Surprise took the spyglass from Irving. One glance was all

he needed. She was a brig with all square sails set, scudding along on the starboard tack like she owned the world.

'British,' he said. 'August, you in charge of the fort. Don't fire unless you have to. Use your head. We putting out in the *Bateau* – you only fire *after* we have and if you are *sure* you can hit and help us. Ned Saltus, you stay. Irving, Bossie, Henry and John – and you, too, George – come with me.'

'The Governor, Henry, should stay with the fort,' Ned said.

'Anyone who disobeys my orders,' Surprise snapped, 'will be slammed in the mouth – and right now.'

He scuttled down the hill. Damn fools : she was British lines, British rig and flying the Royal Navy flags, pennant and ensign.

The British yellow pigs, they come again, they do not take Surprise.

It was a good thing all the women, including the Saltus girls, had been practised at loading the guns. If there was a battle, August would have his hands full – but August was the man for the job. Their first line of defence – and their surprise – was the *Bateau* : and they needed six men to sail her and man the cannon and the Buccaneers.

IV

'Hoist the main.' The anchor was already aboard. It was a good thing the jibs were all pinned with Senex's cedar pins. March 1844

'Break out the jibs – then stand to the sheets.'

The *Bateau Bermudien* spun around, in the first puff of wind, turning, with Surprise's guidance, almost within her own length.

Only good thing, Surprise thought, about these new settlers, is that George what's-'is-name, is a born natural at laying and loading a cannon. If he was good for nothing else, he was a natural born gun man.

It was time that Surprise had hoped for, time to get an answer to his letter to President Tyler. Time to have Captain Macdonald return and bring them news. Well, it was now but a month short of a year, and they had heard nothing.

179

'Mount the Buccanners, port and starboard.' He need not have given the command: Irving was coming on deck with one, Bossie with the other.

'John: stay by my side.' The boy was with him, had been and wouldn't move. 'George: load the cannon with a full charge but *no more* – and careful – and ram the shot – the best shot – home good. But first you wrap it – wrap it with cloth, like we practised.'

The Buccaneers were already loaded. Only powder needed to be tapped into their pans.

Surprise handled the helm between his legs, leaving his hands free to work the main sheet. Henry was on the jibs' sheets – and now Irving was going for'ard to help him.

Time, I need time, Surprise thought. The wind was out of the north-east, and strong enough to move the British brig good, especially if she be handled good or even captained good. Worst of all, the bitches were already to windward.

Surprise wanted, somehow, to gain the windward gauge on her: to gain that advantage so important if he was forced to fight.

He figured he had a quarter of a mile he could sail before they'd see him – for that long the *Bateau* would be hidden by the island and the hill. With a little luck the British hold their course steady – and that was carrying them to leeward all the time.

There were two things he did not like about the brig's looks: one, she looked to be sailing fair and good and confident and, two, she clearly mounted at least eight guns.

But there was a good thing about her looks too: she had all sails set, and, a good captain who thought he might run into a fight, would never have more than working sails flying.

'Like I've said before, men: our advantage lies in our ability to move quick and tack like lightning. So every man be ready to *skip*.'

The *Bateau*, with the strong breeze now catching her clear of the hill, heeled over and then, with a sharp bone of a wave in her mouth, got up cut to windward, like a cross between a gull and a shark.

Forward, where Surprise watched the fill and luff of the jibs, half up the bowsprit, stood the small quite vertical flagstaff he had newly made – now it was empty, but their blue and

180

white ensign floated and whipped off the mainsail, itself snapping along the luff in taut perfection.

'What the wind blowing, John?'

'I dunno, Captain.'

'It blowing twenty, gusting to twenty-five. It called a strong breeze; not moderate, not fresh, but strong. You mark what the ship and the sails do, next time you know.'

'Aye, Captain.'

'You got nothing to be afraid of, lad – you been in a furious hurricane. The British ain't nothing in comparison to a hurricane.'

The boy's teeth were chattering – but the wind was colder now that they were clearing the land and, dodging reefs, beginning to feel the ocean's roll.

Then he saw her clear. He cleated the main sheet a turn more than he had and pulled out his spyglass.

No common jack brig she: four square sails set on each mast, two jibs. Peculiarly, she had her big fore 'n' aft sail furled (and, if she was expecting a fight, that sail would do the most good to her with the least attention and effort) – that was in the *Bateau*'s favour. But the brig was well to windward of them – and if continuing on her course, it would take them, eventually, north-east along the island.

Why, Surprise wondered, would the man keep that spanker furled? And it was too big to be called a spanker, it was a right mainsail, if he let it out.

Surprise held his course away from them, cutting to windward, glad of every second of time and sea and windward gain before the British sighted them.

It sure was a British design ship though – a Bermudian or a Yankee would have twice the size fore 'n' aft sail and thus perform better on all points of the compass, especially to windward.

But, through his glass he counted the gun ports. Not four, but five on each side. What size, he wondered?

Wouldn't matter: even if they were only four pounders – which they sure as hell weren't – they could split the *Bateau Bermudien* with one broadside. Properly aimed, one broadside to cut down all her rigging and one more to shatter her to smithereens. They were likely nine pounders, maybe even twelves.

181

The British ship looked a good sixty to sixty-five feet on the gundeck alone, and what brig o' war would fear a little sloop of twenty-eight feet and she only mounting, it appeared, two swivel guns – and them, maybe, just decorations.

The brig had seen them and was changing course to try to keep the weather gauge.

Now, to the south, their blue and white flag fluttered proudly from the fort.

Surprise put his arm on the taffrail and made his elbow measure the angle of his ship, the brig and the breeze: the line he could lay if he came about.

No, you can't do it, you Limey bastard, I've got you.

'Stand by to come about – hard-a-lee.'

The *Bateau*, in coming about, took no longer than the thrown helm, a count of four, and then the sails were full again. In motion, she rode on the one tack up one wave, tacked over on the crest of that wave, and when she pitched into the trough, her sails were full on the opposite tack.

It was so fast a manœuvre that August, watching from the hill, thought, for a moment, that the *Bateau* had not tacked at all, but always been cutting to windward with the starboard rail down the way she was now.

As soon as the *Bateau* was footing at full pace, Surprise shouted: 'All forward and furl the big jib.'

'Wha'?' Henry said.

'You heard, First Mate – move!'

Surprise knew he had already gained the windward: now he did not want the British to know how fast the *Bateau* was.

They wrestled, four of them, with the spanking sail, but quickly had it furled.

Surprise put his glass on the British: typical, they were now pointing as high as they could (doubtless realising the relative positions of both craft) but it was not much above thirty degrees, nigh a quarter of the compass off the wind and the *Bateau* was cutting almost into the eye of it.

Surprise knew that nothing mattered at all if the British decided to fire first and talk later: any time they wanted, and the *Bateau* be showing them her length, they could blast her out of the water, long before they were within range of his swivels, never mind their hidden stern gun.

Time. Time. Time, is what I need.

'First Mate – as I ease up, let down your main and reef her in all you can.' Surprise hoped the British would not notice this, or not care much if they did: reefed and with the big jib off, the *Bateau* had a considerable surge of speed in store.

The two vessels were converging fast now.

'John. Check the flash pans of the Buccaneers to be sure they have good dry black powder.'

'What is that damn craft, Bainbridge?'

'A sloop, sir. As I said – she put out from behind the island.'

'Well, let's have a look at her, Bainbridge.'

'We are, sir – we are converging.'

'I mean through your glass, man.' The captain, dressed in his blue and gold coat, with his white skin-tight ducks, looked through the glass: 'How many guns, Bainbridge? How many men? And what nationality is she?'

'No guns, sir. About twenty men perhaps. Can't tell what nationality, sir.'

'Course you can, Bainbridge. What flag is that?'

'Don't know, sir – was going to ask you, sir.'

'Don't be bloody impudent. Beat to quarters.'

'But the marines are already standing by the boats for a landing party, sir.'

'I don't give a damn – beat to quarters.'

'Aye, aye, sir.'

'Smith!'

'Sir!'

'What bloody flag is that, Smith?'

Silence.

'Don't know, sir.'

'Beat to quarters.'

'We are, sir.'

'I know we are – '

'I think they want to talk, sir.' Bainbridge.

'Bloody waste of time. One of Her Majesty's ships, with marines ready to land – standing-to one hundred and fifty jack tars to palava with a blasted West Indian fishing boat.'

'Aye, sir. But the flag she's flying is the same as that on the island, sir.'

'When I want your comments, Bainbridge, I'll ask for 'em.'

'Aye, aye, sir.'

'If she doesn't hurry up, I'll blast her out of the water.'

'Could be American, sir.'

'Why, Smith?'

'She's flying the United States ensign from the bow.'

'Impossible. Kindly give the order to come about when you're ready, Mr Bainbridge.'

'John. Climb the bowsprit and break out this flag. Can you manage that?'

'Aye, Captain. Course I can.'

' 'Tis slippery and a long way out, so be careful.'

The American flag, Surprise thought, might buy them a little time. Besides, to go into battle with the Stars and Stripes flying in the bow as a courtesy flag was to carry a good talisman : the United States had had the guts to take on the British at sea, and lick 'em. . . .

He saw the Royal Navy brig start to come about. In less than a minute they'd be within hailing distance.

'Look idle, men – look easy. And be ready to shake out *all* sail.' Surprise lowered his voice. 'Henry, come by me a moment, please.'

Henry came up on the quarter-deck.

'If talk won't work, Henry – I want you to get back here as soon as we've all sails set, see. Get back here and take the helm.'

'Aye, Surprise.'

'Keep everybody easy now – look idle – look *stupid* – look anything but warlike.'

'Aye.'

The vessels now both lay on the same tack. Surprise had to ease sheets to point the same and stay as slow. But the brig looked girt indeed with her towering mass of sails, and totally impregnable in her iron-fastened British oak.

'What ship are you?'

It was a gold-braided lieutenant hailing – and, behind him, Surprise could see the pudgy captain. Most of all, Surprise was aware of the sheer weight of British seamen, British guns, British power all symbolised in the great fluttering red and white ensign.

'*Bateau Bermudien*, of New Bermuda.'

A pause while the lieutenant conferred.

'What place?'

Surprise instantly despaired of explaining. 'Right yonder. That place. New Bermuda.'

More conferring.

'We be from the new Republic of New Bermuda. And we wish peace to all. And enquire what the British Navy desire in these waters?'

'That island is Barbuda,' the lieutenant hailed. 'And ours – British.'

'That island the Republic of New Bermuda. An established republic now waiting the arrival of its envoy from the President of the United States.' Man, Surprise thought, what a mess of tricky words. . . .

More conferring. Surprise slackened his main still more, but kept good and powerful way on his little ship.

'What port are *you* from, sire?' Surprise hailed.

'Her Majesty's ship *Vestral*, of the American and West Indies Squadron, Bermuda. Here to seek escaped convicts and criminals – and re-establish the British flag on the British Colony of Barbuda.'

'Barbuda no longer exists. This is the Republic of New Bermuda – whose existence is known to the President of the United States. We have no convicts or criminals here – only free men.'

Surprise saw the captain waddle to the rail and angrily grab the trumpet.

'I don't give a damn about the President of the United States or the president of any nation. I serve the *Queen* of England. . . .'

'Well, sire, what you *want* of a free people on a free island?'

'I *want* nothing: I intend to land and secure Her Majesty's property and apprehend certain criminals.'

'What criminals, sire? What name?' Surprise was playing for time. 'Pass the word. Break out that jib but let her flap,' he said to John. He was thinking: I gotta figure who's the best officer on that ship. Who's the most valuable: these British, you knock over the officers – particularly the *best* officer – and they are half-finished. But he needed time to be closer, and speed to give the *Bateau* a chance of escape.

'Criminals? I'll tell you what criminals.' More flapping and conferring on the Royal Navy quarter-deck.

'Criminals known as Saltus – and six others, wanted for theft. Criminals Billinghurst, Napier – '

'We have none such. We have no criminals. This is a republic and no British may land.'

The captain turned to Lieutenant Bainbridge, pulled his silver snuff box from his waistcoat and said : 'I will step on that gnat, Bainbridge.' He sniffed a pinch of snuff.

'When, sir ?'

'When I'm ready, Bainbridge.' He grabbed the voice trumpet and went to the rail again.

'I'll see you in hell – ' the captain yelled. 'Her Majesty's ships and officers go where they please.'

'Ye may not land on New Bermuda.' To his crew : 'Tighten that jib – break out the main reefs !'

'I'll blast you to hell and hang you from my tallest yardarm !' The captain was red-faced above his white ruffled neckpiece.

Only about sixty yards now separated the two craft. And Surprise, far from sheering off as the British expected, was easing the *Bateau* closer – thus, off the wind, he was also increasing his speed rapidly.

'Ye can't take that fort, sire – not and it mounting vast cannon and numerous militia.' He spat on his palm, raising it off his tiller and put it back. 'Haul high the main. Chief mate – get back here.' He pushed the tiller up hard, swinging the *Bateau* closer, then eased back on a new course parallel to the old.

The gun ports of the brig, on side mountings, flew open. Surprise had taken measure of his enemy and especially of her officers. The *Bateau* was overhauling the brig fast. The time was *now*. Letting go the tiller, he leapt to a Buccaneer, grabbed its mahogany handle and cocked its flint – all in one movement.

He laid the long sixty-inch barrel exactly one head's height above the gold trimmed hat and slightly to port of it, to allow for wind and fired. It was the officer he believed most valuable and most dangerous.

It seemed a long pause and he, Surprise, was moving when he saw the lieutenant double over, clutch his chest and then clutch his face – all in a red blur of seemingly exploded blood.

He leapt towards the second Buccaneer. Henry already had the helm. The *Bateau* was pulling ahead very fast now – in a

186

few moments they might gain safety, but neither then would there be a chance of another shot at the British officers.

He cocked the second Buccaneer – the bright brass barrel seeming to almost reach the fat cockaded target – and fired.

'Reload. Irving and Bossie reload the Buccaneers.' He took the helm and steered the *Bateau* (only then registering the acid reality of what had been etched on his eye: the Royal Navy captain, taking the one pound shot full against his right shoulder, had been dismembered as if he were a carcass hanging on a hook cut by a mighty butcher's cleaver) so close to the brig that the water, concertina'd between them, raged, splashed and squirted high here and there in vertical streaks of foam.

'Shoot that man!' he yelled at Henry, who had a pistol levelled. 'Not that one – that *fat* one with the gold stripes on him – gold stripes on his arm.'

Henry fired.

Now they were drawing quite level with the brig's bow and bowsprit – lee-bowing her. Moving as fast as the clappers of hell's bells.

Now they were clear of her big guns. One of which, senselessly, fired. Then another.

Soon they were clear of all the ship – save the marines running with muskets to the *Vestral*'s bow. Enough marines to kill them all.

Surprise kept cool – the old steel cold of emergency and battle and all manner of disaster endured, came over him.

'Bossie and Irving. Hear me. Fire *only* Bossie. Only Bossie. Only one. Fire at a sure fat target. Then reload. Irving, do not fire until Bossie is reloaded.'

'What we hit?' Henry said, ready with powder.

'You hear! Fire – *one* only! Keep their heads down – always always keep their heads down. Keep them scared. Busy. Ducking.'

Bossie fired.

Surprise knew that if he wanted a shot at the brig with his six pounder, a shot that counted, now was the time to level it. One shot at the water line, and, with an emperor's luck, the whole girt ship could sink by the bow.

Or should he wait?

'Slack the main a little, Henry. Now take the helm.'

He leapt down the steps off the little quarter-deck, grabbed the rail, snapped his weight against it to turn his body toward the companionway to the after cabin so sharply he heard it crack.

In the dark cabin George was ready – you could feel the pent-up terror and expectation of the boy fill the place.

'Roll her out!'

He himself slammed the cedar port up and out of the way: then helped haul the big black cannon into place.

'All charged?' He did not wait for an answer but began banging wood wedges under her. He wanted the six pounder pointing steep down right at that water line – the one he could not see, through the open port, surging but twenty to twenty-five feet behind them.

'We're laying it!' George said.

Now, impossibly, now, and *now or never* was the time: 'Light that fuse.'

The barrel was steep down: pointed right at the vast oak as it cut the water.

'To hell with the fuse, man. Light the very top, the touch-hole, now. Now!'

He jumped at George, making to grab the torch, but George, quick as in practice, had done it – done it all, as if by instinct.

The six pounder roared, bucked, smashed back down her runners clear to the bow of the cabin – ran the full length she was allowed and crashed against the after bulkhead. The room filled with the bitter smell, smoke and taste of flashed sulphur, saltpetre and charcoal powder.

'Jesus.'

'Reload the bitch.' He moved, like a cat, to the port, but could see nothing but smoke and spray. He ran up on deck.

'Henry – haul arse! Lay on all we got, men. Put water between us and these British bascombes – and right now.'

He looked, keeping low against the British marine muskets, over the stern. Nothing. Then the brig rose up on a wave as the *Bateau* went down.

They had holed her, all right, but it looked such a small hole.

'Fire when you see 'em, you Buccaneers.'

'Shit,' Irving said. 'Captain. I fired twice and hit one bitch

188

for sure – but now they won't show theirselfs. Won't show at all.'

'Shit – me, too. Bossie all ready and damn all left to fire at. T'ain't fair. Put a head up, Limey. Put a head up for Mrs Rudd's boy.' Bossie saw Surprise move forward. 'That's it – fuck, Surprise, get outa the way.'

The Buccaneer barked, bucked back, spun on its gunlock out of Bossie's hand.

'Lookee – he's going overboard,' Bossie squealed and made to load again.

They were pulling away sure, deep and steady. Surprise measured the distance – nigh on a hundred yards. Bossie's shot was damn good or damn lucky – but a Buccaneer was a vicious weapon, especially one with a barrel as long as a man.

He wondered what Captain Darrell would think : his man, Surprise Billinghurst, his Master Helmsman, killing British sailors, in southern climes – hell, killing two British officers in two minutes, and one of them a captain in Her Britannic Majesty's Navy. And, shit, if he'd ever been afraid of being hunted as a murderer – labelled as such by them – now that was a surety.

When they had pulled three hundred yards ahead of the *Vestral*, Surprise tightened his helm to windward in order to get a slightly better view of her – but not so far as to allow any of her guns to bear, even allowing for the *Vestral* making a good and quick fighting manœuvre – which would be to put helm up or helm down, square off and fire a broadside, right now.

But the more they could see, the more did HMS *Vestral* seem in confusion.

'Surprise – you did kill that Captain !' Henry kept yelling. 'I did see it with my own eyes.'

John was round-eyed with wonder and amazement.

'And he killed the sharp mouth, too – he killed both the talkers,' Irving said. 'And I killed three at least.'

'Shit you did,' Bossie said. 'Maybe two. Bossie only got *one* for sure – *maybe* two. So you *never* killed no three.'

'I hit the blue jacket with the gold stripes, Surprise. Did you see me ?' Henry.

'Aye. Look. What you think now ?'

The *Vestral* was indeed all confusion, and, to add to her loss of first and second in command, she was now getting heavy by the bow.

Surprise was thinking that they could tack, double back on her bow to bow, tack again, bow to bow, fire when the *Bateau*'s stern came to bear, and maybe sink her.

He'd lost his glass. 'Take her, Henry, keep easing her up. Someone tighten that jib! Damn, this is a ship, not a rum party.'

He found his glass a way down inside his tight trouser leg and undid his buttons.

When he looked over at the *Vestral*, officers and men were running every which way. One or two clumps seemed to have some order about them : and one of these clumps of men was working to swing out a longboat.

He could see two men on the quarter-deck. Perhaps both officers – though only one seemed to be gold braided.

All was chaos.

It crossed his mind, only to be dismissed as impossible, that he might have defeated this ship – they might strike their colours or even just abandon. Impossible. He began to lay other plans – to make sure that HMS *Vestral* cut out of these waters to lick her wounds and, maybe, head for English Harbour for a refit.

But, if there had been any doubt in any mind on board the British ship as to what they should best do – such doubt was to be instantly dispelled.

A white puff came from the top of the highest point of New Bermuda, a puff that stood out, blossomed like a little cloud, momentarily obscured most of the fluttering blue ensign on the flag pole, and then wafted away a little to the sou'-ard. . . .

Bang!

And the strange echo, bang.

A spurt of water, only yards from the *Vestral*'s port bow, went up, ten, twenty, thirty feet in the air.

Through his glass, Surprise saw chaos become panic and pandemonium. They peeled over the ship's side, some full-dressed, some stripped to the waist, some seeming naked – peeling over as if they were seamen in a whaler's longboat flipped by a great leviathan.

190

One ship's boat banged into the water; another went down stern first – tipping its men into the sea like fry spilled out of a fisherman's hand net.

The shouts of men reached them across the water even against the wind.

Surprise watched in breathless and almost unbelieving rapture : if there was one iota of order on that British man-o'-war, it was only from he who hauled the flag to the deck so that it resembled a sea-bird diving for its prey.

'Put about, Surprise.'

'Aye. Coming about – stand by. Ready about !'

When they drew close to HMS *Vestral*, she was square to the wind – sails set, literally moving sideways, crabwise, her length against the sea, her sails and rudder trapped by the wind into a ridiculous parody of a sailing ship.

Her bow was down now, heavy, deep. Another six inches or a foot and water would be flowing in the foremost of her still open starboard gun ports.

Two of her boats had got clear. One even had a leg-o'-mutton sail up, running to leeward, to the south. Heads were bobbing in the water – swimming towards the boat without the sail. Then he saw there were three boats away, two taking in swimmers.

Some, Surprise knew, would swim for shore. Would August and his band have the sense to capture them? Dare he try to salvage the *Vestral*?

'I going to board and salvage that ship – '

'You'll never do it, Surprise – she too beeg – and spooked by the British.'

'I'm going to board and salvage her. Hear me, men.'

'The British laid to blow her up I bet.' Irving.

'Hear me : Henry, Bossie and George come with me – Irving, you in charge of the *Bateau*, you hear? You captain of the *Bateau* and you get her safe home with only the boy. You get her safe home or Surprise will put you in hell. . . .'

'Aye. I can get her home.'

'Then we laying alongside – make ready to jump. Get a pistol, Henry – and be sure it loaded! George! Get on deck, George.'

In the moments that it took to bring the *Bateau* around

191

and glide her towards the *Vestral*'s lee, Surprise said: 'Henry, you *know*. You know there's only one way to do it – get a big sail over her bow – and then get her under way and keep her moving until we hit her high on the beach. Right?'

'Aye, my Captain, we can but try.'

'Aye. It's a matter of getting the sail over and down deep while she *still* – then get her moving and the movement and the sea wrap that sail over that hole.'

'Aye.'

Coming alongside the *Vestral*'s starboard, Surprise had left the helm to Irving, making ready to jump, and Irving cut too close. The *Bateau* had considerable way on still – and the *Vestral* was sailing, not drifting sideways – and she fouled their ratlines on the second open gunport and gun.

Surprise and Henry jumped. Surprise had his pistol out – but the *Vestral*'s deck was deserted of men, only a mass of abandoned rope. . . .

'Get the *Bateau* clear!' He could see that one of the stay lines was cut – the rest, he hoped, would hold. The bowsprit had smashed head and side into the *Vestral* – amazingly it seemed intact.

'Irving – fling your helm over. Pump it. Shove off that bowsprit George.'

Surprise grabbed up a great sweep off the deck, ran forward, made to give the *Bateau*'s bowsprit a shove to lee – but Irving and young John had got her clear and somehow got sufficient breath of air, despite the lee of the big ship, to pull her underway. . . .

'Watch your stern!' Surprise turned, saw a young British seaman come on deck fastening his britches.

'Get overboard. Get overboard or I'll kill you.' He didn't want to fire: he had only one shot and he might need it.

The seaman, without hesitating, doubtless terror-struck by the appearance of a big, seemingly crazed Negro, ran to the gunwale, scrambled up and bailed himself over the side.

Turning, Surprise yelled: 'Cut down that forecourse – that's the one. Bossie, Henry, let's go.'

Surprise went to climb the ratlines, but Henry, finding an axe, swung it madly against the foremast, severing, with the second blow, the halyard and the yardarm braces, and bringing the whole giant sail and yardarm down over and about them like a maddened cloud fallen from the heavens.

They secured the sail on the port side – cleating great hunks of it to cleats, anchor head, anything they could lay hands to.

Bossie was madly furling the port side of it – cutting the ropes off the yardarm with his knife as he went.

Then, using a lead and rope, they got a line under the bowsprit and began hauling the great mass and weight of sail toward the port side.

'I go and get her under way. When I get her luffed back up and dead in the water – you get her down.'

He ran, over ropes, pumps, pump handles, gratings, dodged masts, capstans, even doormats. Man, what a long girt ship after the *Bateau*.

The quarter-deck was very high and Surprise, for an instant, marvelled at the glistening, golden shine of the brass tread-rail on every step.

He grabbed the girt wheel and spun her to port. No wonder she had double spokes and a whole double wheel – it took near all his strength to move it.

He had her hard over. Nothing happened. The ship just drifted, sailed, sideways as before.

Shit, he was just thinking: I gotta do something with a sail – maybe break-out that fore 'n' aft – when, quietly, heavily, she began, ever so slightly, to fall to leeward by the bow.

He could see the island and the hill clearly, to the south – where the bow was slowly moving.

At last he got her under way and, as soon as her vast tonnage was footing what he judged sufficient, he hauled the wheel to starboard, spoke by heavy spoke.

In comparison to the *Bateau* it was like trying to steer a wine barrel with a kitchen spoon in a sea of molasses.

Shit. He hauled and hauled. She came up agonisingly slowly. Then he realised, that, though she was probably heavy-helmed anyway, she was now vastly hampered by having herself so heavy with water and down by the bow, that her rudder must be lifted half out of the water.

It took her minutes to point to windward. He centred the helm – she staggered forward for a painfully long time. . . .

'Henry, Bossie – did anyone close those forward ports?' He yelled as loud as he could.

There was no answer.

He looked back at the island. Yes, if they could get the sail over the bow, and she steer and stay afloat, he could just get her around the point below the fort – just get her there, the way she was laying and the wind laying.

Trouble was, the reefs: with this cumbersome great tub, dodging the reefs would not be easy. Maybe the girt bitch would just knock one or two over. . . .

Shit, he was thinking what she'd have on board. (He could smell the cooking coming back at him now – he'd have to tell them, as soon as they'd finished the sail and the closing of the for'-ard ports, to douse fires.) All manner of powder and guns and instruments and flags and clothes and money and gold. . . .

But he could tell, already, that for all the shine of the steps, the binnacle and the wheel-spoke caps, she was an old, old ship.

Bossie came aft: 'Try easing her to leeward now, Surprise.'

'Good, Bossie. The for'ard ports – water will pour in.'

'Aye – one thing at a time, Captain. Ease her.'

'And douse fires!'

He spun the wheel, waited the long water-logged pause, then the wind caught her topsails – then gradually filled the other square sails and he began moving the helm, testing her responses, as they got under way to leeward toward the point of New Bermuda, behind which lay the beach.

Just give me three to three and a half knots, Surprise thought, and I can lay her in between those two strips of rock and drive her high and dry on our beach and we can strip her like ants stripping a cockroach.

But what a mess she was. Some sails swept free, others careened as they liked. The helm, now the ship was moving, was lighter – that is, it did not quite take *all* his strength to move it.

'Get the ports closed! Get a man back here to help me!' He was not sure they could hear him, though the wind carried his voice now.

He looked about for the *Bateau Bermudien*. He couldn't see her. Maybe it had all been a mistake: maybe he'd bitten off more than he should. What if he lost his beloved ship – ? But this prize had seemed too impossibly easy to take, too easy to pass up.

He brought the *Vestral* up to windward a bit, remembering one prominent reef.

Then he swung her back to port again.

Henry came aft. 'We can't close the for'ard port, Surprise. The gun is jammed.'

'Not three of you?'

'Hell, no. It's busted clear askew. Take six of us and hours.'

'When will she take on water?'

'Hard to say.'

'You done good, Chief Mate. How's that hole stopper – that's the big point?'

'It over – and over the whole bow. I reckon it ain't coming in bad now.'

'Henry – give me a hand on this wheel – will you? It's heavy as hell.'

'We need more speed, Surprise.'

'Aye.'

'Bossie – secure all the sheets you can. Let's get her sailing.' He turned to Surprise. 'You aim to beach her, don't you?'

'Aye – drive her as high and dry as we can.'

'Right – I be back.'

They scudded around the point with almost every sail set and drawing good.

Surprise, for a moment, had his attention caught by the crumpled, abandoned but still so elegant, British white ensign, lying on the deck – dirty footprints on part of its pure-looking white.

'Fires all out?' he asked Bossie.

'Aye, aye, Captain. Fires out, the ship's flying good, the British Navy engaged and defeated and their vessel – what's-'er-name? – captured.'

'*Vestral*.'

'What it mean?'

'How the hell should I know.' Surprise looked about the sea and sky. 'Must have meant something to somebody once – I suppose. You sure we can't close that port?'

'Surprise, Captain, us and two horses couldn't move that

195

gun – but I stuffed her with canvas. We'll make home. you wait and see.'

'And the other ports?'

'Two closed.'

'Good. You did good – better'n good, Bossie.'

'Uh-huh.'

Surprise looked at him. Bossie was smiling his own particular smile which always seemed to say : good today, bad tomorrow, that's the way it goes and I'll take it as it comes.

'You see the *Bateau*? I can't see for sails – and this quarter-deck stuck up in the air like the arse on a swayback mule.'

'There – she was under there.'

Surprise ducked down. He saw her away ahead, anchored off the beach, all sails furled and shipshape – only the Stars and Stripes still fluttering on the little staff half up the bow-sprit.

He sighed a great sigh of relief.

'What's the matter? You think Irving can't sail? Irving could handle a boat in his sleep, man.'

'I know. The *Bateau* – she's like a mistress to me.'

'You think Bossie don't know that? – you must think Bossie blind and fullish.'

'All right – help me here. We lay her right in between the strips of rocks – right?'

'Sure.'

After a while, as if the crash of beaching was not even ahead of them, never mind imminent, Bossie said : 'What the British send next, Surprise? Their whole army?'

'Don't know.'

' 'Spect so. Them Limeys going to send Nelson, Wellington and King William, too – that's what I figure.'

Surprise smiled – he'd always liked Bossie Rudd and counted on his great humour and optimism. He wondered why the man had voted against him, but he said : 'She getting awful heavy by the bow now.'

'Aye, Surprise. No matter – she ain't got far to go and she can lay her head down like a'old dawg.'

Surprise moved the wheel to port, laid the *Vestral*, still doing three knots and more, between the last strips of rock.

'Brace yourselves!'

She touched, but, strangely, drove on and on and up and

196

up on to the beach. Her stopping was peculiarly unviolent, and, due probably to the cushioning sand, almost soundless. Then, suddenly, there was a rending, splitting crash from aloft : the top-gallant mast, the top section of the mainmast, snapped and came down to the deck, through the rigging, trailing the pennant above the falling mass.

'Gawd-almighty – she quit hollering now,' Bossie said and sauntered off up the deck.

'Bossie !'

'Yeah.'

'Where you going ?'

'Get drunk – to get pissed, Surprise.'

'Not such a bad idea, either – first I check the Captain's cabin.'

'Shit, man. Don't you ever quit – it ain't going no place you know ?'

'Well – I'll just check.'

'Man. The British ain't sending two ships in one day. Come on, let's you and me go get pissed, Surprise. Like the old folks say, man, let your hair down. If you don't let your hair down and cool out, man, you'll blow like a cannon. Come on. Your missus and the children like to celebrate, too.'

'You're right, Bossie. Let's cool out. To hell with it. That's enough for today.'

'You can say that again.'

From the sounds from the bow, the whole colony was climbing aboard.

Henry came up. Surprise let out a great sigh.

'We got to get this canvas off, Surprise.'

'Aye. Bossie and I were talking of getting drunk – but we can't leave the sails on. And, there's liable to be British sailors crawling all over our island.'

'True.' Henry looked peculiarly saddened, deflated. 'Surprise, you want to see something as would break your heart ?'

'What ?'

'Take a look down here.'

Surprise followed him.

Just forward of the mainmast, half-covered by the fallen top-gallant was a small clinkerbuilt British dinghy.

'Well, what ?'

'Look close.'

197

'I don't see nothing.'

'Look at this.' Henry put his hand on a thin box-like thing in the centre of the dinghy.

'It a keel?'

'Yeah. In a box. See. The Limeys can raise and lower it here, see. It *in* a box – can't leak.'

'Well, I never. . . .'

'Never would have noticed it myself – hadn't that spar fell and damn near killed me. What the hell would Saul Billinghurst make of that?'

Surprise didn't answer. The Limey bastards, they thought of everything.

'It sure make our fin keel look stupid . . . silly.'

There were shouts on the shore.

Henry and Surprise went to the rail.

On the beach, in a line, sat about forty British seamen. Bernice stood overlooking them, armed with a great fish gaff.

'Look like Bernice captured the whole Royal Navy.'

Bernice had her free arm on her hip. One Englishman started to move, as if to get up.

Bernice menaced him with the gaff, her big arms flaying about in the sun. The Englishman sat back.

Then they noticed that Jennie was there, too, standing behind the prisoners. In her good arm was an axe.

'Sometimes,' Henry said, 'I swear to Gawd women don't even need men at all – 'cept for the necessary.'

'Aye.'

V

March
1844 It was decided that Surprise would take the prisoners immediately to Nevis and drop them on the nearest shore. He figured he could make Nevis, without tacking on a broad reach, and back on a tight reach, all within twenty-four hours.

They'd tow the longboat, with eleven British in her, with Ned Saltus aboard with a pistol.

'Don't take any shit from them,' Surprise said so that they

could hear. 'They give you any trouble – shoot one. Then we'll make 'em all swim, just like they used to dump black people. We'll dump 'em right where we are. If they don't behave, to hell with the whole lot of 'em.'

In the *Bateau*, he'd have twenty-six British and Irving and John and George.

Four of the British seamen claimed to be Americans pressed into the Royal Navy and asked for asylum on the island until an American ship came by.

Surprise was suspicious and questioned them one by one. Three of them he believed; the last he had questioned thus :

'Who is the President of the United States?'

' – '

'Who?'

'George Washingborough.'

'What is capital of the United States?'

'Boston.'

'Throw this Limey on the *Bateau*.'

August and all remaining would get the canvas off the *Vestral*, anchor her aft – although that certainly didn't seem necessary, she being so high out of water – and take stock of their spoils of war.

Delia had rushed towards Surprise the moment he jumped ashore. Young Johnson was holding her skirt, falling over and picking himself up; the baby, small for his eight months, was in her arms, his head lolling over her shoulder.

She kissed Surprise and hugged at him with her free hand. He kissed her, put his arm around her head, kissed the baby. Then he picked up little Johnson.

The elder boy was talking now as well as walking : but, being a child of great feeling, he was shy, and, in moments like these, could only express himself by enormous stares from his startled and wondering eyes and clamp his little arms around his father's neck and bury his head.

'I'll be back soon – this nonsense nearly all over.' He held Johnson away from him a moment and looked him in the eyes. 'Daddy be back soon – you hear?'

Johnson nodded seriously, like a little man. Surprise had the sudden horror that he was a dwarf : that he was a little man and would never grow bigger. Then he realised it was pure fantasy, just the perpetual anxiety of parenthood.

Delia was nuzzling against him again. 'A lot of nonsense nearly over – you hear me, man?'

'Yes.'

The trip to Nevis went without mishap – save that Ned slightly holed the longboat, putting a wounded Englishman ashore on the rocks.

Surprise had spoken to the only officer, a young midshipman named Jimson.

'You tell your masters how we return you the same day – and all safe and in good order, save the three Americans who beg to stay. You tell them we only want peace. We the Republic of New Bermuda. We not want to fight the British or anybody – just want to live in peace and harvest salt and fish and – live. But that if anyone think they going to take New Bermuda – then *they* in trouble. For we fight like blood-crazed sharks if we attacked at our home. And you tell them New Bermuda got cannon and powder a'plenty – and men as can man them good.'

'And what name shall I give them, sir?'

Surprise was startled, not so much by the title as by the midshipman's incredibly blue eyes and his blatant youth – the red blush of the girlish cheeks.

'Le Negre. I am called Le Negre.'

'And you are from Bermuda, sir?'

'No, sir. You hear this good. I am from *New* Bermuda – and from there only.'

'Aye, aye, sir.'

'And you tell them we have sent an envoy to President Tyler of the United States and that we daily expect to hear that we are under the Monroe Document.'

'The what, sir?'

'You write it down. The captains and admirals will know. President Monroe promised protection to all free people.'

'Yes, sir.'

And Delia came to him when it was dark and the children were asleep on shore and they could be alone on the *Bateau*.

'I a damn silly girl –'

'Oh, shut up – forget it.'

'No, Surprise. When you close on that girt British ship I

suddenly knew you were going to die – then I realised that if you killed it would kill me.'

'Don't talk such.'

'And you might have died with me still being a silly girl – but that change now.'

The talk was blurred, then drowned in passion, and, to Surprise, an ecstasy made more poignant because it was familiar and true. Delia was his girl, his woman and the heft of her – body and spirit – had always fit him right.

They held a meeting about the three American seamen.

Surprise had already promised the men that they could leave on the first American ship that put in to the island – or be taken in the *Bateau* on their next trip to a French port.

'I say they be warned that they can't *stay* with us,' Irving said. 'This a Negro colony – and we want no white.'

'Aye.'

'Aye.'

'You damn right.'

'And they be warned,' Ned Saltus said, 'not to touch any of our womenfolk under pain of death.'

Surprise agreed to tell them. 'They all seem like decent folk. I don't think they give us any trouble.'

'Maybe,' Henry said, 'but you tell them just the same. And for their food, they must work.'

'Shit,' Bossie said, 'them three already proved themselves working fools.'

Apart from the cannon – the *Vestral* mounted six nine pounders and two twelve pounders – the massive stores of shot and powder and provisions, what Surprise liked best from their prize was the big brass barometer, which was mate to a big brass clock.

He'd always relied on their home-style, old-fashioned shark oil barometer (and he didn't figure to be without that in the future – for oil from a shark's liver was a mighty fortune teller of weather) but this new-fashion London-made piece of weather-telling scientific machinery was fine indeed. He mounted it right in his captain's cabin.

He liked too the big ship's bell. They mounted that by the door of the new Long House, that Ned Saltus had built, and they rang it for emergencies, meetings and every noon hour to tell all the time. The label, HMS *Vestral*, engraved deep in the brass, they turned, hidden, towards the wall. The *Vestral's* brass clock was set, in a place of honour, inside the Long House – and many suitable furnishings from the ship were put there, too : tables, chairs, gun rack of muskets and swords, two drums and much else.

The maritime fittings Surprise put on the *Bateau*. Indeed, by the time he had finished, the *Bateau Bermudien* was the only Negro-owned sloop in the Caribbean – probably in the whole world, he figured – with the décor and luxury of appointments, appurtenances and accoutrements, of a Royal Navy ship – a royal yacht. His beloved *Bateau* had at last received the crowning trimmings her graceful lines had always deserved.

Yes, he figured the British would charge him with murder and piracy, but he figured, too, he had time to prepare for their next coming (and a mighty fort New Bermuda would be) and he had the hope that Captain Macdonald would return with news from President Tyler.

He also had some alternate plans for his people, should the British attack – and he just wanted time to rest and work them out.

Then, too, he wanted to have it out with Ned Saltus : what the hell was this theft the British had against him? And maybe it was nothing, like him and Delia and the compass, but if it was, why hadn't he told them of it?

In the meantime, they dismantled the spars, yards and all rigging of the *Vestral*. Then, despairing of hauling her hull clear on shore (there was just no way they could move her, save by a hurricane tide) where it would make a fine building – even a fort – they began breaking her up, saving every timber, fastening and nail.

May 1844 In May, an American schooner, a big one, put in and she was from Savannah, Georgia, and Surprise didn't like that at first. But the Captain was friendly and he wanted two holds full of salt – which was very nearly all their stock – and he paid in advance in silver (and Surprise pocketed the money and figured he'd have this splitting up shit out with Saltus and the others as soon as the Americans left). But, most important of all, he said he'd been sent there by the *Thomas Jefferson*, Captain Johnson Macdonald, Master, from the port of New York.

No, he didn't know where the *Thomas Jefferson* was now or when Captain Macdonald was coming to the island. They'd met up in New York, staying at the same inn.

The Savannah Captain agreed to take the three American seamen back with him. The schooner had white officers and a crew of all Negroes and the Negroes said the Captain was a 'real fair and kind man' and shook their heads, only, about the others.

The way the Captain talked, Surprise figured he must be English, but it didn't worry him much, maybe he had once been English, anyway, it didn't seem to trouble the three American seamen. Besides, to Surprise, news of Captain Macdonald and that they were not forgotten, made him sort of swell with hope, relief and expectation.

He half-hoped three of the Negro Americans might elect to settle, but nothing ever came of it. Neither did Surprise push the matter: for even if the Captain was a friend of Macdonald's his home port was Savannah, and them people were old-fashioned to say the least.

And then they were good and busy, too: not only a whole new harvest of salt must be completed as soon as possible (for it would not do for any ship to come and they turn them away empty) but the fort had to be enlarged, immensely, to take the two twelve pounders in commanding positions. It was a vast job to even haul them up the hill – though the *Vestral*'s stores of rope, blocks and tackle were a big help.

Indeed, Surprise figured on two more small gun posts at a slightly lower level on the hill. And, also, he was thinking of a secret gun post – another surprise – to be hidden away down below the salt beds.

The loss of the three American seamen, the loss of the weight of their manpower, seemed disproportionately great to them all. Surprise realised it was just their small number that caused it: they had really benefited from the addition of three strong male backs.

They were but seven men and a boy: Surprise, August, Henry, Irving, Bossie, Ned, George and John, now aged twelve.

And six women: Delia, Bernice, Jennie and the Saltus girls, who were named Theah, Leah and Zeah – Surprise could never figure out that puzzle and always got the names wrong. After a while he just called 'Hey you' to them all and figured it sure took a pig-headed man like Saltus to name three children all the same – or nearly. But the girls were childbearing age – and, as Senex would observe, with legs set like fowls, too.

Even if we all set to breeding right away, Surprise thought, it be ten long years before we got useful citizens. Trouble was, breeding didn't look about to happen and, anyway, they needed manpower right now.

He called a meeting in the Long House.

'I address our Governor,' he nodded at Henry, diplomatically, 'and all present.

'We got a girt problem and it faces us *right now* – not next year. We got to expect and be ready for a bigger attack by the British than ever before.'

'Aye,' Bossie said, for there were murmurs of disagreement and impatience. 'Listen to the man – he talking nothing but the truth. Surprise win us a *big* battle. But the British coming. They not take this defeat lying down. Next time they come, I figure they going to bring Wellington and Admiral Nelson and King William, too.'

'They all dead, man,' Bernice said. 'Least, Admiral Nelson is, everybody know that.'

'Well,' Bossie said, 'you know what I mean – they coming and they bringing their big people.'

Surprise got up and paced in front of them. 'Listen, this be a republic. Everybody got the right to speak and be heard. First I want to say this: my father, Senex, the wise one, he taught me that those who rebel against the whites are destroyed by whites. But I do not believe he was right for this time: that liberty place in Africa is still free – as far as we know – and there be a Negro republic on Hispaniola. That I know. I have come to believe that only those *who rebel* – like us – are *not* destroyed. Those back in the old country – except they rebel are destroyed. I believe that only those who rebel and fight and are *strong* – like in Hispaniola – only those do the whites respect.

'I thought about it long and deep. And I, like all of you, fight long and deep. I know the British, our enemy, respect

204

nothing but power. And power is cannon and shot and powder
– but one thing else it is most of all : it is *men*. Numbers of
men.

'To have sufficient power, New Bermuda needs fifty more
people. Twenty-five young men and twenty-five young
women.'

'Where we going to get them?' Delia said.

'St Kitts,' Jennie suggested. 'Lots of people on St Kitts –
and poor, too.'

'And Guadeloupe,' Delia added.

'I don't know about West Indians,' Henry said. 'I tell you,
West Indians are a dark and *deep* lot of people. They funny.
I ain't sure I want to be with a lot of West Indians – and I
damn sure I don't want to be *out*-numbered by West Indians.'

'Aye to that,' said Irving.

The agreement was pretty general.

'I don't see nothing wrong with good black West Indians –
least, we could try to get a few.'

'A few, yes – many, no,' Henry said, nodding sagely.

Again the agreement was a clear majority.

'And now the question of money.' Surprise paced again.
'It been passed by this republic before that money from salt
be divided evenly. I feel this is wrong. I feel the money *belongs*
to all – all of it – but the money must be kept to buy the needs
of the whole colony. I believe *part* of the money should be
parcelled out to all – to those as need some – but that the big
mass of it must be kept by one person, for all.'

'Who?'

'And where is the money from that Savannah schooner?'
Ned Saltus said.

'It on the *Bateau*,' Surprise said. 'I have it all safe.'

'*You* have it. You mean, you *take* it – that thiefing.'

Surprise turned on Ned. 'Everyone here know Surprise not
steal from New Bermuda – from the people. Everyone know
that what is mine I give to the colony – '

'Shit,' August said, 'you talk fullish, Saltus. Afore you
came, we once have no colony at all, save it belong to Surprise.
Our colony be the ship, the *Bateau Bermudien*, and the ship
belongs to Surprise. You a damn newcomer, Saltus – '

'Well – why he *take* the money – the silver for the salt? That
thiefing.'

'It all safe – everyone knows how much it was. I got it, but it not mine, it belong to all.'

'Shit. That's what you say – '

'And this what I say to you in front of all, Ned Saltus. Why do the British want you? Why? All on the *Bateau* in the last fight heard the British captain say, you and all your party wanted for theft. Now you tell us what that be about? What theft? What you steal?'

'I be innocent.'

'That may be so – but what they accuse you of? What theft they want you for?'

'I – I don't know – '

'What?'

They heard the sound of a conch shell being blown. It was the lookout in the upper fort.

'Alarm! Ship coming.' Surprise ran to the door. 'Everybody to their post.'

At last it was the *Thomas Jefferson*. The news was good and bad. Good because Captain Macdonald wanted his hold lined with salt. Bad because the Captain had no news from President Tyler.

'I put in to Baltimore but two months ago, Monsieur Le Negre. From there I took a coach to Washington and did wait at the President's house for three days – all the time asking for a reply for your letter. But I could get nowhere. No one knew anything and the place was swarming with office seekers, favour seekers and blasted money-lenders.'

'What be office seekers?'

'Many men seeking jobs that pay big for no work – mostly.'

'Then I write another letter. But Henry must sign, he Governor of New Bermuda now.'

Macdonald nodded.

While Captain Macdonald visited with Delia and the children, Surprise withdrew and wrote his second letter.

It was dated 23 May 1844. He wrote much that he had written in the first letter and added:

'. . . the British claim they own this island but they were not here when we got here and they are not here now, we are.

'And the British send a mighty Royal Navy ship with

206

upwards of one hundred and fifty men, sailors and marines. This only weeks ago and this colony did defeat this Royal Navy ship, called HMS *Vestral*, capture her and all her guns and supplies, and capture many souls, who we returned, of our free will, to the British island of Nevis.'

He wrote the President, also, of the Americans taken and restored, and again asked for the protection promised in the 'Monroe Document'.

He took the letter to Henry to sign. Henry asked Surprise to read it to him.

'It be good, Surprise. But I not put my mark on it – that be *bad*. President Tyler think we all a band of dumb niggers if he see my mark. Only you can write – you put, Surprise, Governor and Leader. Me being leader is sheer fullishness – '

' – '

'Do what I say. I tell them all later. And another thing, Surprise – we gotta see to it that the children of this colony can read and write – that what we gotta do.'

'Aye, Henry – we sure have gotta do that.'

'Anything happen to you, man – we be lost in ignorance. And that be very bad. I figure you better teach us all – and right now.'

Surprise took the letter to Captain Macdonald and again Macdonald made some corrections and suggestions.

'Will this letter get to President Tyler, sure?'

'Yes – it will be delivered to him. Whether he does anything, is another matter. I'm afraid I cannot go again to Washington – it takes more time than I can afford. But I'll have it sent – and reliably.'

'I understand, Captain. And we not charge you for the salt, either.'

'No. I'll pay the fair price.'

'Not so, Captain,' Delia said. 'No money do we take from you. We owe you – and much.'

'Yes. We be lost without you, Captain Macdonald. You be our colony's first friend – just about all we got.'

Ned Saltus heard that the salt for the *Thomas Jefferson* was to be a gift and objected. Surprise and Delia, away from

Macdonald's hearing, said they'd pay the colony from their own silver. Ned Saltus, grumbling, assented to that.

Captain Macdonald had a look over all the island. Surprise showed him, with barely controllable pride, all the fortifications – existing and planned.

The Captain was impressed but clearly worried. Finally he said: 'But you don't have hardly one man for each cannon?'

'No, Captain. We don't. We have eleven cannon and only six men. That's our problem. We need twenty-five more men.'

'Oh, aye. And then you'll need twenty and more gals – won't you?'

'Yes, Captain. But how we going to get them?'

'Simple,' the Captain said. 'Buy 'em.'

'What – we want no slavers here.'

'Who said anything about slaves – to get settlers, you got to give them an incentive, a reward.'

'To be free is reward enough, Captain.'

'You tell my seamen that. Old Macdonald got the best sailors – the best seamen in New England. You know how he get 'em?'

'Offer them more money?'

'Aye, laddie – I *buy* them – with better pay – and something else, too – something that make a man put his heart as well as his back into a venture. You know what it is?'

'No.'

'A share on the ship's profit. On board the *Thomas Jefferson* – as would please her namesake – every man shares in the ship's profit. Even the ship's cook – even the bilge boys.'

'But where I get settlers? And how, Captain, can I *go* for them – since I must needs be here to defend us against the British – and they may come at any time.'

'Let me think on it.'

'Delia always says, sleep on it.'

'Wise – may surprise you, Monsieur Le Negre, but we say very similar in New England.'

Surprise and Captain Macdonald, together, composed an advertisement that the Captain promised to post in every port he visited in his journey down the islands: Guadeloupe, Martinique, Bonaire and Curacao. If any settlers came forward, he would bring them on his homeward passage.

'New Settlers Needed.

50 silver pieces right away and 50 pieces per year to any man or woman, respectful and able-bodied, as would care to join the new Free Negro Republic of New Bermuda, formerly known as Barbuda Island. Share in profitable salt industry assured to the industrious. No man or woman afeared of hard work nor defence of liberty of said island need apply. Preference given to those able to read and write. Apply the *Thos. Jefferson*, now at this port for – – days only. Capt. J. Macdonald, Master.'

The rest of the colony agreed but added the provision that no more than six men and five women be permitted. There was no way Surprise could budge the majority from this resolve.

Surprise went aboard the *Thomas Jefferson* just before she sailed.

'Please tell your Missus, Monsieur, how pleased I am with the way her breadfruits are doing – I told her, but tell her again. May come a time when your colony need them, for a human can live off breadfruit alone.'

'Yes, Captain. And if we get new settlers, we might dearly need a food reserve.'

'Which reminds me, Monsieur. I can only take on settlers for you if the island governments agree to let them go. The French are probably lax – especially at Guadeloupe – but the Dutch are something else entirely.'

Surprise pushed into the Captain's hand one of the purple velvet wrapped embossed silver watches.

'This be my covenant with you, sire. This be my father's watch and I wish you to have it.' He didn't know why he had told such an untruth – but somehow it seemed true enough. Some untruths were truer than truth, as the old folks said.

Macdonald examined it carefully, minutely, turning it over, listening to it. 'But I do not want to take something that your father gave you, Monsieur.'

'Yes. You take it.'

'But your father....'

o

'Everybody – somebody got to give it to me, otherwise how I get it? Now I give it to you.'

'But I protest – it is too valuable.'

'Then you say it be a present from little Johnson.'

'In that case, I can only accept with the sincerest thanks, Monsieur Le Negre.'

Surprise, well satisfied with his allegiance with his friend, set about drilling the colonists against every eventuality of a British attack he could imagine.

He had sand buckets set everywhere to put out fires; he trained all in the use of muskets and in fast loading. He carefully explained the purpose of the great ten-foot trench in the upper redoubt.

'If we ever have to flee from an enormous force of British, flee in the *Bateau* and other boats – this trench is to hold the brass cannon only. It and twenty-four shot and two kegs of powder. All other cannon they can have to take or break – but this be hidden for our secret return.

'Likewise we now make a graveyard in the trees. On each grave I mark a name and date and put "Died of Yellow Fever" – but each grave contain powder and shot and muskets.'

The colonists marvelled at his wisdom. The British were terrified of yellow fever – and rightly so, for it bad on Negroes but it kill whites like flies.

'What we do if they poison our water?' Delia asked.

'We test – a little taste, by one at the time. If one get sick – we find a new well.'

He tried, also, after the noon meal, to teach reading and writing, using the quills, ink and paper from the *Vestral*. Except for Delia, who knew a little already, and for Jennie, who persisted stubbornly, they made little progress.

Surprise found himself an impatient teacher, and when all three Rudds said reading and writing was too hard for them to learn at their age, that it was as heavy work as farming, he agreed in anger.

He tried hard with George and George made some progress – mainly through Delia's intercession. It was impossible to teach John: if Surprise even raised his voice in anger, John froze and wept. His mother cuffed him, but it did no good.

210

'He a natural born working man,' Surprise said. 'That's all.'
John's face immediately wreathed in a great smile.

Most important, Surprise drilled all, particularly his leaders –
Henry, August, Bossie, Ned and young George, too – in the
attack defence he thought most likely they would need.

He reasoned that the British, if they came, would now send
a mighty ship. Probably a ship of the line, but certainly a
frigate – a vessel Surprise, August and the Rudds knew would
have upwards of forty guns and probably five hundred men.

'If they send one ship we fight – if more than one, we run,'
he said. He kept to himself the knowledge that if a ship of the
line, mounting eighteen and twenty-four pounders – and they
be long guns – came, the colony must flee or be destroyed
from superior range.

But he well remembered Captain Darrell saying that a wise
man had written that there be two big dangers in war, to
under-estimate your enemy's strength and wisdom and to over-
estimate it.

'And one of these dangers be most prevalent – most often
happen in history, Surprise, and which one do you think
it is?'

And he, Surprise, would never forget that he had answered :
'Obviously to think too little of your enemy, Master.'

And Beau Nat had said : 'Aye, that's what I thought, too,
Surprise. But history proves it is not so. Many, many more
battles, particularly at sea – have been lost by commanders
over-estimating their enemy's strength and ability to think –
to plan. Now, isn't that strange?'

It was, but, if you thought it out good, it figured.

Surprise figured the British would send one ship : for they
had plenty of knowledge that New Bermuda could fight, but
even more knowledge (lest they be insane) that the colonists
be few.

If he was the British admiral, he thought, he'd send two
fast ships to attack at once, staggered, one to pass on one
side of the island, one the other. . . . But that was over-
estimating their wisdom. He guessed they'd send one ship,
and that a seventy-five or a sixty-five or a frigate, and, in
order not to under-estimate, the captain of her be smart and
young and ferocious.

211

He thought it over again and again. They had two twelve pounders on the hill and their range he tested and had marked with small red buoys. Then he tested the nines – and he settled that that was where New Bermuda's power lay : in the seven nine pounders and the two twelves firing with reduced elevation and charge. Properly laid and loaded these cannon could be fired by only four men, if necessary – certainly for the first firing.

He used up four and a half barrels of powder getting their exact range marked by very small buoys – which he and his men could see with a spyglass, because they knew where to look, the British, he thought, would not likely notice them – at least, not until too late.

'The secret going to be,' he told them, 'to set a trap and lure the British in. The trap, I figure, be the *Bateau* firing at them and they pursue her. The *Bateau* then draw them close where our fixed cannon – being on dry land and a steady platform – can outshoot them.

'And if the wind and sea be in any way rough – that all in our favour. For a ship shoot bad in a rough sea. But the fort – all island guns – must not fire at all until the British ship lured into range – right there where we know the exact charge – where we could kill 'em with *rocks* if we had to.'

And he gave a special order to the women, too : 'When the alarm be sounded and we *know* it's the British, you all take and cut saplings and small trees and bring them and lay them all about the fort and guns – so that the fort and guns be hidden – so that they look all harmless growing trees.'

Irving, after examining the little British dinghy, got all fired hot about building such a keel box for the *Bateau*.

'I make it deeper than the fin is now – she be better.'

Surprise agreed only on the guarantee, on Irving's assurance, that the fin could be raised quickly and by one man. And on the demonstration that the British keel box did in no way leak.

Surprise was truly awed by the little dinghy's keel box. 'It be *one* thing,' he told Delia, 'to *copy* such a keel. Such an invention. That be a good, good shipwright like Irving – better than me, he be as good as Senex.

'But to be the man who *think* of that *first*, that be something else. That be *real* thinking.'

212

'How you mean, man?'

'I mean – you imagine that you an Indian or somebody, on an island and there be *no* boats. No boats *ever* built. Just people maybe hanging on to dead trees. Then you be the man first *think* of a boat. That is real thinking.'

'Uh-huh.'

'A thing is simple when it already done – to make a thing from nothing – that is real man wisdom.'

What he didn't tell her was how he feared the British – and the Americans – all white people. For he knew how a gun worked, but he didn't know the why – and you could invent nothing – less you knew the why.

Like a match. He knew it struck against dry wood or rock – but why, how? And he himself could remember the first matches that came to Bermuda when he was a boy. First one he saw scared him half fullish – a tinder box was one thing, this flame on a magic stick quite another.

What wonders there be, he thought. What wonders yet to come? A man maybe see around corners; a man fly in the sky in a sky boat. Why not? He knew they had boats, in America, that go under the water. Just imagining what could be imagined fair made him dizzy. . . .

'You finish that fin keel thing as quick as you can, Irving. We got to have our *Bateau Bermudien* – without her we are trapped.'

'I'm going as fast as I can. Quicker than three men.'

'Well, just remember – she our *first* colony. She have to be our only colony, if need be.'

'Aye. Then give me August.'

'You can have him and another, too – if you want.'

'August only. No one else knows his trade good enough – save you.'

'Uh-huh. You have August and right now.'

The next ship to put in for salt was a French barque and she carried a pleasant and needed surprise for them all. Domino was aboard and he had come to stay.

'I not say forever, Surprise,' he said when he found out that he was welcome and that no one was angry over his past leaving. 'For I suppose I said *that* when I was young and fullish and didn't know who and what kind of a fella I am.

213

But now I know I'm a natural born wanderer – so I just say I stay for a while.'

'Then you best promise,' Delia said, 'to give us fair warning *when* you going. Last time you scared me out of a year's growth.'

'Girl – you ain't grown none since you was twelve – and what you now? Sixteen?'

'Seventeen – real old. And you, Domino? You must be twenty-one now, huh?' She danced around him with little Jack in her arms.

Surprise felt a strange constriction in his throat. It must be, he thought, him having no real kinfolk save Senex and him gone – but he had Delia and the children. Why do I grieve, he wondered.

King Jack was alive and kicking, but 'not so much – he got the British complaint – the goat'.

'Gout,' Surprise said.

'Goat.'

'All right – and what of Saul, my father?'

'Never heard tell – oh, yes, I did. Seems to me I heard tell he died.'

God-almighty, the lack of feeling of some people, Surprise thought and turned away.

'I'm sorry, Surprise. Real sorry. I forgot. It's been so long, see – you understand? Seems to me King Jack say he fell down and then came over poorly.'

But if Domino was young and thoughtless of people's feelings, his youth was sorely needed. Further, he had a friend, Paul, named Paw-Paw, a Bahamian, who agreed to leave the barque and stay a while, too.

Best of all, to Surprise, was the sweet fact that Paw-Paw and Domino wasted no time in making moves towards two of the Saltus girls.

Ned objected to Paw-Paw's open courting, but Paw-Paw paid him no mind at all, except to go into peals of laughter.

He danced, the first night, around the middle girl, Leah. 'My, my,' he said, stamping his foot, 'a little boat built like that, she has *got* to sail. Yes, sir, she got to have a *rudder*. Uh-huh – '

'Shut up and be still,' Ned said.

'Uh-huh. She need a *rudder*, that sweet ship – or how else we going to stir up a *crew*.'

He enticed Leah to dance with him and, before long, was steering her away into the dark.

Ned put a stop to it, that night. But a few nights later (Domino taking up too with the younger, Zeah), when Paw-Paw made to leave – 'I never did see such a sweet sailboat and she ain't got no *rudder*, never *known* no *rudder* at all –'

Ned grabbed him : 'What's the matter with you, young man – you got no respect, no honour?'

Paw-Paw roared with laughter and shook him off. 'In the island I come from, Pop, we only got two kinds of honour : get on 'er and stay on 'er.'

Surprise turned away, laughing, to walk in happiness and contentment with himself. This keep up, he thought, maybe we raise that new generation, that whole new colony.

Already there be Johnson and Jack and Marie and soon they be more. Maybe George or even Bossie would take up with the eldest Saltus girl, the uppity one, whatever her damn name was.

VI

It was August (1844) when the British came again. And when they first hove in sight, a cloud of sails on the horizon, Surprise guessed who they were – and, the weather being mild, cloudless, almost, with a contrary wind out of the south, nigh on due south, he figured they were in for a tough fight.

Only good thing was that the barometers, both the brass one and the shark's oil, were registering for a change – and most likely for a rough change. If it come soon enough.

It was the rigging and the pennant made him sound the alarm, and, within an hour and a half, around half-nine in the morning, he was proved right. The white ensign was visible almost to the naked eye; and she was exactly what he expected, a frigate of forty guns and more.

Watching her, even from afar, he could tell she was a tight good ship with a crack captain and a sharp crew : nothing else could beat to windward the way she was and tack almost like an islander.

And though their rehearsals made this reality run like the innards of a clock – so much so that he had little need to work himself, no need of giving commands, and deep time to plan and think – yet he had a fearful foreboding, for this would be the first time ever he gave up command of the *Bateau* to another and she be setting sail into danger.

There was nothing else for it, no other course left to him, but to give up his beloved ship, his *Bateau Bermudien*, the ship of his father, himself, and he believed, the ship of his son, Johnson, little Surprise, pained him worse than he could remember.

Domino would have command of her. Domino on the helm and Paw-Paw on the main sheet; George, as usual, on the cannon; Irving on the jibs and Buccaneers with Bossie (and those two men to add wisdom to that crew).

Not that Domino couldn't sail a ship : he could have had no two better teachers, Surprise believed, than himself and King Jack. Also he was a natural : put a sail on a cow and he could have got her to windward. Hot-headed, yes, but that was what Irving and Bossie were for.

So the *Bateau* had five where she really needed six – but that was all they could spare for the decoy, the lure. They were short-handed enough with their main fighting force : a fort (and a sprawled about one, at that) with one six pounder, seven nine pounders and two twelves. Ten cannon in all, but only five men : Surprise, young John, August, Henry and Ned. It was the women they had to count on : the three Saltus girls for fetching powder and shot; Delia, Jennie and Bernice would load and generally do the work of men – save that Jennie had but the one arm and Delia had to keep one eye cocked for the three children (though little Johnson, a manly lad for two years and two months – was put in charge).

Bernice was a powerful woman and she had, she'd proved, a considerable aptitude and liking for the behaviour of cannon and shot. She and Jennie worked as a team and could move from cannon to cannon. Delia's other task was to watch over the fetching and carrying of material by the Saltus girls.

But Surprise, with John as his runner, was the brain, the captain of it all. However hard he tried to see it otherwise, he

216

had to give up his ship and be on the land at the head of the upper redoubt.

As the fast British frigate beat to windward and New Bermuda there was a deal of nervous laughter and a deal of random squatting, to make water, done by the woman.

Surprise himself did a deal of praying : first to the unknown God of all weather and storm and power and sea, then, as the ship drew closer and he could see even her jack through his glass (peering from behind the trees and bushes the women had placed all about) his God became his departed father.

Senex, smile down upon us this day. . . .

But when the frigate had beat a way clear over to the eastward, and he could see she was damn near going to lay the line of the island and the fort on the next tack, and he had given John the order to blow the conch, to start the *Bateau*, he stopped praying to any but himself, and became all over his body and mind, a cold being, almost like a clock.

Maybe, he knew, they'd bet too much on their big first blast of cannon – the blast that would make each shot land almost upon the other. Maybe they'd put too much on getting that British ship to pass that very spot – well, he'd taken care of that : his brass nine pounder, laid by himself, would fire first, and if she hit, all would fire – if not, certain changes could be made – but no drastic changes. Drastic changes like changing the complete angle of a cannon, would cut them down to three guns only – and lucky if they could bring them to bear.

It was hoped, but wasn't likely, he figured, that Domino could lay one six pound ball in the frigate's bow. But he'd told him, no close, close stuff : 'That a frigate and she can likely move a gun forward and shoot you forward out of the water. And, Domino, never forget – that no brig – that frigate can sail faster than you any time she want.'

'She can't lay as close on the wind.'

'It ain't going to pay no-never-mind, Domino. You the bait – you lead that shark into the pot. That all you got to do.'

The *Bateau*, with all sails set, cut out from under the harbour and the hill, cut out and haul-arsed sharp to the west with the starboard rail down.

'Ease the sheet, you fool,' Surprise said to himself – for the

217

wind was freshening now and the *Bateau* didn't favour being sailed rail under on any quarter.

He watched them come about.

'Now nobody make a sound – you hear – pass the word. A flooky breeze might carry a sound, as they draw closer.'

August
1844 Captain Horace Sturton, of HMS *Bellerophon*, had his orders : to engage and destroy the rebellious and piratical sloop of war operating out of the island of Barbuda. And this he intended to do; he also had plenty of personal motive. He was forty-two years old, and, fourteen years before, he'd beached and hogged a frigate, his second command, on the Misteriosa Bank, chasing a ship he believed a slaver bound for Cuba. He never caught the slaver, the frigate was condemned and broken up at Kingston, Jamaica, and, what was worse, the Court of Vice Admiralty did not believe the Misteriosa Bank existed and he hadn't had a command since.

Such a length of time without a ship would have been understandable to an officer without means, connections or talent, but Sturton was rich "as a sugar baron" and his father-in-law was one of the Lords of the Admiralty. And he was a good officer : much more than competent at seamanship, navigation and gunnery, and in the Royal Navy he was, almost unbelievably, that contradiction in terms, a captain who inspired devotion from his men.

He achieved the latter distinction by simply being humane – a quality that had more to do, he rightly guessed, with his long lack of a command, than the goddamned Misteriosa Bank, which never mind the charts nor the admirals, existed, moved, and had hogged his ship.

The second part of his orders were : to capture all the rebellious natives of the said island of Barbuda, to burn their dwellings and any forts or breastworks, etc., and to carry them away for trial at the Court of Grand Sessions, St Kitts.

The orders were signed both by the Admiral at Bermuda and by the 'Governor in Chief in and over all Her Majesty's Leeward Charibee Islands in America, Chancellor, Vice-Admiral, the Ordinary of the Same, Sir Charles Leigh, Bart. . . .'

Captain Sturton watched the island closely, saw a sloop start out, had the ship beat to quarters and then went below to catch another glance at his charts to make sure, for the fourth time, there were no sand banks or reefs near – and to get a chance to use the commode, for he was a nervous man and plagued by loose bowels in an emergency.

But, as the British had a way of saying, he had done his homework: he knew, from his careful interview with Midshipman, now Lieutenant Smythe, the only officer surviving from the loss of the *Vestral*, that this sloop was the one: no other in these waters carried the Bermudian rig and the strange mainsail – not to mention the blue flag.

He would, he felt, be absolutely sure when he could make out her flag – if it was a pale blue ensign, that was his man – Le Negre, by name.

Like all sane men, the future opened up a hundred possible roads and decisions he could take: he knew only one thing for certain and that was that he wasn't going to let that little wasp of a sloop get under his bow and pierce his hull at the waterline.

And, he laughed with anguish, as he sat down on the cold porcelain of the commode – half-tripping on his lowered trousers and sword – he wasn't going to run into shallow water.

Best, he thought, to try to pummel the sloop to pieces from long range. Yes, that was best.

Domino yelled: 'Ready about – yoh!' and swung the *Bateau*'s helm over and headed dead towards the British man-o'-war on a closing course.

'Come to Poppa,' he said. 'Let me just give you a smell of sweet pussy, Englishman – and you chase it to your grave. Like the old folks say, you gonna catch a lobster put a mirror in the bay. . . .' He was whistling.

Irving wished Surprise was with them.

Bossie wished to hell he was on shore and it all over.

'Don't get too close now,' said Paw-Paw. 'That British can move – and remember, you gotta zig-zag and that mean he overhaul you quicker.'

'I know. I know.'

'You do like the bossman say, Domino – 'cause there's one thing this mama's boy don't want to do today and that is go swimming – you hear?'

Bossie knew he meant he didn't want to die, and he was glad the lad was talking to Domino – because be damned if he wanted to die either, and not by any damn fullishness from no St David's Island buck.

The *Bateau*, moving north-east, on a reach, was closing damn fast.

'I say you had better come about, you hear?' Irving yelled.

'Aye.' Domino whistled again. 'Just a little further – he gotta smell us.'

Surprise had his glass on the British. She was long and graceful and her square sails tight hauled and she cut good to windward. She was about the sweetest looking piece of British sail he'd ever seen – for a second he even wondered who the man was that designed her.

But the *Bateau Bermudien*, leaping through the water like a young porpoise, was getting too, too close. He sweated in an agony: there was no way he had of signalling save to fire a shot and that would give all away.

Captain Horace Sturton recognised the pale blue ensign. Le Negre all right, and no mistake.

'Wainwright, mind your range on the starboard guns.'

The word was passed. Sturton believed the sloop would expect him to bear off the wind and fire with his port guns.

Not so, he'd luff up and fire the starboard. The rehearsals were all over: the starboard guns would fire a broadside of mixed elevations and, even if they all missed, the *Bellerophon* would be to windward and could afford to bear off and fire the entire port broadside.

Sturton, aware as he was that a captain of his seniority should have, by now, a steamship, was more determined than ever before to use his ship to the utmost of her sailing abilities.

And those were considerable. The *Bellerophon* was old, but it was not for nothing that she had once been King William the Fourth's favourite plaything; and, during the past several months of his command, Sturton had enjoyed, on a number of occasions, flying past Royal Naval steamships, for the *Bellerophon*, at her best, could log twelve knots.

'Helmsman – bring her up. Gentlemen, fire when the guns come on the target.'

Surprise watched in horror. The British ship was luffing her bow to the south – clearly bringing her guns to bear – and Domino had not tacked.

On that reach, the *Bateau* was now a long, if small and thin target – and her sails were totally vulnerable.

He even considered asking August and Henry if he should fire. . . .

But it was too late. The sounds cracked across the water and smacked against the hillside.

Bang! Bang! Bang! Bang! Bang!

And then a Boom, as at least ten guns fired at once.

The British ship was all but obscured in white and grey smoke and when he looked again she was coming about, tacking back through that smoke.

The *Bateau*, stripped entirely of her mainsail – save for tatters hanging off the broken boom and little pieces like shirts flapping from her spar – was finally tacking.

Bossie was yelling at Domino : 'Get her tight on the wind – lay the island.'

Irving shouted : 'She sail as good with the beeg jib as with anything – lay her to windward.'

Bossie ran up on the quarter-deck realising that he was shouting at no one.

In a shiver of his spine and bowels and legs, a shiver of shock and terror, he grabbed the tiller, and set the *Bateau* on the wind himself.

There was nothing left of Domino. Paw-Paw's trousers slumped against the taffrail. Bossie numbly watched Irving tightening all the jibs and then he realised that the trousers, so close to him, contained Paw-Paw's lower trunk and legs. Bossie shivered again and shook himself.

Irving came up on the quarter-deck. 'We laying good, Bossie – hold her there. That's it – right for the island. Pass by close to the hill and keep on out to sea.'

Irving saw the bloody mess. Went over, reached down, threw it overboard and then vomited.

221

'George! Fire that cannon!'

The *Bateau* kept moving good, now cutting to windward, presenting a far smaller target.

No sound of the cannon.

Irving rushed below to find out what was wrong. That cannon must fire – they maybe even hit her now – and even if they didn't, the firing *must* entice the British on.

Surprise watched and sweated. The *Bateau* was at last a smaller target, but she was stripped of at least a third of her speed and the frigate was bearing off to fire again.

'We fire?' Henry yelled.

'Shut-up and wait,' Surprise hissed.

He thought he'd seen the *Bateau* hit in her hull – men hit. But now he could see Domino at the helm all right.

Haul-arse – that's it.

'Helmsman – be so kind as to bear off now. Gentlemen, fire when your port guns are on target.'

It was a decision that Captain Sturton came to reluctantly : for his *Bellerophon* would be, for those moments of firing, a leeward target square to the little wasp's stinger.

He watched her carefully through his spyglass. He let the glass, for a moment, play over the island and up the small hill : all quiet there. Smythe had mentioned shore guns – but he'd looked damned hard and long earlier and he couldn't see a one. It was Le Negre that worried him : Le Negre's sloop sank HMS *Vestral*.

Irving found George knocked cold by something – a shot had entered the cabin, passed through it, and left by the opposite side, making a small extra port on the entering and a girt one on the departing.

He raised the cedar cover of the after port. He grabbed a bucket of water, threw it over George.

Then he grabbed the torch that still flared in its holder by the writing Surprise had carved in the cedar on the forward cabin wall.

'Get up – help me run it out.'

George only stirred.

Irving put the torch back and began wrestling with the six

222

pounder himself. He'd once run it out by himself, but that was with two crowbars and now he couldn't find a one.

'Get up, George! Get up!'

George was shaking himself like a wetted dog.

Bang! Bang! Bang! Bang! Bang!

Boom!

It sounded, to Surprise, all too like the Royal Navy target practice he used to hear off North Rock, echoing in sharp cracks, all the way back to the Western Isles, when he was a child.

'We fire?'

'Shut-up – hold your fire. You know my orders.'

The *Bateau*, through his spyglass, was stripped of the upper part of her spar – the pennant simply ceased to exist – and the forward section of the bowsprit, including the Stars and Stripes.

Somehow she moved on through a sea that was so spouting with shot that it looked like a road puddle into which someone had thrown a handful of pebbles.

Somehow, too, she kept moving on and on, passing now to leeward of them, passing under the very guns of the fort.

Surprise took a breath and wondered how long he'd been holding it.

Bang!

A puff went up from the *Bateau*'s stern. Could it be her own gun? Or was it another hit?

He swung his glass on the frigate. She was sharpening up on the wind again. Reloading, he knew, both her broadsides. Doubtless her starboard guns were already loaded.

Plop.

A shot fell short of the frigate.

His spyglass came back on the *Bateau*. The little craft limped forward, dragging broken rigging, sails and most of the bowsprit – a seabird with her beak hanging and tattered.

Only the smallest jib and a part of the next, had any drawing power. Now she was exactly by the red buoys where their fort guns were trained.

'Keep her moving, Bossie. Keep her moving.' Irving was on the quarter-deck, leaving George to reload the six pounder.

'Um hardly got way on,' Bossie said.

'Just keep her moving.' Irving moved himself to one of the Buccaneers and cocked the flint and checked the pan for powder.

He laid the gun in the highest elevation he could get it towards the closing frigate and fired.

Then he moved to the other Buccaneer.

'Wainwright,' Captain Sturton said with mock wit, a humour that always comforted him, especially if he put his too easily trembling hands in his waist pockets. 'I don't expect to run that bloody sloop down for you, hit it, man.'

Surprise knew what was going to happen next: he said it, quite calmly to himself: they are going to smash the *Bateau* to splinters.

The cracks of the Buccaneers were little comfort – though he saw a hole torn in the main course of the frigate.

What use a two-foot hole in a sail, still left really unharmed and there be fourteen others drawing good?

Bossie heard the shot falling and even heard the rending crash and felt everything around him falling.

Irving knew nothing until he found himself in the water – and, to his surprise, swimming towards the island.

'Helmsman, steady as you go. No closer to the island – steady. There's reefs in close.'

'Sir – a man in the water. Shall we fire on him?'

'Heavens, no. Whatever for? Do you think the poor chap has a gun he can fire at us. Really, Wainwright.

'Steady, man. Steady.'

Surprise's first imagining was of the carving of his father's name, SENEX, being obliterated for ever – then his shock intensified his battle-purpose. What was left was the only true reality and the reality was that the British frigate was laying a course that would bring her exactly to their red buoys.

'John,' he said, gently moving a largish tree branch from in front of his brass nine pounder. 'Pass the word by whisper: fire if I hit. As planned, *only* if I hit.'

'Aye, Captain.'

224

Surprise had, in his steely shock, a simple certitude. By the time he counted thirty that sleek Limey was going to pass clear over the spot where he'd laid so many shots in practice he knew he could lay one now if he was blind and deaf and only had John – now returning to his side like a faithful puppy – to tap him to tell him where to light the fuse.

The marines were ready, lined up by the boats. He had only to give the command. He'd wait until they'd lost way entirely. He was not taking his ship, *Bellerophon*, any further in these shallow waters.

Already, his slick crew were alive aloft, taking in canvas like the highly skilled monkeys they were. And there would be no slipping aloft from the yardarms of his ship – no falling from aloft to a teak death below. He had stopped the standard Admiralty orders that all yards be oiled daily – orders that had killed so many, especially in the heat of these climes.

The wind had fallen, as if in expectation, almost to nothing.

Surprise struck his match. Lined his eye along his brass barrel for one last sure time and lit the fuse.

He jumped aside from the cannon and gained a spot to watch the shot fall.

'Ram and load, John.'

The shot dropped dead amidships, hitting the frigate's bulwarks, and smashing a deep gash down her topsides.

'Fire – everyone. *Now!*'

All along the two gun platforms of the fort, the nine pounders roared. The noise was sweetly deafening.

Then the two twelves crashed off, too, and shook the whole hill. Surprise thought, if this hill be an old volcano, we going to make her blow again.

Shouts from all around and about and below him.

John tugging at his arm.

'She all loaded, Captain.'

But Surprise moved, the better to see, through the branches hiding them all, what damage was being reaped on their enemy.

He stood high on a small knoll and put his glass to his eye – but he had not, never in his born days, expected the result.

The spyglass smashed, knocked against his eye, like someone had punched him in a fist fight.

When he had come quite to his senses, he watched in awe and wonder.

The frigate's spars and sails seemed to be collapsing inwards towards each other. Then, in an out-blasting series of girt explosions, the spars were being blown apart – away from each other, flaming.

Even counting on, as he did, that every shot of their ten cannon had hit its mark – nothing from their fort could have caused this.

The series of crescending roars went on and on and on. Finally, the wind itself seemed stilled in a great red and yellow vomitting upward of the water and ship.

The heat of the blast hit the fort so ferociously that Surprise feared lest their powder stores be caught and blown.

Then he knew, staggered at his slowness of wit: they had exploded the Britisher's stores of powder – the magazine.

Surprise stood in the heat of the morning – it was now past eleven of the clock – and watched with the shouts and clamour of his friends around him. Heat there was, for the wind had died out entirely. He stood and watched: where there had been a girt British frigate there was no ship at all, not even a man: it was as simple as that: what was, was not.

A sense of hot elation passed through his body, tingling on to the nerves of his skin: they had destroyed the British conquerors entirely.

Then his elation passed as surely as if they'd taken him and put him in a sack with shot and thrown him into the depths of the sea –

The price he'd paid was his *Bateau Bermudien*, and, numbly he knew that the price was too high.

Someone fired another cannon – the six pounder, by the sound of it.

'John,' he said softly. 'Go and tell them to stop firing – it's all over.'

He climbed up again the better to see the ocean – then he looked back, peculiarly, he thought, thinking of Delia and the children for the first time.

226

They were safe – even playing, little Jack was, playing, in her arms, with his tiny fingers on her face. His beloved Johnson looked a bit blasted himself – so much so that Surprise cried out at him, cheerfully, and waved.

Johnson recognised him, started a smile and a small upward movement of his chubby arms, and then burst into tears. Surprise waited until he saw Delia going to comfort the boy.

Then he looked out to sea. A small breeze had got up now – contrary bastard – and was blowing almost due north.

The sea was flecked with all manner of small floating wreckage: flotsam, flotsam, flotsam and jetsam.

The sunset was bright on the water – the sunset as bright as the sunsets at home in Bermuda when the water was glassy-still west of the Western Isles and the sun setting at evening time.

He found his spyglass and looked again: it was bodies and blood and chips of oak and hunks of clinker-fastened boats and dinghies – all small hunks. And the sunset was blood.

So much blood he looked for sharks, but saw none.

He swept the water where the *Bateau* had once been: there floating, was the biggest piece of anything left that day: the stern section, he could see the glittering gold of the longtail he'd fashioned so long ago from the American eagle of a wrecked brig – from Baltimore, wasn't it?

Irving came dripping up to him, his face part torn, his eyes blackened and bloodshot and drooping with anguish.

They fell into each other's arms and wept.

In the afternoon and the night and the day that followed, the slight north wind blew the flotsam into the harbour and all along the little beach.

Blood changed the colour of the sand, and pieces of human bodies rotted and the stench of death clung to the little colony.

VII

At first, as if from within a stunned numbness, the colony carried on.

Irving, using the makeshift slipway on which they used to haul the *Bateau*, began laying down a new sloop. Surprise's interest was half-hearted : a sloop built from the remains of a British brig, of oak, was not to his taste. Still, they had to have something better than the longboat, the open Bermuda fishing boat and the little British dinghy.

The legacy of Domino and Paw-Paw was that two of the Saltus girls had morning sickness. Little Johnson ran a high fever.

Ned volunteered to take his Paget fisherman to Nevis for salts for the bowels, astringents and some other small needs. Surprise said he'd be better to go around Antigua to Guadeloupe : Ned said he didn't want to go that far and Surprise felt he couldn't blame him – besides, it wasn't as if their presence was any secret to the British.

Henry worked with Irving – indeed, the two brothers became almost inseparable. Bernice grumbled.

Surprise kept dreaming, as before, that little Johnson died – was killed. It was unbearable to him : the light of lights going out of the bright brown eyes. . . .

With Jennie and John, Surprise dug two deep trenches down by the northern edge of the salt beds.

He showed them to Delia. 'These be the redoubt – the last redoubt – for the children and the women, if the British come again.'

'I stay with you, Surprise.'

'I've no time for arguing, Delia. You have to do as I say : when the British come, all women and children are to lie in these holes. Now, you help me by seeing there's plenty of water kept here – and fresh – all the time.'

The *Thos Jefferson* stopped briefly in September.

Captain Macdonald had had considerable trouble with the authorities on all the islands. He brought but one settler : Samuel Codrington, a man of thirty-seven, who said he was born on Barbuda and was of 'the family that once owned it all'.

The second letter to President Tyler, Captain Macdonald had thought best to give to the American Consul at Curacao.

Surprise wrote a third letter to President Tyler, referring him to his previous letters and telling of the colony's defeat of the second British attempt to destroy them. He emphasised that he expected a third attack at any time and again reminded him of the Monroe Document.

Captain Macdonald took Delia aside and offered to take her and the children back to Bermuda.

'Captain, we do that and there be no New Bermuda. If Surprise Le Negre lose his dream, it not be by Delia. But I thank you.'

He promised he'd come again soon, but he was off to many northern ports.

Ned was gone for five days, which seemed a powerful long time.

Little Johnson's fever had abated and Captain Macdonald had examined him and pronounced him well : he'd also given them salts and told Surprise something he'd never known before, that a person's urine was the best medicine to wash that person's cut or sores and that rum and urine was the best thing for treating any wound.

Macdonald had sailed before Ned got back. Surprise watched Ned with an only half-interested loathing : there was something smug and self-righteous about the man. Self-righteous people, he'd always known, were invariably dishonest and capable of the basest deceits. And whatever was that theft the British wanted him for ?

Delia tried to comfort Surprise. But he would say little. Once he did say : "And I never did sail her with the new lowering keel – never did. . . .'

By October, Irving and Henry had built the frames on to the keel of the new sloop. Their hammering and sawing seemed, save for the children, the only heartbeat of the island. Though

August, and the new man, Codrington, worked hard at the salt beds.

A ship came for salt in October and two came in November. Surprise wrote a letter to President Tyler and gave one to each master, bidding them deliver the letters to the American consuls wherever they could.

On the evening of December 14th 1844, Vice-Admiral Streatham, who carried his flag on the ironclad, HMS *Achilles*, wrote a letter, at sea, to his wife:

'. . . down here off Barbuda to put down a rebellion of blacks, who claim they are a republic. Of course, they are really just the descendants of the slaves of the Codrington family, to whom the island legally still belongs (and to England of course). It's a hellish place, anyway. . . .'

Little Jack still slept in the tiny dinghy on rockers that Senex had made of Bermuda cedar, what seemed now many many years ago, for Johnson.

Surprise had come down from the upper redoubt to the trenches to bid the children goodnight. He'd been watching the stopped and still distant British ship for long hours with Henry and Irving.

He gave the crib a little rock. 'It is the little *Bateau Bermudien*, eh?'

She kissed him. They made no fuss so as not to frighten the children.

'I'll be back,' he said.

'What do you make of her, *really*? Henry asked.

'Simple – just what we all see before nightfall. She a girt British steamship, painted grey. She so saucy she anchor off and not even care whether we see her.' Surprise had on his green jerkin with the brass buttons; he even had the top button done up as if he was cold.

'I don't reckon our cannon could harm her at all,' Irving said.

'Me either.'

'Perhaps not,' Surprise said.

'You know what I don't like most, Surprise?'

230

'What, Irving?' Henry asked, taking a big pull on a rum bottle.

'That goddamn Ned. Him disappearing this morning – like I said. Him disappearing just before the British come.'

Surprise said : 'Yeah. A man like Saltus. I seen 'em before. I tell you, a man like him ought to be shot with a ball of his own shit.'

'You reckon he tell the British about our fort – everything?'

'Tomorrow will tell.'

'A fine man,' Henry said, 'go off and leave his three children.'

'But what this British ship got for guns, Surprise?'

'Long-range ones, I expect. We can only hope they come in a lot closer.'

HMS *Achilles* was an ironclad steamship of over two hundred and fifty feet in length. She had three tall, enormous spars, complete with yardarms – but she had no need of them.

She was higher out of the water than the length of the *Bateau Bermudien* and all along the two hundred and fifty feet of that height, there bristled guns.

Neither were they the type of gun that Surprise and the Rudds had ever experienced. They were 'Paixhans Guns', which fired explosive shells. She had many thirty-two pounders with explosive shells; but her main armament was eight-inch sixty-four pounders with explosive shells – she had thirty-eight in number of those on each side.

She was also armed with rockets and one giant howitzer on her main deck. (Though each Paixhans Gun was itself a howitzer.) She was painted overall, even the spars and rigging, a dull slate grey.

When she was launched a correspondent for the London *Daily Graphic* wrote : 'Alas, poor humanity might well sigh and say, What next !?'

Her complement was two thousand and nine men.

In the early morning, when they prepared to move in, the senior gunnery commander on board the *Achilles* did an unprecedented thing : he virtually forced his way into the Admiral's quarters to see his commanding officer.

Astounded, Vice-Admiral Streatham asked what he wanted.

'Sir. I've seen women and children on that island – and I beg you, sir, to send a messenger warning the people there what our guns can do and explaining their position is worse than hopeless.'

'Commander what-ever-your-name-is, those *people*, as you call them, have sunk two of Her Majesty's ships – one with all hands – and if you think I'm going to treat them like humans, you are sadly mistaken.'

'But, I beg you, sir. Only we – only perhaps I, know what our guns and rockets can do. No one has experienced them before – '

'Get out, Commander.'

'I beg you, sir – '

'Get out, sir, I said. Throw the man out.'

In the dawn light, lighting up the grey of the *Achilles*, Surprise said to himself : They come again, the British yellow pigs – they do not take Surprise.

But it was only an incantation of habit. He was awed to emotional numbness by the sheer size of the monster as it manœuvred closer.

He hauled their pale blue ensign with the white longtail up on the flagstaff, as usual. He'd told all the others to go to the trenches.

August, Henry and Irving said they'd fire the guns with him.

Before, hours before, Irving had said : 'Why don't we run for it in the boats?'

Surprise shook his head. 'We have only the longboat. It not safe in any open boat for children. Besides, we are too many and too few rowers – besides, we would not escape them, and, on land, the children have a better chance.'

'Yeah,' Henry joked. 'Time to leave was with Ned.'

Surprise watched the green of dawn change to the tender tint of blue. The sun shafted pale yellow streaks into the sky before it actually rose.

Then the incredibly beautiful rockets went off and up. Surprise was transfixed with the simple revelation : everything

. . . everything is beautiful that is alive – *IT'S ALL A BRIEF BURST OF LIGHT*.

Then the guns opened up.

The British bombardment lasted exactly seven minutes.

The first rockets set the upper and lower redoubts burning, and also the Long House and one of the other houses. A good deal of their powder was set off.

The Paixhans Guns' first shells exploded over, on and below the redoubts and reduced them to, mostly, tossed and burned sand.

Then they hit the other building, the boats, the salt beds. Nothing was left standing, after the seven-minute bombardment, hardly a tree. Indeed, there was hardly anything left after two minutes – but they kept on firing at the same targets, their own explosions.

August, Henry and Irving were all killed outright. After it was over, Delia, climbing the west side of the hill, past the well, gained where the upper redoubt used to be and found Surprise still alive, blown into the trench he'd dug so long ago.

It took him a long time to die. The British were coming ashore – she could hear them, but she knew Jennie and Bernice would care for the children.

Surprise was all blood and sand stuck to it. He was all mashed up but he could both see and talk. His green jerkin was all holed and caved-in looking.

'Don't touch me.'

A long while later he said : 'All I wanted to do was create the *Bateau* – '

'You want water, Surprise?'

'No. Listen to me. All I wanted to do was to create the *Bateau* and sail in her – to be a sailor – all else was a mistake. . . .' He started coughing, and then said 'Senex. . . .'

Then she thought he was dead, but stayed, scared, with him and then, a long while later, he said, 'I wish . . . I wish I was home . . . in Bermuda. . . .'

Sometime after that he died, she didn't know when, it was an awful long time. She just looked down and he was not there : just a lot of dead skin and flesh and old clothes with

233

blood on them. Her man had gone, he just wasn't there anymore.

The Admiral, being told the transport brig had hove in sight,
said : 'Send this message : "Ship them all back to Bermuda
but first take all the men and put them on Andros Island in
the Bahamas and then all the women back to Bermuda." ' He
turned to the other officers. 'Oh, yes, they breed like rabbits –
separate 'em right away.'

Confusion for a moment. The gunnery commander was
breaking in again.

'Don't send that last, you fool.' a lieutenant said to the
signalman. 'Message ends, "Bermuda".'

'Captain of Marines,' the Admiral said. 'Bring me Le Negre,
alive or dead.'

'Yes, sir.'

'What the blazes do you want now, Commander?'

'Forgive me, I request that of those few who are living –
of the children that is, that the boys as well as the girls be
allowed to stay with their mothers – sir.'

'Commander. You'll be the death of me. You're a madman.'

'Yes, sir. I am a madman.'

'Do what you like with the children. Get out of here !'

'Yessir.'

The Admiral turned away. 'Where's that explosives
engineer?'

'Here, sir. Alexander, sir.'

'Mr Alexander, do you think you could blow up that hill?
Just a bit?'

'Well, sir, I could certainly round it off a trifle.'

'Do so.'

Delia and her two children were alive. Jennie and her Marie
were alive – so was John, though blinded.

Samuel Codrington was alive and unhurt. So was Theah
Saltus. Leah, Paw-Paw's pregnant girl, was killed by shrapnel.
Zeah, Domino's girl, was unhurt. Bernice was unhurt.

The British Marines rounded them up. Delia suddenly found
that Johnson was missing.

Then she saw him, a few yards away.

A young lieutenant of the Marines was hit by a stone thrown from a tiny hand.

He turned and grabbed the child:

'What is your name?' he asked good-naturedly.

'Surprise!'

Les Bateaux
Bermudiens,
the little ones,
they float no more
upon the deep
yet are
the air
we breathe.

There was once
a brave man
who sailed a brave boat;
the boat is smashed,
the man is dead,
the bravery
remains.